Mr Bennet
leaves his study

A Regency Romance based on P&P

Sydney Salier

This is a work of fiction. The characters, locations, and events portrayed in this book are fictitious or are used fictitiously. Any similarity to real persons, living or dead is purely coincidental and not intended by the author.

To Michael

with love

My thanks also to all those lovely readers
on FF who helped to improve this story.

A special thanks to David Six, who
suggested the title.

Content

1 Prologue

1810

'It is not fair that Kitty should be allowed to go out and have fun, while I am stuck at home by myself,' whined Lydia Bennet.

'Lydia, my love, I know that you are beautiful and lively, but at fourteen years of age you are simply too young to be out in society. You are still a child.' Mrs Bennet attempted to calm her youngest daughter, who was not of a mind to accept that her sister, who had just turned sixteen, would be allowed to enter society while she had to languish at home.

'I am taller than Kitty and I have a more womanly figure than she has. That makes me more grown up than she is. Perhaps she should stay at home while I go dancing,' Lydia challenged her mother again.

Mrs Bennet tried a different approach. 'Lydia, I know that any gentleman who meets you would be unable to resist you, but I have no wish to lose my favourite daughter at such a tender age.'

Lydia refused to be mollified. She let out a blood curdling shriek and stomped her foot. 'I will not stay at home. I will attend that assembly with you all...'

'NO, you will not,' roared Mr Bennet, who had been disturbed by the ongoing argument and shouting, and walked into the room in time to hear Lydia's last statement. 'You are an unmannered child who has no business to be out in society. You belong in the schoolroom, not in a ballroom. Until you learn to behave with propriety and decorum, you will remain in the nursery, even if it should take ten years.'

'Mama, you cannot let him talk to me like that,' whined Lydia. While she had been shocked to hear her father shout, she refused to give up and sought the support of her mother.

Before Mrs Bennet could answer, her husband declared coldly, 'I am the Master in this house and I will not tolerate the antics of ill-mannered children any longer. Mrs Bennet, I would speak with you in my library.'

Mr Bennet courteously extended his hand to his wife and led her out of the room.

~~B~~

When they were in private, Mr Bennet told his wife, 'I am sorry, Fanny, but I can no longer sit by and do nothing while you try to deal with the monster you created. I let you have your way for too long. This has to stop now.'

'She is but a lively child...'

'She is ill-mannered and spoiled rotten. If we do not pull her into line now, she will ruin all her sisters within six months. While Kitty is not quite as bad as Lydia, particularly when she is away from our youngest, I think it would be better to wait another year to launch her.'

'But, Mr Bennet, the girls must have every chance to find husbands. They cannot do that if they languish at home.'

'Jane has just reached her majority and is still unmarried despite having been out in society for five years, and the beauty you extol to all and sundry. If even she cannot attract a suitor, what chance will our youngest two have?'

'Jane could have married by now, but that hoyden drives away any gentleman who is interested in her sister,' complained a petulant Mrs Bennet.

'Fanny, this too has to stop. Lizzy is a lovely and intelligent girl. I cannot tolerate you belittling her any longer. Especially since I know to which incident you are referring. Mr Coopers was not an honourable man, and I am grateful to Lizzy that she told Jane that the man had already buried three wives, and there had been questions raised about how they had died. Apart from that, he was my age and he was... odiferous... to put it politely.'

Mr Bennet sighed, and took his wife's hands. 'It pains me to tell you, but you have become so obsessed with the need to see your daughters married, that you cannot consider their happiness, or at least their well-being.'

Mrs Bennet's face crumpled as she burst into tears. 'I am so very worried about what will happen to all of us because of that ghastly entail, if you should die. You have told me about that horrid Mr Collins, who I am sure will throw us into the hedgerows before your body is even cold.'

Mr Bennet silently admitted to himself that there was some substance to his wife's fears. His cousin, Mr Collins, was indeed an unpleasant man, who had coveted Longbourn ever since Mr Bennet inherited the estate. Since Mr Collins had a son, which had been denied to his cousin, he kept wishing Mr Bennet into an early grave, so that he could supplant the Bennets at Longbourn.

'My dear, how often do I have to tell you? You have your portion and my mother set some money aside for the girls, which has been invested for the past fourteen years. Between what you and the girls have, even in the four-percents that gives you about six-hundred pounds a year to live on. While that is not as much as the income from Longbourn, you can have a nice cottage and a comfortable life.'

'But I am only getting two hundred pounds a year. What is happening to the other four hundred?'

'The interest which the girl's money accrues is being reinvested to earn more interest.

'Why, their inheritance must have grown to about ten thousand pounds, if the interest is four hundred.' Mrs Bennet beamed at the realisation.

'Precisely. And your brother will ensure that the interest is made available to the girls, should they need it. But I am in excellent health and have no intention of departing this world for a long time yet.'

Mrs Bennet gave her husband a tremulous smile. 'If only I had been able to give you a son.'

'We are not so old yet. Anything could yet happen.' Mr Bennet pulled his wife into a comforting hug. 'But stop worrying. All will be well. I assure you. In the meantime, I believe that I should write to Edward and ask him to help us find a governess for the youngest girls. Preferably one who is proficient on the pianoforte, to also assist Mary to improve.'

'Perhaps you have the right of it,' sighed Mrs Bennet, not certain which part of his speech she agreed with.

~~B~~

Mrs Bennet had gone to rest after the fraught morning she had spent, while Mr Bennet wrote the promised letter to Edward Gardiner, his wife's brother, who had become a successful tradesman in London.

Mr Bennet had reluctantly inherited Longbourn at a young age, when his father died in an accident. Since he would have preferred to be a scholar, he spent the minimum time he could, to attend to estate duties, and the rest in his study, which turned into a library over the years.

Within a year of inheriting, Mr Bennet had married Miss Frances Gardiner, at which time her brother had become a frequent visitor to Longbourn, and a doting uncle to his nieces.

Mr Bennet's mother had been impressed with the young man. Most particularly with his sensibility and business acumen, both of which were sadly lacking in his sister.

In the early days, Thomas Bennet had been head over heels in love with his lively wife and could deny her nothing. But after a few years, Mr Bennet realised that liveliness without sensibility can become wearying, and he retreated to his library whenever his duties allowed. By the time his mother died, shortly after Lydia's birth, which had been difficult and the outlook for another child became remote, his wife became ever more shrill, worrying about the entail.

During those early days, unbeknownst to him, his mother had kept her daughter-in-law's spending in check, and she did not trust her son or his wife to provide adequately for her granddaughters.

To ensure that the girls would not be penniless, Mrs Bennet Senior had bequeathed her marriage portion to the sisters. But instead of giving the girls the money immediately, she had invested the six thousand pounds, to be distributed to them when they married or if they needed to set up their own establishment.

The surprising aspect was that Mrs Bennet had nominated Mr Edward Gardiner as the trustee for that fund, giving him complete control, including the authority of withholding the money if a girl was being targeted by an unsuitable man.

Mr Bennet had been somewhat offended by that provision, but he knew full well that he had never been able to deny his wife whatever she wanted, since he had come to value his peace. If Fanny had had access to that money, she would have insisted on spending it on the girls, and within five years there would have been nothing left.

So, while his pride was hurt, the sensible part of him applauded his mother for her wisdom.

~~B~~

'I received a letter from Gardiner today,' announced Mr Bennet a few days later at dinner. 'He has found a governess for Kitty and Lydia, to teach them how to become accomplished and well-mannered ladies. She is also qualified to assist Mary with lessons on the pianoforte.'

The reaction of the ladies was exactly as he expected. Mrs Bennet appeared resigned to the necessity. Jane and Elizabeth, while their expressions only displayed pleasant smiles, were obviously pleased, judging by the twinkle in their eyes. Mary broke into a happy smile after the first surprise wore off.

Kitty seemed uncertain if a governess was a boon or a bane. Lydia objected vociferously. 'I do not need a governess. Mama has taught me everything I need to know. I do not need a governess to teach me how to flirt to capture a handsome husband.'

Mrs Bennet tried to soothe her daughter. 'If you become more accomplished, you will have a much better chance to engage the interest of a man who can give you a good life.'

'But you always said that I just need to be beautiful and lively,' protested Lydia.

'I have come to realise that I was excessively fortunate to have married Mr Bennet, despite the fact that I had few accomplishments. It has been brought home to me that most men wish their wives to know more than how to dance and flirt. At least men, who wish to marry.' Mrs Bennet sighed. 'I am sorry, Lydia, but you will have to learn how to become a genteel and accomplished lady.'

'I do not want to be boring. I want a husband who looks handsome in regimentals.'

'By the time an officer can afford to support a wife, he must be at least a Colonel. To reach that rank, he will usually be well into his thirties. Do you truly wish for an old husband?'

'But...'

'No more, Lydia. You will attend your governess and you will learn.' Mr Bennet cut her off. 'The sooner you learn to behave with propriety, the sooner you will be allowed into society.'

Lydia glared at her father. But since she was merely spoiled, not stupid, she considered the last statement. She did not like the idea of being stuck in the schoolroom. But it seemed that this time she had no choice. Her father appeared completely resolved to have his way.

But he had given her an opportunity to minimise the time. The quicker she learnt, the quicker she would be allowed to have fun. Very well. She would amaze her parent by the speed with which she acquired her accomplishments.

~~B~~ ~~B~~ ~~B~~

1811

'Netherfield is let at last,' cried Mrs Phillips excitedly, as she bustled into the parlour at Longbourn, to inform her sister, Mrs Bennet. The lady had married Mr Phillips, soon after he had come to work as a clerk in her father's office. Mr Phillips, due to his intelligence and diligence, had become a solicitor in his own right, and taken over his father-in-law's business.

Mrs Bennet was seated in the most comfortable chair in the room, in the company of all her five daughters and Mrs Taylor, the girl's governess of the past year; each of them was engaged in some form of needlework.

Mrs Bennet had been feeling poorly lately. Due to her condition, she was confined to Longbourn, and had been unable to go visiting in recent weeks. Therefore, she was thrilled to catch up on the latest gossip. 'Has it indeed? And who are to be our new neighbours?'

'A young *single* man of fortune has taken the lease.' Mrs Phillips emphasised the important point. 'His servants have already arrived to make the house ready, and he will follow within a week.'

'How wonderful. I hope he has the good taste to fall madly in love with my beautiful Jane,' Mrs Bennet exclaimed. She smiled fondly at her oldest daughter, who was indeed classically beautiful, and had a tall willowy figure. But despite her beauty, at the age of two and twenty, Jane was still single, as were all her sisters.

Mrs Bennet was getting quite worried, due to Longbourn's entail to the male line, and at present the only eligible male heir was the distant cousin, whose father had been a thoroughly unpleasant man before he had died earlier that year. No one knew anything about the son, but Mrs Bennet feared he would be like his father.

Mrs Phillips agreed. 'How could he not fall in love with such a kind and thoughtful young woman. I hope he arrives in time for the next assembly.'

'Oh, how I wish I could attend,' mourned Mrs Bennet. 'I must speak to Mr Bennet. I know how he despises balls, but he simply must escort his daughters, since I cannot.'

'I am certain, dear sister, that Mr Bennet will be agreeable,' replied Mrs Phillips, unaware of her double-entendre.

~~B~~

Mr Bennet had gone to call on Mr Bingley, the day after the young man arrived at Netherfield. Although he pretended to go only at the urging of his wife, as the leading land-owner of the area, he felt that it was incumbent on him to welcome Mr Bingley to the neighbourhood.

Mr Bingley had already heard that Mr Bennet's daughters were the prettiest girls in the neighbourhood. He looked forward to meeting them, when a few days later he returned Mr Bennet's visit. Alas, he was disappointed, since the three oldest girls had all gone to have tea with Mrs Phillips, while the youngest two were sequestered in the schoolroom with their governess.

While during the past year Mr Bennet had tried to curb his penchant for making sport of his neighbours, he was still vastly amused at Mr Bingley's disappointment.

The past year had wrought many changes in the Bennet household, starting with Mr Bennet himself.

The Master of Longbourn was full of contradictions. He had been reluctant to take on the responsibility for the estate at the death of his father, preferring to focus on his studies. Although his studies were not confined to books. His stablemaster had been a sergeant in the army, and could still give the master a good workout with a small sword or a sabre, and with bare hands he was even more formidable, especially as his tactics were not gentlemanly.

Until the events of the previous year, Mr Bennet had preferred to take the easy path, and ignore anything that would disturb his peace. But he did love his family, and once he had roused himself to intervene, he involved himself with the lives and concerns of his ladies.

After the arrival of Mrs Taylor, the house became much quieter. With Kitty and Lydia under the care of the lady, Mr Bennet made an effort to spend more time with all his ladies, not just Elizabeth.

Mr Bennet also attempted, more or less successfully, to curb his sarcasm, particularly against his wife, who responded to his increased attention by suffering fewer attacks of nerves, and becoming a much more agreeable company.

At present Mrs Bennet was cautiously optimistic and hopeful about the future. Knowing that she and her daughters would not be penniless and homeless, had helped Mrs Bennet to become a little less frantic. She still hoped to marry her daughters to men who could provide well for them, but she was a little less vocal and more restrained about her efforts.

Another good change in the house was Mary's increased proficiency on the pianoforte. Mrs Taylor had even taught Mary to make the most of what little voice his daughter had, although now she generally confined herself to playing while Elizabeth and Jane sang. Mr Bennet was rather pleased with the sounds emanating from the music room these days.

Mary, at the age of eighteen, was a quiet and studious girl, who used to dress plainly and in unbecoming colours, to avoid her mother's penchant for matchmaking. With her, Mrs Taylor achieved two small miracles, although Mrs Bennet's greater restraint assisted her efforts. She, assisted by Mr Bennet, had managed to expand Mary's horizons when it came to reading, and her student now also dressed in more becoming colours and styles. While Mary would never match her older sisters in beauty, she turned out to be a rather handsome young woman.

Jane remained as she always was. Apparently calm and serene, she managed to soothe Mrs Bennet when no one else could. Although she too seemed happier these days, since the need for her role as peacemaker had been greatly reduced.

Although Elizabeth remained the apple of her father's eye. She was twenty years old, and in shape and colouring her older sister's opposite. Mrs Bennet often bemoaned the fact that Lizzy's brown curls could not be tamed, and neither could her inquisitive spirit, although Mrs Bennet was inclined to call her impertinent rather than inquisitive. Elizabeth had inherited her father's love of learning, which had made her his favourite.

While Lydia was disappointed that she did not learn all the things Mrs Taylor expected her to learn, as quickly as she had hoped, Mr Bennet was still amazed at the progress his youngest daughter was making. An added bonus to Lydia being too busy studying, was that she did not have time to get Kitty into mischief.

Kitty, being a shy and timid girl, was grateful that her father had prevented her mother to push her out into society when she was barely sixteen. A large part of her reason for following Lydia, was that she used her sister as a shield, since she wanted to be overlooked. Although she was pleased that Lydia was no longer allowed to liberate her ribbons or bonnets, which contributed to the harmony at Longbourn.

Now Mr Bennet had the peace and time to look forward to a happy event.

~~B~~

2   Assembly

Since Mrs Bennet was unable to attend the assembly, she insisted that her husband escort her three oldest daughters. It was not to be borne that Jane should miss out on a chance to meet and dance with Mr Bingley.

'Young men, who are both rich and single, do not come frequently to Meryton,' she explained to her apparently reluctant husband. 'Jane is already two and twenty, and is in danger of becoming a spinster. She must have every opportunity to find the right sort of husband.'

'What makes you think that Mr Bingley is the right sort of husband for Jane?'

'He is rich and single and must be in want of a wife. Why should not our daughter be the lucky lady? After all, she is the most beautiful young woman in the neighbourhood.'

She sighed. 'It is a pity that you still do not think that Lydia is ready for society. If Mr Bingley should have the bad taste not to be interested in Jane, he would perhaps prefer a girl who is just as beautiful, but more lively.'

Mr Bennet bowed to his wife's wishes about the assembly, mostly since he knew how much Lizzy loved dancing, and he would not deprive her of the opportunity to enjoy herself. That Jane and Mary benefitted was an additional incentive. Lydia and Kitty would of course stay at home.

~~B~~

They had barely arrived at the assembly, when several gentlemen approached and requested dances of Jane and Elizabeth, and their old friend John Lucas even asked Mary for a set later in the evening. To ensure Mary would not feel left out, Mr Bennet requested the first set of the youngest of the sisters.

Mr Bennet leaves his study

Soon the couples lined up for the first dances. Jane and Elizabeth had pleasant partners, who had been their friends since childhood, which added to their enjoyment of the dance. Mr Bennet was pleased to see that several gentlemen seemed to notice how well his Mary danced. Although he was her father, Mr Bennet moved with grace and energy, and his daughter was swept up in the fun he was having.

The second dance of the first set had just finished, when there was a stir at the door. It seemed that the party from Netherfield was making an appearance after all.

Charlotte Lucas had sought out Elizabeth and her family, and pointed out the various members of the party. Charlotte was the daughter of Sir William Lucas, and Elizabeth's best friend outside her family, despite the fact that Charlotte was seven years older.

'The gentleman in the front is Mr Bingley. The ladies with him are his sisters, Mrs Hurst and Miss Caroline Bingley, who is the younger lady clinging to Mr Darcy. Mr Hurst is the shorter of the gentlemen with his wife.'

'Mr Bingley appears to be a pleasant and amiable young man, judging by his ready smile. Although the ladies and Mr Darcy do not appear pleased with the company.' Elizabeth commented with a smirk, noting the almost pained expression on the exceedingly handsome man's face. She wondered if it was caused by Miss Bingley or by the inhabitants of Meryton.

'I shall attempt to discover the cause. But I had better join my father.' Charlotte excused herself, and sought out Sir William, who had invited the party from Netherfield, and was now making introductions.

~~B~~

As expected, Mr Bingley danced, first with Charlotte Lucas and later with all the Bennet sisters, while the rest of his party avoided the exercise. After several sets, Bingley thought to encourage his friend to join the fun, with the sister of his dance-partner. His attempt was a miserable failure.

'She is tolerable I suppose, but not handsome enough to tempt me. I am in no mood to give consequence to ladies who have been slighted by other men.' After a quick look at Elizabeth, Mr Fitzwilliam Darcy said angrily to his friend.

'What makes you think that you have enough consequence anywhere to insult my favourite daughter, you lout?' came the quietly angry voice of a gentleman, who was carrying two cups of punch and had come within earshot, just in time to hear the disparaging remark.

Darcy's head whipped around to face the accusing voice, and saw a tall, well-dressed gentleman who appeared almost too young to have a grown-up daughter. There was only a little grey at his temples amongst the dark hair. The man was only an inch shorter than Darcy, and in excellent shape, and he moved with the grace of a dancer, or worse... a fighter.

'Cat got your tongue?' the man enquired with a sardonic smirk when Darcy, too stunned at being taken to task, was slow in answering the first question.

'My apologies, Sir, I had not meant any insult to your daughter. I only wished for my friend to stop pestering me to dance.'

'Mayhap Mr Bingley should not have pestered you, but did you think it gentlemanlike to insult a lady in furtherance of your unsociability? And by the bye, said lady was not being slighted, she refused several offers to dance, to spend some time with her crotchety, but doting father. So, you see, you were wrong, as well as insulting, on several counts. It just proves what they say about what happens when you *assume*.'

Before Darcy could answer the charge, Mr Bingley intervened. 'Mr Bennet, I am the one who must apologise. I know that my friend dislikes to dance, unless he is well acquainted with his partner, and I should not have importuned him to do so.'

'Perhaps. But that still does not give your friend the right to insult a lady. I am of a mind to give him a good thrashing to teach him that lesson.'

'Father, instead of fighting yet again, you should rescue your daughter from dying of thirst,' the young lady, who was the bone of contention, interjected with a smile, as she approached Mr Bennet.

'My dear, forgive your old father. You well know that I am easily distracted.' He smiled fondly at his daughter and handed her one of the cups he was holding.

Darcy, who was slowly gathering his scattered wits and his manners, requested of his friend, 'Bingley, would you do me the honour to introduce me to the gentleman?'

'Mr Bennet, would you allow me to introduce my friend?'

'I suppose I should know the name of the man whom I am going to thrash,' Mr Bennet shrugged carelessly.

'Mr Bennet, this unsociable lout is Mr Fitzwilliam Darcy, of Pemberley in Derbyshire. Darcy, Mr Bennet of Longbourn is our neighbour, and has graciously offered me his assistance in becoming acquainted with my other neighbours.'

'Mr Bennet, it is an honour to meet you. Please allow me to most humbly apologise for my earlier and most ill-considered words. The verbal thrashing you have already delivered will be more than sufficient to indelibly brand your reprimand in my mind.'

'Mr Darcy, I will reserve judgment if your acquaintance is a pleasure. But I believe Reggie would be put out with me if I injured his godson.'

'You know my godfather, the Duke of Barrington?' gasped Darcy.

'I went to school with his youngest brother.' Mr Bennet again gave a negligent shrug. 'But on second thought, I remember him complaining about how arrogant and conceited you have become in recent years. Maybe he would thank me for teaching you a lesson?'

'Mr Bennet, I assure you, no further instruction will be necessary,' Darcy protested. To prove his point, he asked, 'would you do me the honour of introducing me to this lovely lady?'

Mr Bennet raised a quizzical eyebrow at his daughter, who mirrored the gesture with a smirk and said, 'I suppose it would be *tolerable* to meet your new acquaintance, Father.'

Darcy flinched and blushed, even as a grimaced at the realisation that Mr Bennet's daughter had also overheard his slight.

Mr Bennet grinned as he said, 'Lizzy, this *gentleman* is Mr Darcy, Reggie's godson. Mr Darcy, I have the honour to introduce my second and favourite daughter, Miss Elizabeth Bennet.'

Darcy bowed deeply as he addressed the lady. 'Miss Bennet, it is an honour to meet you, and I pray that you will allow me to apologise for my earlier behaviour. I will endeavour to remember to act in a more gentlemanlike manner from now on.'

'Mr Darcy, it is a pleasure to meet you, and I am tempted to accept your apology.' Miss Elizabeth dipped into a small curtsy.

'You are all that is gracious, Miss Bennet. I would be most grateful if I could also tempt you to dance with me, if you have a set still available.'

'I am sorry, Mr Darcy, but all my dances are spoken for. The current set was the only one I was able to reserve, to allow my feet to recover.'

Mr Bennet gave his daughter a look which Mr Darcy could not decipher, whereupon the lady shook her head.

'Now, if you will excuse me, Mr Darcy, I will return to my seat to rest my weary feet and enjoy my father's conversation, since my next dance-partner will keep me on my toes.'

Darcy bowed with a murmured, 'of course', while Mr Bennet led his daughter back to her seat.

When Darcy looked around for his friend, he noticed that Bingley had returned to his dance-partner, since it had looked like the gentlemen would resolve their issues without bloodshed. Because he was again on his own, Darcy found another spot against the wall, and considered all that had happened.

~~B~~

Darcy had come to Meryton because his friend leased an estate, to learn not only the management of an estate before purchasing one, but also to see if being the Master of an estate suited him. Bingley was the son of a successful tradesman, who had hoped that his children could make the step up into the landed gentry. Leasing Netherfield Park was the first step in that direction.

Because Darcy had been in charge of his own estate since his father's death, five years previously, he had the experience to advise his friend and to help him become a good manager.

Unfortunately, Darcy had arrived only earlier that day, and had been in an unsettled mood due to a family difficulty. He had not wanted to attend the assembly, but Bingley had accepted the invitation for all of his party. Remaining behind would have meant that his friend's unmarried sister, who acted as his hostess, would also remain to keep him company. For several years, Miss Caroline Bingley had been determined to become Mrs Darcy, and more importantly to her, the Mistress of Pemberley, a fate which Darcy was equally as determined to avoid.

He had had no choice but to attend. He arrived with his party, but immediately after being greeted by their host, Sir William Lucas, using Miss Bingley's momentary distraction to disengage her hand from his arm, Darcy had made a strategic retreat to the side of the hall, which he slowly circumnavigated to stay out of the clutches of Miss Bingley, and all the matchmaking mothers, which he had expected to be present. Within minutes of his arrival, he heard whispers of *five thousand a year* with respect to Bingley, and *ten thousand a year* as an estimate of his own income.

Darcy was tall, handsome, rich, as well as the nephew of the Earl of Matlock, and the godson of the Duke of Barrington. All these factors combined to make him a favourite prey of the ladies in London, who were looking for an eligible husband.

The fact that he always had to be on his guard to avoid being compromised by the most determined fortune-hunters, had made the already shy and reticent man even more withdrawn in unfamiliar company. He had not realised that his manners had become gradually more rude towards all whom he considered beneath him; but to him, fortune-hunters were not worth his notice, irrespective of their status, and Darcy did not care if they felt slighted. On the contrary, he hoped that his manner would keep everyone at bay.

Therefore, on those occasions when he could not avoid a function such as a ball, Darcy practiced that haughty mien, to deter anyone approaching him.

Bingley on the other hand, loved company and kept trying to coax his friend to join in the merriment. Tonight, with devastating results.

Darcy had paid scant attention to what he told his friend, when Bingley prompted him to dance. He had said similar things on numerous occasions, and if anyone had heard him, no one had ever taken him to task about it.

He had quite literally been shocked speechless when Mr Bennet had reprimanded him.

It had never occurred to Darcy that anyone in this backwater could have the kind of connections that Mr Bennet appeared to have. He thought that the people in this neighbourhood were only marginally above savages. It was quite inexplicable that Mr Bennet not only knew of his godfather, but was friends with the Duke.

And Darcy had unwittingly insulted Miss Elizabeth Bennet. Even worse, during their introduction, Darcy had realised that while Miss Bennet was not conventionally beautiful, she was quite pretty and had the most captivating eyes, which sparkled with intelligence and humour.

The amused look in her eyes had been the reason Darcy asked her to dance, rather than because he was trying to make amends. Now he wondered if he had missed a wonderful opportunity.

~~B~~

The new set of dances was about to start, and Darcy carefully watched Miss Elizabeth to see which gentleman would be the lucky man to partner her.

When Mr Bennet bowed to his daughter and led her to the floor, Darcy understood the look which had passed between the two. Mr Bennet had wordlessly offered to relinquish his dances to Darcy, if Miss Bennet should wish it.

Miss Elizabeth had obviously preferred to dance with her father. That fact alone was highly unusual for Darcy, since no lady had ever refused to dance with him, on the rare occasion when he made such an offer. It made him wonder about the character of Miss Elizabeth, who did not appear to be interested in his wealth, or trying to catch his attention.

Mr Bennet leaves his study

Observing the couple most carefully, Darcy could understand Miss Elizabeth's preference, and her comment that her dance-partner would keep her on her toes. As Darcy had surmised from watching him move, Mr Bennet was indeed a superb dancer, and his daughter was equally proficient.

Mr Darcy spent the rest of the evening regretting his words and his ungentlemanlike manner.

~~B~~

3   Conclusions

The Netherfield party had barely entered their carriage when Miss Bingley started her complaints.

'Charles, how could you drag us to this barbaric backwater. The locals have no style and no sense of fashion, they are almost savages.'

'I thought the ladies were lovely,' her brother protested.

'I concur,' said Mr Darcy. 'Whilst they might not be up with the latest fashions, I found most of the ladies elegant and their dresses becoming. Which is a relief after being assaulted by those eye-searing creations which ladies in town are wearing this season.'

'But those dresses the ladies wore, are years out of date and quite out of fashion,' protested Miss Bingley, trying to defend the brightly coloured fashionable gown she was wearing.

'I always felt that good taste has very little to do with fashion,' Darcy tried to sound casual and not look too pointedly at Miss Bingley's gown.

'I quite agree, Darcy. I can never understand why ladies would want to cover their dresses in feathers. And why throw away a perfectly good gown, just because the sleeves are the wrong length this season? But I must say, the gown which Miss Bennet wore, was most becoming, and she looked quite charming. Was she not an angel? I cannot remember ever seeing a lady who is her equal.' Bingley was rapturous.

'She was a sweet girl, I suppose, but nothing compared to the elegant ladies in London.' Miss Bingley was diverted from considering her wardrobe, which was exceedingly fashionable, but apparently not to Mr Darcy's taste. This was most disappointing, since she had just spent her whole year's allowance on the dresses which she had brought with her, to impress the gentleman, and encourage him to offer for her at last.

~~B~~

Mr Bennet leaves his study

Mr Bennet was happy that he had accompanied his daughters to the assembly this night. While his wife had improved over the past year, he suspected that she would have agreed with Darcy about Lizzy's looks.

Instead, he had been there to deal with the man's slight to his favourite daughter. Although Mr Bennet had discovered that he loved all his daughters, Elizabeth's intelligence and lively wit drew him to her. He delighted in their debates about a variety of esoteric subjects, and he was not about to let some arrogant puppy insult her.

Admittedly, since he had become more involved in the lives of his family, he had noticed that Mary too had the ability to learn, which he had ignored for much of her life. On the other hand, in Jane he had discovered an iron core of determination. While she tried to see the best in everyone, she could only be pushed as far as she allowed.

Now, on the way back to Longbourn, he was content to listen to the sisters discuss the evening.

'Mr Bingley seemed quite taken with you, Jane,' commented Elizabeth.

'He is a charming gentleman. But I noticed he danced with you as well, and he seemed to be enjoying himself.'

'But he only danced with me once, while you had the pleasure of his company twice.'

Jane was grateful for the dim light in the carriage to hide her blush. 'But he also danced with Mary. Did you enjoy his company?' Jane turned to their youngest sister.

'I did indeed find him amiable, but he is perhaps a little shallow for my taste,' Mary replied. She too had had a surprisingly pleasant evening. She had been asked to dance for at least half the dances, a fact she attributed to her father singling her out for the first set. 'But I noticed Elizabeth speaking to Mr Bingley's friend. I believe that apart from Sir William, you and father were the only people he spoke to, outside his own party.'

Elizabeth giggled. 'I did notice him avoiding Miss Bingley.' She turned the conversation, since she was not inclined to explain the reason for the introduction, or dwell on the man's insult.

'I think Miss Bingley and Mrs Hurst are the most fashionable ladies whom we have ever seen in Meryton.' Jane, ever kind and the peacemaker, had no wish to laugh at anyone.

'I am just pleased that none of you insist on being as fashionable as those ladies,' Mr Bennet commented dryly. Unbeknownst to him, he quite agreed with Mr Darcy's ideas about fashion. He thought the ladies would have been better served with a simpler style of clothing, rather than London's high fashion. 'I would appreciate it if you did not go into too much detail about their dresses with you mother. She has too many ideas about the proper amount of embellishments as it is.'

The sisters, whose taste in dresses was much simpler and more elegant than their mother's, laughingly agreed. 'Very well, Father, we will spare you discussions about feathers and lace.'

~~B~~

Elizabeth was relieved when she could go to bed, where she would have the needed peace and quiet to consider the events of the evening.

At the end of the first set, which she had danced with John Lucas, she had noted the arrival of the party from Netherfield. When she caught sight of the tall and exceedingly handsome gentleman, she had been struck by how uncomfortable he looked. At the time she felt sorry for him. Elizabeth had seen how Miss Bingley was gripping his arm possessively, and his subtle movements, as if he was trying to extricate himself from her clutches.

She had almost laughed out loud, when he managed to scrape off the lady during the introduction with Sir William, and he had fled to the opposite side of the room.

Soon after, her neighbours embarrassed her by discussing the purported wealth of the two gentlemen. Elizabeth was grateful that her mother had not been able to attend. She was certain that Mrs Bennet's voice would have rung out above all the others, exclaiming *ten thousand a year*.

As it was, Elizabeth wondered if it was like this wherever Mr Darcy went. If women saw his wealth as an incentive to pursue him. It was not to be wondered at that he tried to put everyone off by adopting a discouraging mien.

For some unfathomable reason, she had remained aware of him for the rest of the evening. She attributed this awareness to his undeniable good looks. Meryton did not have his equivalent.

She had been amused when he had stopped in her vicinity, while she waited for her father to fetch her a cup of punch, and heard Mr Bingley trying to persuade him to dance. Elizabeth stopped being amused when he uttered his insult.

But then her father had intervened and Mr Darcy had apologised. He had not tried to make excuses, simply admitted that his behaviour had been ungentlemanly. He even tried to make amends by asking her to dance.

When her father had wordlessly offered to concede his promised set to Mr Darcy, she had been tempted to accept, but decided that the man must be too used to having his own way, and needed to learn different.

Elizabeth had thoroughly enjoyed her dances with her father, but she remained aware that Mr Darcy was watching her intently.

Now she considered if she wanted to know him better.

He was certainly very pleasing to look at, but did his character match his handsome looks?

Yes, he had appeared exceedingly arrogant towards her neighbours. But was that his true character, or a defensive mechanism to keep sycophants at bay?

She could not make it out on such a short acquaintance. Elizabeth resolved to spend time sketching his character, but would not worry about anything that might or might not happen in the future, especially as there was a small, niggling doubt in her mind.

The insult he had voiced, echoed Mrs Bennet's comments to Elizabeth – not pretty enough to tempt a man to offer for her. Could a man as handsome as Mr Darcy overlook her less than impressive looks? Would he want to?

~~B~~

Mr Darcy too, had a restless night, thinking about everything that had happened this evening.

He had come to Meryton to help Bingley, expecting to meet nothing but country bumpkins, who would be beneath his notice.

Darcy had been raised to be proud of his heritage. His mother was the daughter of an Earl, and while the Darcys did not have a title, the family had a long and noble history. He had prided himself on his manners, and thought that he was a perfect gentleman of the first circles.

When Darcy was in Town, his family and wealth had been respected, and he was highly sought after as a match for the daughters of the best families. In his opinion he had been *too* highly sought after, since he found the machinations to get his attention exceedingly exasperating.

Ever since he entered society nearly a decade ago, he had been considered eligible, but once his father died, leaving him as Master of Pemberley, his popularity had increased exponentially. Most young men were dependent on their families for many years after they married.

For a man as young as Darcy to be master of his own fate, seemed to make him irresistible to the matchmaking mothers and their daughters.

Even though he was shy and uncomfortable in unfamiliar company, in his early years, Darcy had made an effort to meet young ladies. Back in those days, he had had the assistance of his cousin, Richard Fitzwilliam, the second son of the Earl of Matlock, to smooth over Darcy's ineptness at conversation.

During that time, Darcy discovered that the young ladies he met, had all been trained to be the perfect wives... by society's standards. Unfortunately, Darcy was not interested in fashion and gossip. And the only interest he had in the weather was in regard to how it would affect the crops at Pemberley. Any time he tried to introduce subjects that he was interested in, he received disconcerted looks, followed by uncomprehending, but fawning agreement.

By the time his cousin joined the army, Darcy was thoroughly sick of simpering females, and he adopted his scowling mien to keep them away.

After his father's death, despite his obvious reluctance, the efforts to gain his hand in marriage had increased substantially, making him withdraw ever further into his shell.

Mr Bennet leaves his study

In retrospect, Darcy realised that he must have become quite rude in recent years, to utter such an insult as he did tonight, without even thinking about it, as if it were an everyday occurrence.

While it was acceptable for a gentleman to be reserved, even standoffish, to realise how low he had sunk to display such disdain and complete disregard for the feelings of others, was mortifying to him.

Although, he most certainly had not expected to be taken to task by one of the locals for his manners, he was grateful to Mr Bennet for his reprimand. He had needed this prompt to examine his conduct in recent times, and Darcy was not at all proud of the man he had become.

A Darcy was polite to all, and he would be so again.

Perhaps, if he mended his manners, Miss Elizabeth would be prepared to dance with him, if the opportunity presented itself.

In the meantime, he hoped to become better acquainted with this most unusual young lady.

He eventually fell asleep, dreaming of a pair of sparkling eyes.

~~B~~

Before going to sleep, Mr Bennet composed part of a letter which he was going to write to his friend Reggie in the morning.

Last night I had the dubious pleasure of meeting your godson.

You were correct in saying that he has become an arrogant puppy. Would you believe he had the temerity of insulting Lizzy... to her face. He claimed that she was not handsome enough to tempt him to dance, and he would not give consequence to ladies who were slighted by other men.

No, this was not in some London ballroom where he is known. This happened right here in Meryton, where he has no consequence to speak of.

Although he changed his tune quickly enough when I threatened to thrash him, especially after I told him that you would probably approve of my actions, since no one has taught him the manners of a gentleman.

Even though he apologised, I have not yet withdrawn my threat to chastise him, and to teach him some manners. But before I do, I thought I would ask for your ideas on the subject.

~~B~~

4   Review

As was customary for the ladies of Meryton, the day after an assembly they would meet and discuss in detail all the happenings of the night before.

Lady Lucas and her daughters were the first visitors at Longbourn.

Mrs Bennet was eager to hear all the news, since her daughters never provided enough particulars of these events.

'Jane tells me that Mr Bingley singled out Charlotte for his first dance.'

'He did indeed, but I suspect it was because Sir William introduced him to Charlotte first. After that, he danced twice with Jane. The only lady to whom he paid such a compliment.'

'I overheard Mr Bingley speaking to Mr Robinson,' Charlotte added. 'When Mr Robinson asked, who Mr Bingley thought was the prettiest girl at the assembly, he replied *the eldest Miss Bennet, beyond a doubt; there cannot be two opinions on that point.*'

'Did he indeed. That was very decided. I wonder if anything might come of this.' Mrs Bennet was pleased to be provided with such encouraging intelligence.

'Mr Bingley was exceedingly amiable and gregarious. He danced every single dance. The same cannot be said about his friend, Mr Darcy. He appeared very put upon having to attend our ball, and never danced even once, despite the dearth of gentlemen. Although he did speak briefly with your husband and Eliza.'

'Lizzy, why did you not tell me? What about did you speak?'

'He was speaking to father about Uncle Reggie, who it appears is Mr Darcy's godfather, and since he missed being introduced earlier, he asked father to introduce us.'

'I heard that Mr Darcy actually asked you to dance.'

'He did, but I had to decline, since all my dances were already spoken for.'

'Since when are you so popular, Lizzy?'

'Lizzy has always been popular, Mama, but there is always such a crush at these assemblies that it is hard to see who is dancing.' Jane, always the peacemaker tried to cover the fact that her mother did not pay much attention to her second and least favourite daughter.

Mrs Bennet, remembering her husband's strictures about denigrating his favourite, replied. 'You are quite correct, dear Jane. It had quite slipped my mind. I do not know what is happening to my mind of late.'

'Do not distress yourself, my friend. I know what it is like to be in your situation.'

'Mama, since you have Lady Lucas for company, perhaps Charlotte would like to take a stroll through the garden with Lizzy and me?' suggested Jane.

The matrons found the suggestion eminently acceptable, since it gave them a chance to speak freely without having to consider what would be suitable for their daughters to hear.

~~B~~

'Now that our mothers are not listening, tell me, what did you think of Mr Bingley?' Charlotte asked Jane.

'He is just what a young man ought to be, sensible, good-humoured, lively; and I never saw such happy manners. He is so much at ease with everyone,' enthused Jane.

'He is also handsome, which a young man ought to be to make him perfect,' Elizabeth teased.

'I gather you like him a great deal?' Charlotte asked.

Jane blushed. 'I do, but I will not get my hopes up that he feels anything other than happy with pleasant company.'

'Would you like him to feel more then?' Charlotte was curious. It was unlike Jane to be so affected by a gentleman. She was very reserved and guarded her heart. Charlotte suspected it was due to her mother's determined efforts to see her married.

'I do not yet know. After all, we only danced twice. I know nothing of his character and cannot say whether we would suit each other.'

'At least he is much more pleasant than your previous suitors,' Elizabeth commented. Unbeknownst to their mother, Jane had already received two proposals, other than Mr Cooper's, both of which she had politely declined.

'Sometimes I wonder if there is any man out there whom I can love, and who will love me in return,' sighed Jane. At the age of two and twenty, although she was five years younger than Charlotte, she was starting to get concerned about her future prospects. But she was not yet ready to give up her dream of marrying for love.

'You never know, but perhaps Mr Bingley will be your knight in shining armour, who will sweep you off your feet, and carry you off to his castle. He certainly looked at you as if he would like to do just that.' Charlotte was adamant. 'But tell me, Eliza, why did you refuse to dance with Mr Darcy? I saw you speaking to him before your dances with your father, and I am convinced that Mr Bennet would have allowed you to change partners.'

Elizabeth hesitated. She had not yet told anyone about what had prompted her introduction to Mr Darcy. But, deciding that she could trust her dearest sister and her dearest friend, she related the events of the previous evening.

'How dare he,' fumed Jane. 'Insulting you like that. I shall...'

'...do nothing, dearest sister. All is well. Truly. Mr Darcy apologised and even asked me to dance. I simply felt that he is too used to getting his way, and needed to feel like the rest of us mortals. Apart from that, I have not yet seen Mr Darcy dance. Why would I trade a known, exquisite dancer for a potential disaster? I gather Mr Darcy does not often dance. It could very well be that he simply does not like dancing, or he does not dance because he is not proficient.'

'I must confess, many young ladies envy you your father, Eliza. Not many of their parents are so light on their feet.'

That comment raised appreciative chuckles from the sisters.

~~B~~

Despite getting to bed late the night before, Mr Darcy woke at the break of dawn as was his habit. Knowing that his hosts kept town-hours, he luxuriated in the comfortable bed for a few minutes, before leisurely rising and getting ready for the day.

Parker, his valet, assisted him into his riding outfit, since Darcy planned to give his stallion a good run after breakfast.

When Darcy entered the dining room, a selection of his favourite dishes awaited him on the sideboard, since Parker had alerted the staff at Netherfield to his preferences, which included rising early.

Mr Darcy was just finishing a final scone with raspberry preserve, when Mr Bingley walked bleary eyed into the room.

'Good heavens, Bingley, what is the matter with you? exclaimed Darcy in amazement.

'Nothing is wrong with me, I am simply still half asleep,' mumbled his friend as he poured himself a cup of coffee.

'I was not speaking about how you look, but the fact that you are already out of bed.'

'You told me that the best time to get things done is early in the morning. If I am to learn how to be a good manager, I suppose I must learn to deal with country hours.'

'I commend you for your conscientiousness,' Darcy complimented his friend. Seeing that Bingley had made the effort to rise early, Darcy changed his plans and decided to wait for his friend. He poured himself another cup of coffee and watched his friend devour his meal.

Darcy noticed that Bingley kept glancing at him. 'Is something the matter, Bingley? Do I have preserve on my face?'

'No, there is nothing on your face. I simply wondered if you would wish to leave?'

'As a matter of fact, I have planned to go for a ride after breakfast.'

'No, I meant back to town.'

'Why would I go back to Town? I only arrived yesterday.'

'I thought that after being taken to task by Mr Bennet you might wish to remove yourself from this area.'

Darcy closed his eyes briefly at the reminder of how badly he had behaved the previous evening. 'Bingley, Mr Bennet was completely within his rights to speak to me the way he did. I was abominably rude.' He gave his friend an apologetic smile. 'And not only to the people of Meryton, but also to you. I have become more of a grouch every year, and I apologise for taking it out on you.'

'Please Darcy, do not fret. I know that I should not have pushed you to dance, since I am fully aware how you despise the activity.'

'As it happens, I do not despise dancing, but I do object to the majority of potential dance-partners. I am afraid that I raise expectations whenever I ask a lady to dance.'

'You know, Darcy,' Bingley said around a mouthful of ham, 'if you danced more often, it would not be such a noteworthy event. Then you could enjoy yourself without raising expectations. Look at me. I dance almost every dance, but no one expects anything of me.'

'Unless, of course, you ask a lady for a second dance.'

'Well, there is that. But I only ask for a second dance, if the lady is exceptional.' Bingley decided to change the subject. 'But to get back to the question I was asking before. Are you quite content to remain and teach me to manage the estate?'

'I see no reason to leave. While Mr Bennet, rightfully, objected to my behaviour, he was discreet enough not to make it public. Remaining will also give me the opportunity to relearn my manners without the scrutiny of Town.'

'In that case, what are our plans for today?'

'I thought we could go for a ride until you are fully awake, and then continue on, to inspect the estate.'

'Thank you for giving me a chance to wake up properly before expecting me to pay attention to anything. I believe your temper is already improving.'

Darcy smiled, but refrained from saying, *my temper always improves when your sister is asleep.*

'Louisa, you must help me. We simply must get Charles out of this savage town and back to London where we belong,' Caroline Bingley demanded of her sister.

'But you know that our father wanted Charles to purchase an estate and raise our social position. But before he does so, he must learn how to manage an estate.'

'All he needs is a trustworthy steward. All the best people in town are doing so. They do not waste their time languishing in the country.'

'Some of them do that. But have you noticed who those people are?'

'Not particularly.'

'Then it has probably escaped you that the ones who rely on a steward, are either so very rich that even with mismanagement the estates produce sufficient income for them not to care. The others are selling their estates bit by bit to fund their lifestyle. Then they try to find a wife with a large dowry to squander.'

'How would you know? Charles has never mentioned anything like this to me.'

'I do occasionally speak to my husband. His parents are managing their estate themselves, to ensure that there will be something for Mr Hurst to inherit. Many of the landowners, who rely entirely on stewards, usually only leave debts to their children.'

'Mr Darcy has a steward.'

'Indeed, but his is an exceptionally large estate, and he is in frequent contact with the man, *and* he spends many months each year at Pemberley.'

'Well, once we are married, I shall insist that we shall reside in town for most of the year. In summer, of course, the London air becomes unpleasant. At that time, it will be just as well to be at Pemberley, and give house parties.'

'Caroline, how long have you known Mr Darcy?'

'It must be just on five years. I met him during my second season. Why do you ask?'

'During those five years, Mr Darcy had plenty of opportunity to court you and offer for you. He has not done so. Why do you think that is?'

'You know that he is shy. I believe he is just waiting for the right opportunity.'

'Caroline, you are deluding yourself. Mr Darcy has had years to offer for you, and he has not done so, because he never will. I know that he would never marry the daughter of a tradesman.'

'But our family is no longer in trade.'

'Our uncle still is. At present we are simply nouveau riche. Apart from that he despises your character and your supposed sense of fashion. You heard him last night. He praised the local ladies for their good taste.'

'You know perfectly well that men know nothing of fashion, but I am certain that I can teach him.' Miss Bingley, as usual, ignored everything she did not wish to hear and flounced off to the dining room, hoping to catch the gentleman at his meal.

But she was doomed to disappointment. Mr Darcy had finished his breakfast, as had her brother, and both gentlemen had gone out to inspect the estate.

After all, Mr Darcy was one landowner who took his duties seriously, and he was teaching his friend to do the same.

~~B~~

Dinner at Netherfield was a most uncomfortable affair for the gentlemen.

Miss Bingley was in full flight airing her complaints about the estate which needed redecorating, to make a fashionable home; the staff of Netherfield were clumsy and did not seem to understand her orders; the town did not have a single fashionable shop; and most of all, the population, who were country mushrooms at best.

And then there were her particular complaints about the Bennet ladies.

While Miss Bennet was pretty enough, Miss Bingley was convinced that she was a fortune-hunter, who only smiled at her brother because he was rich.

Miss Bingley had noticed that Mr Darcy had spent the whole evening at the assembly avoiding her, but had deigned to speak and even smile at Miss Elizabeth Bennet. Therefore, Miss Elizabeth came in for the lion's share of vitriol. How could a woman with such crooked features dare to show her face in public? Her hair was wild and she had no grace. Her dress was not only years out of date, but it was also exceedingly immodest, and clearly designed to attract the worst kind of attention from gentlemen.

It had apparently escaped Miss Bingley that her own bosom was considerably less covered than Miss Elizabeth's had been.

The gentlemen knew that there was no point arguing with Miss Bingley, as she never listened to an opinion which contradicted her own, even when she pretended agreement to flatter Mr Darcy. Therefore, they gritted their teeth and tried to ignore her harangue, so as not to spoil their dinner.

~~B~~

5   Visit

'I say, Darcy, I believe it would only be polite if I called at Longbourn. Mr Bennet and his family were most gracious at welcoming me to the neighbourhood,' Mr Bingley declared at breakfast, which he consumed heartily and again at an exceedingly early hour, by his standards.

Darcy had already been up for an hour and gone for a ride, to while away the time until his host would make an appearance. Bingley's eagerness to visit their neighbours explained why his friend again joined him in the dining room, when Darcy had barely started to eat.

'By all means. I quite agree that Mr Bennet is an exceptional conversationalist,' Darcy teased his friend, who coloured slightly at the obvious misinterpretation of his intent.

Bingley knew that Darcy was observant, and had noticed his interest in Miss Bennet. He decided there was no sense in prevarication. 'I am hoping to become better acquainted with Miss Bennet. She was an exceedingly pleasant dance-partner.'

'Is she to be your latest angel, whom you will abandon again a month from now?' While Darcy valued his friend for his easy going manners, he was getting concerned at the ease and frequency with which he went from one lady to the next. 'Bingley, please do not raise the expectations of yet another lady. Will you not grow up and learn that your behaviour can easily be misconstrued?'

'Am I truly so inconstant?' Bingley was upset that he could have hurt the feelings of any lady. He was even careful not to hurt the feelings of his younger sister, who certainly did not care whom she might hurt.

'Miss Price, Miss Smithers, Miss Cartwright, Miss...'

'Stop, Darcy. you have made your point.'

'Those were the ladies whom you met only this year.'

'Why am I saddled with a friend who has such a cursed good memory?'

'Because one of us needs to be sensible.' Darcy smiled to take the sting out of his words. 'But since we are on an uncomfortable subject, I need to raise another one... Your sister.'

'Has Caroline been making a pest of herself again?'

'At the assembly it took a major effort on my part to pry her hand off my arm. Her grip was so strong that I was afraid I might break her fingers.'

Bingley sighed. 'She is determined to be your wife.'

'You mean she is determined to be Mistress of Pemberley, but that will never happen.' Now it was Darcy's turn to sigh. 'I have to warn you that no matter what she tries, I will never marry her. The very idea of having to touch her...' Darcy shuddered visibly. 'If she attempts a compromise, it will be her reputation that will be ruined. Please make certain that she understands the situation.'

'I will try, but you know that she does not listen to what she does not wish to hear.'

'In that case, I will have to leave. I will not be importuned by her any longer.'

'Maybe if you were to get married... to someone else, of course... she would search further afield.'

Darcy gave his friend an offended look. 'I will not marry for your convenience,' he mock growled, although that comment called to mind a pair of eyes sparkling with humour. 'But since you will not be here to protect me, I believe I shall accompany you on your visit.'

'You want to make certain that I do not raise Miss Bennet's expectations,' accused Bingley.

'Naturally,' Darcy lied with a straight face.

~~B~~

The visitors were warmly welcomed at Longbourn by Jane, Elizabeth and Mr Bennet, who introduced Jane and Darcy, and suggested that it would be acceptable for the gentlemen to address his younger daughter as Miss Elizabeth to avoid confusion. He added cheerfully, 'you must excuse us for not welcoming you properly, but my wife is indisposed at present, and Mary is sitting with her. I am afraid you will have to make do with us.'

'I hope it is nothing serious, but if it is, I could send for my physician from London,' Mr Darcy offered.

'That is exceedingly kind of you Mr Darcy, but it is not necessary. Mrs Bennet will be back to her usual self in no time at all.'

Since her mother was absent, Jane took over the hostess duties and arranged for tea.

Bingley had chosen a seat next to Jane, in an effort to get a chance to speak to her, but once the opportunity presented itself, he became tongue-tied, remembering Darcy's admonishment.

Jane, noticing the gentleman's sudden discomfort tried to make him feel at ease. 'How do you like Netherfield Park, Mr Bingley?'

Relieved to have a neutral subject, Bingley waxed eloquent about the beauties of Hertfordshire in general, and Netherfield Park in particular.

'I am exceedingly lucky that Darcy was available to visit. He is trying to teach me how to manage an estate.'

'I am all astonishment that Mr Darcy is as knowledgeable in this matter. He seems very young to be such an expert.' Jane enquired. While Mr Bennet was aware of Darcy's background, due to his friendship with the Duke, it had never occurred to him to gossip about the man with his family.

'Unfortunately, like myself, Darcy lost his father some five years ago. Since then, he has successfully managed Pemberley, which is probably the largest estate in Derbyshire.'

'That would explain his expertise. You are indeed fortunate to have such a friend.'

Meanwhile this friend was taking the opportunity to converse with Mr Bennet and Elizabeth.

'Mr Bennet, I am grateful to you for your words the other evening. I have given the matter considerable thought, and realised that over the last few years I have developed some rather bad habits. I was raised to be better than that, but I had forgotten my teachings. Thank you for reminding me.'

'We all go astray at times, Mr Darcy, but as long as you try to improve, when you find out that you have made a mistake, people should not hold it against you. We are all imperfect.' Mr Bennet sincerely told his guest, remembering his own epiphany the previous year.

'I do not know if this makes it better or worse, but I have been behaving badly everywhere. Town, country, it makes no difference.'

Elizabeth tilted her head, giving the statement some thought. 'I believe it is both. Both better and worse. Better, because you did not single out our community for your disdain. Worse, because you let yourself become too...'

'Proud?' Darcy supplied.

'No, I would have said arrogant. A certain amount of pride is permissible for a man in your situation, but that should not make you arrogant and disdainful.'

'You make an excellent point, Miss Elizabeth.' Darcy sighed.

'Mr Darcy, at the assembly I had the impression that you did not wish to be there, and you were decidedly uncomfortable.'

The gentleman looked as if he could not decide whether to be uncomfortable at having been so transparent, or relieved that Miss Elizabeth had discerned his true character. 'You are quite correct,' he admitted.

'I suppose comments like *ten thousand a year* must get rather tedious.' Elizabeth mimicked the shrill whispers of the matrons to perfection.

Darcy bowed his head in acknowledgement of her perspicacity. 'As you say. Society appears to take it amiss that I have avoided marriage at my advanced age.'

'Of course, *it is a truth universally acknowledged, that a single man in possession of a good fortune, must be in want of a wife*. How could you possibly resist all the blandishments of the debutants,' Elizabeth teased with a smile.

'Indeed. It is most remiss of me not to fall into every trap those ladies set. They refuse to understand that I do not appreciate being prey, and expect more from a wife than just a pretty face and the ability to pour tea.'

Turning serious again, she asked, 'Mr Darcy, please forgive me for saying so, but is not marriage amongst the first circles a matter of business? I would have expected that a man in your position would weigh up the candidates based on their eligibility, rather than their personality.'

Darcy blushed. He had evaluated the available ladies based on their wealth and status, but those who met those criteria, had personalities which he found intolerable. The idea of producing an heir for Pemberley with any of them had been repugnant, but that was not a topic to discuss with a young lady. Especially with one who was anything but repugnant. Even more so, since her father was listening to their conversation.

Eventually he offered, 'my parents married for affection. I remember that, when my mother was still alive, I observed a level of comfort and understanding between them, which I would like to have for myself.'

'I wish you luck in your search, Mr Darcy. But if I might be allowed to make a suggestion...'

'Suggest away.'

'You might be more successful if you did not scowl at everyone. While you push everyone away, you will never meet anyone who will respect your wish to be left in peace... because they will respect your wish, and they will leave you in peace. As a consequence, you only meet ladies who are not put off by your demeanour, since they do not care about you, but only your wealth and position.' Elizabeth smiled as she raised a challenging eyebrow, daring him to argue with her evaluation.

Darcy stared at her for a moment as he absorbed her advice. 'Hoist with my own petard, it seems,' he groaned.

Elizabeth's smile became even more brilliant. 'Precisely.'

Darcy's chagrin was interrupted by Mr Bennet's laugh. 'I should have warned you, Mr Darcy. My daughter has a very analytical mind. She is always trying to work out why something happened the way it did.'

'I consider that an admirable attribute in anyone, Mr Bennet.'

'Do you indeed, Mr Darcy?'

'I do, although I find it a rare attribute, even amongst gentlemen. To find a lady with such an accomplishment, is a rare pleasure. Perhaps Miss Elizabeth would be kind enough to assist me.' Darcy turned his attention back to Elizabeth.

'Miss Elizabeth, do you have any other suggestions?'

'You might try conversing with ladies. Politely, of course.'

'Therein lies the difficulty. I never know what to say.' Darcy gave her a sheepish smile.

'You could always ask the lady about her own interests; you might find that you have something in common.'

'And what are your interests, Miss Elizabeth?' Darcy asked with a small smile, which could have been perceived as mischievous on anyone, who was not as serious as this gentleman.

Not wanting to stifle the gentleman's attempt at following her suggestion, Elizabeth answered with a smile. 'I enjoy books and taking long walks in the country.'

'Miss Elizabeth, we do indeed have common interests. I enjoy spending most evenings, when I am at Pemberley, ensconced in the library with a book. My sister often sits with me, and while we frequently each read a different book, at other times one of us will read aloud to the other.'

'What kinds of books do you enjoy reading, Mr Darcy?'

'I have rather eclectic tastes, although I do still enjoy reading Robinson Crusoe.'

'Why, Mr Darcy, so do I. As it happens, I only just read it again last month, when we had several days of rain, and my parents would not countenance me to go for my usual walks.'

They fell into an animated conversation about their favourite scenes from the book, while Mr Bennet sat back and listened for a time. Their lively debate soon attracted the attention of Bingley and Jane, who were also familiar with the story, and added their opinions on the book.

Mr Bennet leaves his study

The group enjoyed their conversation, and did not realise how quickly time passed, and they well and truly exceeded the time for a polite visit.

They were eventually interrupted by Mrs Hill, who announced, 'Miss Lucas is here to see you.'

At that point Darcy and Bingley realised how long they had stayed, and started to apologise.

'Nonsense, we all thoroughly enjoyed this discussion,' declared Mr Bennet, and offered, 'come back anytime, particularly if you want to discuss Plato.'

Darcy bowed and said, 'I will hold you to that, Mr Bennet. Thank you for a most enjoyable visit.'

Bingley added his thanks, before both gentlemen made their farewells.

~~B~~

On their leisurely ride back to Netherfield, Bingley commented, 'I must say, Darcy, that was probably the most enjoyable time I have ever spent in the company of ladies.'

'I too cannot remember a more pleasant visit,' Darcy agreed. He had followed Miss Elizabeth's suggestion on the spur of the moment, and discovered not only that it was an excellent way to start a conversation, but he had also found out that Miss Elizabeth was a delightful conversationalist. She also seemed to enjoy many of the things he did, although she had disagreed with him when she had a different opinion.

'You surprised me though, Darcy. Usually, it is I who draws you into a conversation, but this time it was the reverse. I have never before seen you so animated, unless it was in company of Colonel Fitzwilliam.'

'It should not be so surprising, Bingley. You know I love a good discussion about books. Although I must admit that I was surprised to find such well-read company in this area. I congratulate you on choosing such an excellent location for your country home.'

'Now I just have to try and remember what I can about Plato.' Bingley grimaced. 'You warned me to pay more attention at school. I should have listened to you.'

~~B~~

Even though neither of the gentlemen would have admitted to it, they were both reluctant to endure the company of Miss Bingley after the enjoyable time they had spent at Longbourn.

Instead of returning to Netherfield by the most direct route, Bingley suggested that he wished to inspect more of the estate.

Mr Darcy was more than happy to accompany his friend.

~~B~~

6   Invitations

'I have come to deliver an invitation to Lucas Lodge for a party two days hence,' announced Charlotte Lucas, once she had greeted her friends.

'It is very kind of your mother to extend this invitation, but, as you know, Mrs Bennet will not be able to attend,' Mr Bennet replied reluctantly.

'Surely, she would not wish to deny her daughters the opportunity to enjoy themselves. Especially since my father will deliver an invitation to the gentlemen, who just left your company,' Charlotte cajoled.

'What say you, Jane, Elizabeth? Would you like to spend time with your friend?' Mr Bennet asked his daughters, without clarifying which friend.

Jane blushed, but answered firmly. 'If Mama can spare us for the evening, I would dearly love to spend time in Charlotte's company. And of course, the rest of her family.'

'My father is also inviting several officers of the militia to even up the numbers, in case there is any dancing,' Charlotte informed her friends.

A few days previously, a troop of militia had come into the area, to spend several months training in the Meryton environs. Colonel Forster, their commander, was hoping to integrate his men into the neighbourhood, to give the soldiers some much needed diversion when not on duty.

Elizabeth's eyes lit up. 'Did you say dancing? You know that I cannot resist such a delightful pastime.'

'Do you suppose that Mary would come as well? It would be greatly appreciated if she could share in providing us with music.'

'Ever since Mrs Taylor has helped her to improve on the pianoforte, Mary delights in the opportunity to display her talent.'

'That is wonderful. But now tell me about your visitors. I quite expected Mr Bingley to call on you, but I was surprised to see him accompanied by Mr Darcy. After that gentleman's reticence at the assembly, I did not think he would be prepared to call on their neighbours.'

'Charlotte, please do not judge him too harshly. Did you not hear many of the matrons discussing his and Mr Bingley's wealth within minutes of their arrival?'

Miss Lucas coloured slightly as she remembered the evening. Her mother had been amongst the most vocal matrons. 'I suppose that both gentlemen, but Mr Darcy in particular, have been the target of matchmaking mothers for some time...' She left the question hanging.

'Indeed. Especially since their fathers died. Although, Mr Bingley, as the son of a tradesman is not quite as sought after as Mr Darcy.'

'I suppose, since you refused to dance with him, he felt it was safe to visit.'

'You probably have the right of it,' replied Elizabeth, although her father suspected that the refusal had spurred Mr Darcy's interest in his daughter. 'Now tell us about those officers.'

Charlotte was happy to comply.

~~B~~

Miss Bingley was furious. She had risen at her usual time of eleven o'clock. By rushing through her toilette, so that she could spend as much time as possible in Mr Darcy's company, she had been ready in an hour.

But when she came downstairs, she discovered that her brother and Mr Darcy had gone out. None of the staff knew, or at least admitted to knowing, where the gentlemen had gone.

Instead of being able to impress Mr Darcy with her abilities as a hostess, she spent her time alone, pacing in the drawing-room. Even her sister had deserted her, on the feeble excuse of feeling unwell.

By the time Bingley and Darcy returned in high spirits, Miss Bingley was ready to throw things. Preferably something breakable. At the head of her brother.

'Where have you been?' she hissed at Bingley. When she noticed Mr Darcy trying to suppress a smirk, she moderated her tone. 'You have been gone for hours, and I have been all anxiousness for your well-being. None of the servants knew your whereabouts.'

'Oh, Darcy and I went for a ride, and suddenly decided to stop at Longbourn to pay our respects, before continuing our inspection of the estate.'

'Longbourn? How could you expose Mr Darcy to such a common family, Charles?'

'I think they are perfectly charming.' Her brother defended his actions.

'But they have no refinement or fashion. They are such country mushrooms. Why would you waste your time with such low company as the Bennets? Do you not know that they have relatives in trade?' Miss Bingley had questioned the servants about their neighbours, and found them severely wanting.

When Bingley was looking uncomfortable, Darcy decided to intervene. Since he was getting very tired of Miss Bingley's behaviour, he deliberately used the rudeness he had learnt, and matched the... ah... lady's manner. 'Miss Bingley, for a woman who was educated in one of the finest seminaries in the country, you are remarkably ill informed.'

'I beg your pardon? In what respect is my education lacking? If that is true, and there is any part that was overlooked, I shall send a letter of complaint to the school.'

'You seem to be unaware that in our society, landed gentry are ranked higher than tradesmen.'

'Mr Darcy, I am fully aware of that fact. I do not see how that can be a lack in my education.'

'The point that was obviously not made clear to you, is that as a consequence, the daughter of a landed gentleman ranks higher than the daughter of a tradesman... irrespective of wealth.' Darcy looked at her pointedly.

Miss Bingley turned an interesting shade of puce, but she tried to claw back some advantage. 'But the daughter of a poor gentleman cannot have the advantages of a superior education, such as I received.'

'Did not your superior education include the fact that vicious gossip is only used by social climbers, who are attempting to tear down anyone above them on the social ladder? Those members of the first circles, who are secure in their position of superiority, do not have to resort to such mean and demeaning devices. Therefore, it is a clear indication to all who are aware of it, that only people who are insecure in their position indulge in attacks on their rivals.'

'But Charles is leasing Netherfield and is planning to buy an estate. That makes us landed gentry... wealthy landed gentry.'

'Once he purchases an estate, although that is not yet certain, that circumstance will be to your brother's advantage, but even then, your family will still be ranked lower than a family who have been landed gentry for generations.'

'But the Bennet chits' education...'

'Is substantially better than yours, Miss Bingley. Your brother and I spent a most delightful time in a discourse on literature with Mr Bennet, Miss Bennet and Miss Elizabeth.'

'Literature!'

'A most interesting topic of discussion. While you may consider vicious gossip to be the highest accomplishment, I most certainly do not. Especially if that gossip is untrue. Over the years, every time you denigrated someone, you lost some more of what little respect I had for you. Your latest endeavour has removed the last shred.' Darcy felt partly gratified, and partly guilty at the completely horrified expression on Miss Bingley's countenance.

It was not his habit of lashing out at someone in this fashion, and deliberately setting out to destroy them. But this... female had attempted to destroy Miss Elizabeth with her vitriol. Miss Elizabeth was so much superior to his friend's sister that he felt that Miss Bingley was not even fit to be in the same room with her.

Darcy was at the limit of his tolerance with this woman. He turned to his friend. 'My apologies, Bingley, I am afraid that I let my temper get the better of me, and for having been the cause of such disruption in your household. I will remove myself immediately.'

'You cannot leave.' This cry came from both siblings simultaneously.

'You did not say anything that was not true, and it was long overdue for Caroline to clearly hear it,' added Bingley.

'It is good of you to try and see my abysmal behaviour in such a good light. Nevertheless, I must leave. I would not want to risk our friendship. Remember our conversation this morning?'

'You are afraid that Caroline will be stupid enough to ruin her reputation,' Bingley said, understanding his friend's reasoning.

'Charles, how can you say such a thing? Have you forgotten that I am still here?' Miss Bingley was outraged.

'I wish I could forget, Caroline, but you never shut up long enough to grant me that luxury.' He turned to his sister. 'But you have stretched my patience to breaking point. I will write to our Aunt Mathilda in Scarborough, and ask her to take you in hand.'

'You cannot do that, Charles. What do you expect me to do in Scarborough?'

'Whatever Aunt Mathilda tells you to do.'

'I do not want to go to Scarborough.'

'You should have thought of that before you acted like the vicious harridan that you are. I had hoped that you would take the genteel ladies of this area as an example, and mend your behaviour. But your performance in the last few days has made me realise that this was a forlorn hope.'

'How can you call the women in this neighbourhood genteel ladies. They are nought but country mushrooms.'

'They are polite, courteous and kind. Behaviours you have refused to learn. I am tired of having you embarrass me in polite society, therefore to Scarborough you will go.'

'But Mr Darcy...'

'You are exceedingly fortunate that Darcy is a gentleman, and will not give you an opportunity to try a compromise.'

Mention of his friend's name made Bingley realise that Darcy had taken the opportunity of their distraction to quit the room. He decided to go and find out his friend's plans.

~~B~~

As expected, Bingley found his friend in his rooms, where Darcy's valet had already started packing his master's belongings.

'Darcy, you cannot leave now. You will never make it back to Town before dark.'

'I am not going to Town, but to the White Hart. Parker assures me that they have excellent rooms and good food, albeit a limited menu.'

Darcy looked rather shamefaced when he admitted, 'I truly am sorry that I caused you distress, but I could not stomach listening to your sister denigrating Miss Elizabeth yet again.'

'You rather like the lady... Miss Elizabeth I mean,' Bingley said with a delighted smile. 'It is good to see that you are human after all. I believe she and her sister are two of the finest and most interesting ladies whom I have ever had the pleasure to meet. Personally, I think Miss Bennet is perfect, but I can appreciate that her sister would appeal to you.'

'That is why I am not leaving the area. I hope to get to know her better.'

'You should know that I am planning to write to Aunt Mathilda in Scarborough to take Caroline off my hands. Once she is gone, I hope you will return here.'

'If you are certain that you can tolerate such a cantankerous grouch as myself...'

'That is what friends are for. To like you even when you are not at your best.'

~~B~~

Darcy found that his valet had been correct. The rooms at the White Hart were quite comfortable. To give his valet a chance to unpack without him being underfoot, he went downstairs to a private dining room, and arranged for an early dinner to be served to him.

The food, although simple, also lived up to its reputation. Darcy enjoyed his meal, accompanied by a glass of good wine, which he ate in peace. An enjoyment which was enhanced by the opportunity to read a book without interruptions.

He had just finished his leisurely meal, when the landlord announced a visitor.

'Mr Darcy, I hope I am not interrupting your meal,' Sir William Lucas exclaimed when he saw the dishes on the table.

'Not at all. I have just finished and was simply enjoying a leisurely glass of wine. Would you care to join me?' Darcy offered politely, remembering his resolve to improve his manners.

'Thank you, Sir, but I must decline. My wife expects me home for dinner shortly. I have only stopped by, because Mr Bingley informed me that you have removed yourself from Netherfield temporarily. I had gone there to deliver an invitation to you and Mr Bingley, as well as his family to join us for a party at Lucas Lodge two days hence.' Sir William explained in a rush.

'Thank you, Sir William, you are exceedingly kind. Not just for the invitation, which I will gladly accept, but for going to the trouble to find me here.'

'It was my pleasure. I was sorry to hear that you found the accommodation at Netherfield not to your liking. I did not think that there was anything lacking in such an excellent house.'

'It was no lack on the part of the house.' Darcy hesitated to explain why he preferred to stay at an inn, rather than with his good friend.

Sir William gave him a sly look. 'Perhaps the problem was not any lack, but that there was too much of an expectation...' Watching Darcy's reaction, he suggested, 'considering how proprietarily she acted towards you when you arrived at the assembly, some people wondered...'

'Certainly not. I prefer the company of ladies.' Darcy blurted out. As soon as the words were out of his mouth, he coloured. What was it about this area that his mouth kept running away with him? 'Please, Sir, forget what I just said. Lately I find myself speaking before thinking. I do not know what has caused that tendency...'

Sir William laughed. 'Do not trouble yourself, Mr Darcy. I find it refreshing that I am not the only one, who at times says the wrong thing. But I think it is capital that I can look forward to your company at our little get together. I shall leave you to enjoy your wine.'

~~B~~

The following afternoon, a servant from Longbourn delivered a package to Mr Bingley.

The gentleman was torn between conflicting emotions when he unwrapped the parcel and discovered a copy of Plato's *Republic*.

He could not decide whether to laugh or groan.

~~B~~

Mr Bennet leaves his study

7 Lucas Lodge

Mr Bingley arrived at Lucas Lodge at the appointed time, which was a novel experience for him, since his sister Caroline usually made him late for any function, in an attempt to make a grand entrance.

Since the lady was unaware that Darcy remained in Meryton, and Mr Bingley chose not to enlighten her that his friend would also attend the party, she had opted to stay behind. Surprisingly, Mr Hurst had insisted that he and his wife would accompany Mr Bingley, who suspected that Mr Hurst wished to escape Caroline as much as everyone else did.

Darcy, punctual as ever, had arrived only a minute before Bingley and his party and was still being greeted by their host. 'Mr Darcy, it seems you are being reunited with your friends.'

Mr Hurst laughed when he saw Darcy. 'It appears that Bingley forgot to mention that you did not return to London.'

'Oh dear. I am afraid that my memory is getting worse. It must be all the effort I am expending to read Plato's Republic.'

'I do not remember seeing that book in your library.'

'You remember correctly. I believe that Mr Bennet thought I needed to refresh my memory.

Sir William was still effusively greeting his guests, when they were distracted by another set of arrivals.

Mr Bennet and his three oldest daughters entered the house, to be greeted warmly.

As soon as they had greeted her host, Bingley was ready to escort Miss Bennet wherever she wished to go. In short order, Mr Bennet and Mary had lost the other half of their party, since Darcy too absconded with another sister.

'Miss Elizabeth, I had hoped that you were to be part of this party,' Darcy greeted the lady.

'And here I had thought that Sir William's gregarious nature was the motivation for your attendance,' Elizabeth teased Darcy, to cover the fluttering in her stomach.

'While Sir William is a most congenial gentleman, he is not pretty enough to tempt me to dance with him. I had hoped that if there was dancing tonight, you would honour me with a dance or two.'

'You wish to dance, Mr Darcy? I am all astonishment. I had thought that you abhor the activity.'

'I only dislike dancing with ladies with whom I am not well acquainted. With a charming and intelligent lady like yourself, it would be pure joy,' Darcy replied extravagantly in the same teasing tone.

'As I told you before, Mr Darcy, until you speak to a lady, you cannot become well acquainted. I distinctly remember giving you advice on the subject.'

'Indeed you did. And I believe I followed your advice to the letter. I learnt that you like books and long walks.'

'But one simply cannot discuss books while dancing.'

'In that case, what other interests do you have, Miss Elizabeth? I would be happy to discuss any subject, and if I am not familiar with it, I will be pleased to listen to you explaining it.'

'But what if I should wish to discuss fashion and lace?'

'I would by no means wish to suspend any pleasure of yours,' he teased with a bland smile, although the twinkling of his eyes belied the statement.

'You are fortunate that I have little interest in that subject, although I am tempted to discern the length to which you would go.' Elizabeth gave him a brilliant smile, which made Darcy catch his breath.

'To the ends of the earth,' he murmured, giving her such an intense look that made Elizabeth go weak at the knees.

To cover her confusion, she replied, 'in that case, I can do nought but grant your request, Mr Darcy. But now I must go and greet Charlotte Lucas.'

He offered his arm. 'Might I escort you to your friend?'

Elizabeth was in two minds. Since the gentleman was making her feel exceedingly flustered, she wanted to escape, but at the same time she found it impossible to resist taking his arm. She reached out and gently took hold of the arm, and felt a shock go through her at the touch. She thought, *this must be what it feels like to be struck by lightning.*

'Thank you, Sir. Since you have the advantage of me in height, I would be obliged if you could find my friend.'

Darcy too was affected by her touch. How different it was when Elizabeth delicately held onto his arm, compared to the vicelike grip which Miss Bingley habitually used. It felt right having Miss Elizabeth on his arm, like she belonged there. He was pleased that he could not immediately find Miss Lucas.

~~B~~

Jane was ecstatic when Mr Bingley immediately sought her out. While several gentlemen had shown an interest in her before, none of them had been as personable as Mr Bingley. That he was handsome and moderately wealthy was a bonus.

She felt that she could easily love such an amiable man, if he was truly interested in her, but for the moment she was determined to guard her heart. After all, he might just see her as a pleasant means to spend some time, while he was in the country.

But still, her heart did beat a little faster as he approached.

'Miss Bennet, you look more lovely every time I see you,' Mr Bingley greeted her gallantly.

'It is very kind of you to say so, Mr Bingley, but I must confess that I find it disappointing when everyone I meet focuses on superficial beauty, rather than qualities which I believe are more important.'

'May I enquire as to which qualities you hold most dear?'

'Kindness and consideration. These are qualities that anyone can achieve.' She looked towards Elizabeth. 'While I appreciate my sister's lively wit, I cannot hope to match it.'

'Bingley followed her gaze. 'I do not suppose that there are many who can match Miss Elizabeth in that department... except perhaps Darcy.'

'Our father is at least her equal, but then he was the one who educated Lizzy.'

'That would explain why Darcy likes to argue with her.'

'Mr Bingley, that is called debating. Lizzy would never be so improper as to *argue* with a gentleman,' Jane exclaimed in mock offense.

Bingley noticed the suspicious twinkle in her eyes, and bowed. 'I shall bow to your greater expertise in such matter... but to me it still sounds like an argument.'

That last mutter elicited a peal of laughter from the lady. Bingley was delighted to have caused such a reaction in the exceedingly reserved lady.

~~B~~

Mary had joined Elizabeth and Charlotte, where they enjoyed catching up on the latest news. Since Mrs Taylor had started to teach her, and her father paid attention to her, Mary had come out of her shell.

They were quietly discussing the latest arrivals, when Sir William presented Colonel Forster to them.

Colonel Forster bowed to the ladies. 'Please forgive me if we have interrupted your conversation. In my defence I will admit that it has been some time since I had the chance to spend an evening in the company of genteel ladies. Which is why I requested this introduction.'

'Think nothing of it, Colonel. In a small town like Meryton, we are always pleased to make new acquaintances,' Charlotte reassured him.

'Indeed, Colonel. Considering the dearth of gentlemen in this area, we welcome new additions. I hope that you and your officers are fond of dancing,' Elizabeth added with a mischievous smile.

'I cannot guarantee the abilities of myself and my officers on the dancefloor, but I can assure you of our enthusiasm, if it affords us the opportunity to spend time with such lovely ladies.'

'Surely you have opportunities to mingle with the inhabitants wherever you are stationed.' Mary suggested shyly. 'After all, you and your men are tasked to protect us.'

'Alas, many people are weary of soldiers stationed in their towns. While I will admit that not all officers are gentlemen by birth, they are no worse than other men. I am grateful to Sir William that he has welcomed us so generously.'

'If you wish to make your neighbours more favourably inclined towards you, perhaps you should consider giving a ball.'

'If you think that would help, I will certainly take your suggestion under advisement.'

They chatted pleasantly a while longer, before Charlotte pressed Elizabeth into performing on the pianoforte.

~~B~~

Since the advent of Mrs Taylor to Longbourn, even Elizabeth had been persuaded to practice more on the instrument. As a result, her technique had improved and she did not have to fudge her fingering as much, but she still played with as much feeling as before.

Darcy listened spellbound. While his sister, who practised several hours each day, might be better technically at playing the instrument, he had never heard a better performance. When Elizabeth added her voice to the second song, he was completely bewitched.

When he came out of his trance at the end of the performance, Darcy noticed Sir William standing next to him smiling indulgently. 'Yes, Miss Eliza has that effect on everyone, when she graces us with a performance.'

Sir William watched with interest when Mary took over Elizabeth's position at the pianoforte. 'Capital. I believe we will have some dance music now.' When Mary started to play, he waved at Elizabeth to join them. 'My dear Miss Eliza, why are you not dancing? Mr Darcy, you must allow me to recommend this young lady to you as a very desirable partner. You cannot refuse to dance, I am sure when so much beauty is before you.'

Darcy was grateful of the opportunity. 'I would be honoured if you would grant me this dance, Miss Elizabeth.'

'You are truly tempted to dance, Mr Darcy?'

'Greatly tempted indeed.' He held out his hand to her.

'How could I possibly refuse such an offer?' Elizabeth smiled impishly, although hesitating to take his proffered hand, wondering if touching him would affect her as much as it had earlier.

'Quite easily as I recall,' Darcy returned her smile in the same fashion, waiting expectantly, hoping that this time she would not refuse.

The smile swayed Elizabeth. 'In that case I shall be contrary and accept,' she said, forgetting that earlier, she had already agreed to dance with him. She took Darcy's hand, the warmth of which seemed to spread all the way through her body.

To distract herself from the sensation, she asked, 'I forgot to enquire, Mr Darcy. Since you usually avoid the activity, can you actually dance?'

'You are about to find out, Miss Elizabeth,' he replied as he led her to the floor.

Elizabeth was amazed and delighted when she discovered that Mr Darcy was a superb dancer. He moved with grace and fluidity.

'Mr Darcy, for a man who does not practice the skill, you are a most proficient dancer,' she commented at the end of the first song.

The comment caused Darcy to chuckle. 'Forgive me, Miss Elizabeth. You reminded me of my Aunt Catherine, who always claims she would have been a great proficient, if she had but learnt, whichever skill is being discussed.'

'Does she have any skill at which she is proficient in actuality?'

'She is most eloquent in giving advice or making demands.' At this reminder, Darcy's mien darkened.

'Demands, Mr Darcy?' asked Elizabeth, concerned at the change in mood.

Darcy noticed the look of concern, and hastened to reassure Elizabeth. 'My aunt wishes me to marry her daughter, despite the fact that neither Anne nor I are in the least interested in such an arrangement. Her insistence would be funny, if it were not also irritating, because she refuses to listen.'

'I am afraid that we all have relations who are less than perfect, Mr Darcy. Perhaps you should adopt my philosophy. *Think only of the past as its remembrance gives you pleasure.*'

Darcy smiled. 'That is excellent advice, Miss Elizabeth. I shall attempt to follow it faithfully.'

Now that their pleasant mood was restored, Darcy asked Elizabeth for a second dance, to which she happily agreed. They became so absorbed in the activity and their company that they did not notice the attention directed at them.

~~B~~

Charlotte too had a dance-partner, since Colonel Forster immediately prevailed on her to grant him a dance or two.

A few songs later, Elizabeth took over playing from Mary, to give her a chance to dance as well. When Mary demurred, suggesting that no one would want to dance with her, Mr Darcy and Colonel Forster immediately disabused her of that notion.

After one dance with each of the gentlemen, Mary did not lack for partners.

~~B~~

Mr Bennet watched Elizabeth and Darcy most carefully, and concluded that a bond was forming between the couple.

He was pleased to note that Darcy seemed to make an effort to overcome the first bad impression he had made at the assembly.

While he was afraid the he might soon lose his favourite daughter, he was reassured by the letter he had received earlier in the day from his old friend.

The Duke had told him that while Darcy's manners in recent years had become atrocious, he was essentially a decent and honourable man. As long as he had someone to knock some sense into him, physically or metaphorically, there were no objections to the young man. One phrase had stood out at the end of the missive. *He is even a decent chess player, although he has not yet managed to beat me.*

Although Mr Bennet would never admit it, Darcy dancing with Mary, did in fact give her consequence, even though it was only by the fact that he had not danced previously, and tonight only with Elizabeth.

But despite all the improvements, Mr Bennet was determined to keep a close eye on the situation.

~~B~~

8   Aunt Mathilda

In the afternoon, a plain but excellent carriage rolled to a stop outside Netherfield, from which alighted a middle-aged woman. She was tall and slim, with strong features and a no-nonsense attitude.

Bingley was coming down the stairs, just as a footman opened the door to the visitor. He exclaimed with a huge smile, 'Aunt Mathilda. What a delightful surprise to see you. What brings you to Netherfield?'

'Your atrocious handwriting, Charles. I received your letter, but the only words I could decipher were Caroline, problem and help. Instead of wasting time trying to clarify the problem via correspondence, which I assumed would be a true waste of time, I decided to come and find out directly.'

'I am exceedingly pleased to see you, Aunt. Would you care for some tea while Mrs Nicholls arranges for a room to be readied?'

'Tea would be delightful, as long as you have something stronger to go with it.'

'I do have a rather nice brandy...'

'Excellent. We shall partake of both in your study, where you can tell me what problems Caroline is causing now.'

Mrs Nicholls, who had arrived to see if she was needed due to the new arrival, after being introduced to Miss Mathilda Bingley, assured Bingley that she would see to both tasks immediately. Miss Bingley thanked her graciously, and instructed her nephew to lead the way.

When Mrs Nicholls turned away to carry out the requests, her eyes were brimming with mirth. While she had not deliberately eavesdropped, she heard enough to suspect that Miss Caroline Bingley's days as Mistress of Netherfield were numbered.

She hoped that the new arrival would stay indefinitely.

~~B~~

'Congratulations, Charles. This looks like an excellent house. You have chosen well.' Miss Bingley looked around in approval. 'I hope Caroline has not had a chance to ruin it too badly with her atrocious taste.'

'We have been in residence for only two weeks. She has been making plans to refurbish the public rooms and her chambers.'

'Do you like the house as it is?'

'I do, but I know nothing about fashionable décor.'

'Never mind fashionable. A home should be comfortable, and preferably elegant. Those criteria are not always fashionable, but only an idiot would want to live in a house that is uncomfortable, just to be fashionable.'

Bingley smiled in relief. He had never been able to stand up to Caroline when she had her mind set on something. Aunt Mathilda on the other hand, was stronger than Caroline.

Some people thought his aunt to be irascible and difficult. While it was true that she could intimidate anyone with her forceful personality, she was a kind and considerate woman. She simply had no patience with meanspirited people like his sister.

'Caroline...'

'...is a fool.'

There was a knock on the door, and Mrs Nicholls entered, followed by a footman, carrying a tray which he placed on a small table by the window.

Miss Bingley smiled at the man, and thanked him, before turning to the housekeeper. 'Mrs Nicholls, have my nieces given instructions about redecorating the house?'

'They have given instructions, but there has not yet been time to carry them out.'

'Do you believe those instructions will improve the house?'

When Mrs Nicholls hesitated to answer, Bingley told her, 'please answer my Aunt honestly... without fear of retribution.'

The housekeeper smiled. 'Miss Caroline's instructions will make the house more fashionable, but I do not believe they will improve the comfort of the accommodation.

'In that case, ignore her instructions, and refer any complaints to me.'

'It will be my pleasure, Miss Bingley.'

'I bet it will,' murmured the lady under her breath, before adding in a louder voice, 'thank you, Mrs Nicholls, that will be all for the moment.'

Once the housekeeper had left, and Miss Bingley had poured tea, while her nephew took care of the brandy, she instructed, 'now, tell me what has been going on.'

~~B~~

Mr Bingley spent the next hour telling his aunt all that had happened since his arrival at Netherfield.

Miss Bingley listened attentively, interjecting the occasional question to clarify her understanding.

'I can see why you wrote to me. Caroline is getting completely out of hand. Although I loved my brother dearly, I have to say that he never could control your sisters. And neither can you.'

Bingley looked shamefaced when he agreed. 'I simply do not know how to get her to listen to me. When she gets an idea in her head, nothing can change her mind.'

'Well, I am here now, and I have decades more experience in being stubborn than Caroline.' Aunt Mathilda smiled. 'I have wanted a change of scenery for a while. If you are agreeable, I believe I should stay for a time.'

Mr Bingley looked hopeful and apprehensive in equal measure. 'I would appreciate it if you could get Caroline to mend her ways, but I fear that the process is not going to be quiet.'

'I can do that on one condition... you do not countermand any of my decisions or orders.' When Bingley looked hesitant, she added, 'as regards to your sister, and the running of this household. I will not interfere in anything else, although I do wish to meet the Bennet ladies.'

59

Bingley brightened considerably. 'I will support you in all things concerning Caroline. As regards to the household, will you act as my hostess, Aunt Mathilda?'

'Yes, I think it would be best if I took on the Mistress' duties while I am here.' She patted her nephew's hand with a smile. 'Cheer up, Charles. We will soon have everything running smoothly.'

The lady rose and added. 'Now that I know the situation, I believe I will go to my room and freshen up. Then I will have a conference with Mrs Nicholls. Please inform her of the new arrangement.'

~~B~~

Miss Mathilda Bingley could understand her family's problems, since a similar situation had occurred about twenty years earlier.

Miss Mathilda had been the youngest of the Bingley siblings by more than a decade. As a result, she had been indulged in her interests. Unlike her niece, she had not wished to climb the social ladder, but was interested in the family's business.

She had an excellent head for numbers, and understood how external events shaped the market. She was quick to spot business opportunities. The first time she made a suggestion to her father, he was amused that his young daughter had the audacity to assume that she could better predict where a profit was to be made than he, who had decades of experience.

Mr John Bingley decided to allow Mathilda her opportunity to fail, to teach her to listen to him, and not interfere in his business, but stick to keeping the books. He provided her with the funds to attempt her foray into the business world, and then sat back, waiting to have the last laugh.

To Mr Bingley's amazement and chagrin, Mathilda's scheme was a spectacular success. Being a pragmatic man, interested in maximising his profits, he started to involve his young daughter in his business affairs. He allowed Mathilda to keep the profits she had made on her first venture, and use them for further projects.

By the time Mathilda Bingley came out in society, she had made a small fortune, but then she met with disappointment.

Mr Bennet leaves his study

There were quite a number of gentlemen who were willing to marry her, but each of them was only interested in the money she could bring to the marriage. Not only that, they expected her to hand over her hard-earned profits to them, and then refrain from any further involvement in business. After all she would be too busy to keep house and look after their children.

None of the men she met was prepared to let her make her own decisions, and be useful outside what they perceived to be her proper sphere.

In the course of a year, Mathilda rejected five proposals of marriage. When her family tried to coerce her into accepting, she dug her heels in, explaining that she would rather be a business woman than a wife.

There were many acrimonious discussions, but unlike her niece, Mathilda Bingley did not scream, shout or throw crockery. She simply refused to bow to social and her family's pressure. Since she had enough money to support herself, threats of expulsion from the family proved ineffective.

In the end, her father accepted that she would not be a traditional female. Instead, he made her a partner in his business, and ensured that her brother could not oust her from her position.

Although Charles Bingley Senior was not comfortable with his sister's interest, he recognised that with her help he could amass a great enough fortune, so that he or his children could eventually purchase an estate and leave trade. He had just reached the point where he could make his dream a reality, when an accident claimed his life.

Now Charles Bingley Junior was trying to fulfil his father's dream.

Unfortunately, in the process of preparing to becoming a gentleman, Mr Bingley Senior had sent his daughters to a renowned school for ladies, where Caroline had learnt not only her accomplishments, but had become determined to rise above her station.

While Mathilda Bingley understood Caroline's desire not to be confined to her traditional sphere, she abhorred her niece's methods. It was time to make some changes.

~~B~~

When Miss Mathilda Bingley had freshened up and changed into a clean dress, she asked a maid to send Miss Caroline Bingley to her.

While she waited in the sitting room of the suite Mrs Nicholls had prepared for her, Miss Bingley amused herself with writing a list.

It was several minutes before Caroline entered her aunt's presence. 'Good afternoon, Aunt Mathilda. While it is good to see you, I would have liked to know of your visit, so that I could have a room prepared for you.'

'Good afternoon, Caroline. It was a spur of the moment decision to travel hither, but do not concern yourself, Mrs Nicholls has done well by me, arranging for these *rooms*. Quite a nice house Charles has here.'

'I suppose it will be liveable once I am done redecorating. Although I hope that we will not be in this backwater long enough.'

'Oh, I expect it will be unnecessary to redecorate. I do believe that the house is quite charming from what I have seen so far. I will be quite comfortable here for the next few months.'

'Aunt, while I am pleased to host you, I am afraid that I will be unable to entertain you, and I doubt we will be here much beyond the end of the month. If we are here even that long. You know what Charles is like. He becomes enthusiastic about something, and then just as quickly loses interest'

'I do not expect you to entertain me, dear niece. I can do that quite well for myself. But since I arrived, I have received reports of your deplorable behaviour, and have offered my assistance to your brother to curb your manners.'

'That is just like Charles, hiding behind your skirts,' sneered Caroline.

'Your brother is a gentle soul, who has done his best to look after you. But since you refuse to listen to him, I have come to take you in hand.'

'There is nothing you can do to me,' blustered her niece.

'Charles is the head of this household. If you do not like living by his rules, how would you like to live on your own? I can suggest to Charles to release your dowry to you to set you up in your own establishment.' Aunt Mathilda paused with a malicious smile. 'Naturally that would only be after he deducts your overspending of the last five years from your dowry. If he follows my advice, I suspect you will be left with next to nothing.'

'He would never do such a thing.'

'Charles has agreed to let me handle the situation, no matter how I choose to act.'

Aunt Mathilda had given the matter some thought. She hoped that Caroline had enough native intelligence to learn to behave with decorum, if not with kindness. She banked on Caroline's selfish nature to bring her into line.

'Here is what is going to happen. I will remain at Netherfield and act as Charles' hostess. You will remain as his dependant. If you behave with propriety and decorum, all will be well. If you do not, for each infraction of the rules, ten pounds will be deducted from your allowance.'

'I have already spent my allowance for the year.'

'In that case you had better not squander your allowance for the next year on bad behaviour.' Miss Mathilda Bingley said carelessly. 'You might as well sit down and make yourself comfortable. It will take a while for me to acquaint you with the new rules.'

Caroline glared at her aunt, but sat down, and crossed her arms in a belligerent attitude.

Aunt Mathilda suppressed a smile. Part of her plan was already working.

'Here are the new rules. I will give you a copy in writing, but I thought I give you an opportunity to ask questions.'

She looked at the list she had prepared. 'One. You will be polite to the staff.'

'Why should I? Those people are of no consequence and are only here to serve me.'

'Because good manners demand that a lady is polite to all. See, it was a good idea to give you a chance to ask questions.'

Aunt Mathilda smiled. 'Two. You will be polite and courteous to your family and to your neighbours. At all times.'

'Three. You will not denigrate anybody to anybody, including your sister.'

'Four. You will dress with restraint. Not one of those eye-sores you are currently wearing.'

'That is the latest fashion.'

'The colour is completely unbecoming to your complexion. The combination hurts my eyes. If you cannot dress tastefully, you can stay in your room.'

'Five. You will only be allowed to purchase things for which you can pay in cash. Charles is closing all your accounts, and will not cover any debts which you run up. Any debts will be deducted from your dowry.'

'But I just spent my whole year's allowance on my current wardrobe. I cannot afford to buy the kind of clothes you insist that I should wear.'

Miss Bingley considered the conundrum. 'Very well, as a Christmas present to you, I will gift you with two dresses... to be made locally,' she emphasised when Caroline brightened, assuming that her niece would want to go to London, to order the dresses from a fashionable modiste. She was confirmed in her suspicion when Caroline's face fell.

'But the locals have no style and no sense of fashion,' Caroline whined.

'Then you will fit in perfectly.'

Caroline Bingley rose and stormed out of the room in a huff, slamming the door behind her.

'That will be ten pounds,' her aunt called after her. 'And we have not finished the list. We did not even get to Mr Darcy yet.

~~B~~

9   Meetings

Miss Bingley was tired from her journey, and as a consequence slept late, by her standards. She arrived in the dining room, expecting to find it deserted. Instead, her nephew was already seated at the table with a plate of food, a cup of coffee and a book.

She was uncertain which fact shocked her the most. That Charles was awake at this hour, or that he was reading a book. Both were unheard of in her experience.

'Good morning, Charles. Are you well?'

Bingley looked up with a sigh. 'Good morning, Aunt Mathilda. I am well enough. Why do you ask?'

'It is eight in the morning and you are reading a book.'

'Miss Bennet's father sent me a copy of Plato's Republic. He suggested that he would like to hear my views on the subject.' Bingley admitted with a sheepish grin. 'I believe he realised that I did not pay much attention to the subject when I was at school.'

Once she was reassured that her nephew was not ill, Miss Bingley fixed herself a plate and joined Bingley at the table.

'The young lady must be special indeed, if you are prepared to read Greek philosophy.'

'At least Mr Bennet was considerate enough to send the English translation, not the original.'

'Even so. I am all astonishment at your diligence. Although I must admit that I am pleased that at last something, or at least some *one*, is important enough to you to shake off your laziness.'

'Laziness, Aunt?'

'Indeed. I had almost despaired, because you could never rouse yourself to do anything other than go to parties. You never even made your own decisions. You usually let someone else decide what you should or should not do. First it was your father, then Caroline, and in recent years you relied on Mr Darcy. At least he has a sense of responsibility and does not squander your inheritance.'

Miss Bingley did not mention that even reading the book was at someone else's behest. At least that was an endeavour which required significant effort for her nephew.

Bingley sighed. 'I know, Aunt. What do you think I should do?'

Aunt Mathilda gave him a pointed look. 'I would suggest that you grow up.'

Bingley flushed. 'I meant about Caroline.'

'Caroline is not your problem any more. That is one issue of which I will take care. I will also ensure that meals are on time and that you have clean linen. Everything else is up to you. What would you like to do?'

'I would like to become better acquainted with Miss Bennet, and I would like to learn more about managing an estate. Then, if it turns out that Miss Bennet and I are suited, I would like to marry the lady and purchase an estate. If Miss Bennet and I are not suited, or if she should not feel inclined, I will try to find a lady whom I can love, and who will love me in return.'

'Do you have any specific requirements about the lady whom you wish to marry, apart from mutual love?'

'I want her to be kind and sensible. Not given to histrionics and not a slave to fashion.'

'In other words, a lady as unlike Caroline as possible.'

Bingley gave a slightly shamefaced chuckle. 'You are quite correct, Aunt Mathilda.'

'You did not mention beauty.'

'Miss Bennet is indeed exceedingly beautiful, which I admit caught my attention initially, but she is so much more.'

'Well said, Charles. After breakfast, you and I shall go and visit this paragon.'

Mr Bennet leaves his study

~~B~~

As soon as the time for visiting arrived, Mr Bingley escorted his aunt to Longbourn, where they were greeted by Mrs Bennet and her three oldest daughters. Mr Bennet was absent, as he was spending time in the school-room with his youngest daughters, teaching them about literature, a lesson which Kitty enjoyed and Lydia tolerated.

'Mr Bingley, it is such a delight to see you,' Mrs Bennet greeted the gentleman effusively, while eyeing the lady who accompanied him.

'Mrs Bennet, it is a pleasure to see you looking so well. I would like to introduce my aunt, Miss Mathilda Bingley. Aunt Mathilda, these ladies are Mrs Bennet and her daughters, Miss Jane Bennet, Miss Elizabeth and Miss Mary.'

The ladies greeted each other, before Mrs Bennet asked, 'your aunt you say, Mr Bingley? Does that mean that you plan to remain in Hertfordshire longer?'

Miss Bingley answered instead. 'I am planning to stay here with my nephew and his sisters for some months to come. Charles was most inconsiderate to burden my niece with the duties of being the Mistress of an estate. My being here will allow Caroline to learn her proper role.'

While Mrs Bennet accepted the statement at face-value Elizabeth suppressed a smirk and exchanged glances with Mary, who also understood her sister's mirth.

Jane innocently approved the change. 'Miss Bingley, you are all consideration. I quite understand that Miss Caroline would find the task daunting, since she was not raised on an estate.'

Elizabeth valiantly suppressed the laughter which threatened to escape her, but Miss Bingley noticed her reaction, and responded with a polite smile, but twinkling eyes. 'Indeed, Miss Bennet. My niece did not have the advantages of your genteel upbringing.'

Mrs Bennet was concerned when Mr Bingley nearly convulsed in a coughing fit. 'Allow me to order some tea to soothe your cough, Mr Bingley. I believe the air is exceptionally dry today.'

Mr Bingley gratefully accepted and chose a chair next to Jane, Miss Bingley sat next to Mrs Bennet, while Elizabeth and Mary kept each other company.

Tea was served and Miss Bingley tasted the lemon tarts, which were a favourite of hers. 'These tarts are excellent, Mrs Bennet. Please compliment your cook on these delicate creations. I can see that your reputation as a hostess is well deserved.'

Mrs Bennet preened at the compliment. 'We are lucky indeed to have Mrs Barker. She is such a treasure.'

'Since I am new come to the area, perhaps you could advise where to get the best supplies?

Mrs Bennet was pleased to display her expertise, thinking that Miss Bingley had much to teach her niece, and soon the two ladies chatted pleasantly.

Mr Bingley thought it a perfect opportunity to suggest a walk with Miss Bennet, to which Mrs Bennet added her support, and suggested that Elizabeth and Mary could also use some fresh air. 'I shall be very well in the company of Miss Bingley.'

The younger people did not need further encouragement, and once they had donned their outerwear, Mr Bingley offered his arm to Jane and the group stepped out of the house.

~~B~~

They had not gone far when they encountered Mr Darcy. 'Good morning, ladies, Bingley. I see that we had the same excellent idea. I too hoped to invite Miss Elizabeth to join me for a walk.'

Mr Darcy turned to Elizabeth. 'Miss Elizabeth, you declared your love of walking, and I had hoped that you would be agreeable to show me the sights of the area.'

'Mr Darcy, while I would be pleased to show off the delights of my home county, today we cannot go far, since Miss Bingley is keeping our mother company, and we cannot impose on the lady for too long.'

Darcy, who was unaware of the presence of Miss Mathilda Bingley, thanked his lucky stars to have encountered the group in the garden. Bingley, who knew which Miss Bingley was at Longbourn, was too distracted by Jane to point out the true identity of the lady.

Darcy bowed and offered his arms to Elizabeth and Mary. 'In that case, I would be happy if you allowed me to escort you on your stroll.'

The sisters accepted the offer, and placed their hands on Darcy's arms. While Mary was completely unaffected, Elizabeth again felt that warmth and a sensation of rightness as they walked off, following Bingley and Jane.

Darcy was trying to find a topic of conversation, when inspiration struck. 'Miss Elizabeth, since there is no opportunity to see the sights of Meryton and its environs today, will you tell me about your favourite places?'

'I often walk to Oakham Mount to watch the sunrise. It is such a beautiful and peaceful spot, and on a clear day, the view is quite astonishing.'

'Perhaps I will have the opportunity to see it for myself, one of these days.'

'It is an excellent location for a picnic. Perhaps I should arrange for a few friends to make up a party.'

'That is a splendid idea. At Pemberley Georgiana and I have picnics near the lake whenever we have the opportunity.'

Darcy and Elizabeth started trading stories about their homes, while Mary was content to walk along and listen to their easy conversation.

When they had almost returned to the house, Darcy made his polite farewells, since he did not wish another potential confrontation with Bingley's sister. He was already out of earshot, when Mr Bingley remembered. 'Drat, I meant to introduce Darcy to my aunt.'

~~B~~

On the way back to Netherfield, Bingley asked his aunt, 'how did you like the Bennets?'

'Mrs Bennet is a little excitable and not overly refined, but she has a good heart. I can understand her apprehension under the circumstances. The entail must weigh heavily on her mind.'

Bingley fidgeted before he nervously asked, 'Caroline suggested that Miss Bennet was only interested in me for my wealth and that her mother would force her to accept, should I make an offer, irrespective of her own feelings.'

'That is what Caroline would do. Since she is mercenary, she believes everyone else is too. While I am certain that Mrs Bennet would be happier if her daughters married men, who can provide well for them, I did not think her mercenary.'

'Thank you, Aunt. You greatly relieve my mind.'

'I can see why you like Miss Bennet. She is a charming young lady.'

'I think she is an angel,' Bingley declared with a besotted smile.

'Yes, I can see that.'

~~B~~

Miss Caroline woke up shortly before her relatives returned to Netherfield. Today the lateness of the hour had to do with the fact that she had spent a miserable night.

After dinner, Aunt Mathilda had cornered her in her chambers, with a servant in tow. 'This is Lucy,' the lady introduced the woman. 'She will be your new maid. She is proficient in everything you will need from now on.'

Aunt Mathilda turned to Marie, Caroline's French maid. 'You may serve me if you choose, or you may choose to take employment elsewhere. I shall of course provide you with an excellent reference. What say you?'

Caroline was furious and mortified when Marie beamed, and immediately replaced the hairbrush on the vanity. 'It would be an honour to serve you, Miss Bingley.'

'Excellent. Wait for me in my chambers,' Miss Mathilda Bingley dismissed her new maid. She then turned to Lucy. 'See what you can do with my niece's wardrobe.'

When they were alone, Miss Bingley handed a sheet of paper to Miss Caroline. 'Here are the rules I wish you to follow. I have decided to be generous and adjusted the penalties. The first infraction of a rule will cost you one pound, and every subsequent infraction will increase by one pound. In other words, the second will be two pounds, the third three, and so forth.'

'You cannot do that,' gasped Caroline in horror.

'I can and I will. In addition, any damage you cause will be paid for by you. So, I suggest that you keep your temper under control.' She paused for a moment, considering. 'I believe that you are an intelligent young woman. You can learn, if you so choose. But I must also warn you about Mr Darcy. He has made it abundantly clear that he has no interest in you. Should you try to compromise him, I will conclude that you are mentally unstable, and have you committed to Bedlam.'

Aunt Mathilda handed Caroline the paper. 'You had better memorise this list. Good night, Caroline.'

Caroline studied the list in consternation. When she read rule number eleven, her temper got the better of her and she reflexively picked up the nearest ornament and, without thinking, threw it against the wall.

As soon as she heard the crash, she realised that rule eleven had a triple penalty.

11 - Staff will no longer be available to clean up your messes. If you break anything, apart from the cost of the object being deducted from your allowance, you will have to clean up the mess yourself, or live with the danger of cutting your feet.

That was on top of the fine for breaking the rule.

The list fluttered unheeded to the floor, as Caroline dropped her face into her hands and started to weep.

During her sleepless night, she concluded that she was in for a most unpleasant time.

~~B~~

10 Conversations

The following morning, Darcy walked along the road leading to Longbourn, when he encountered Elizabeth.

'Good morning, Miss Elizabeth. Fancy meeting you here. Is it not rather early to be up and about?' Darcy pretended innocence about the encounter.

'Good morning, Mr Darcy. It is indeed quite a coincidence to see you. Are you just out for a morning constitutional, or are you bound for a specific destination?'

'Your description of Oakham Mount at sunrise was so vivid that I felt I simply had to see it for myself.'

'If you are bound for Oakham Mount, you are heading in the wrong direction.'

'Indeed, Miss Elizabeth? In that case, could I prevail upon you to show me the way?'

Elizabeth gave him a dubious look, taking in the slightly apprehensive, but eager look. 'You are of course aware that what you are asking is most improper, Mr Darcy?'

'What could be improper about a good Samaritan helping a stranger find his way. We are in full view on a public road and have nothing to hide...'

'Very well, Mr Darcy. I shall be a good Samaritan. But if anyone questions your presence, it will be your duty to explain the innocence of our encounter.' Elizabeth laughed quietly as she saw the pleasure of her acceptance on Mr Darcy's countenance.

'Indeed, I shall declare to one and all that you are completely blameless of any impropriety. Shall we?' Darcy offered his arm.

'I hope that you can keep up, Mr Darcy.' Elizabeth smiled in challenge and gently grasped his arm, absently noting the usual warmth suffusing her, before setting off for Oakham Mount at a brisk pace.

Due to the speed at which they walked, they saved their breath and walked in comfortable silence until they reach their destination.

Darcy and Elizabeth arrived just in time to see the sun starting to rise from behind the horizon. They stood silently as the panorama turned from misty grey to a landscape bathed in gold.

Darcy broke the silence. 'While I love the cragginess of Derbyshire, the soft rolling hills of Hertfordshire have a beauty of their own as well.'

'A great compliment indeed, Mr Darcy. My Aunt and Uncle Gardiner are planning a trip to the Lakes District next summer, and have invited me to accompany them. Pray tell, what are the beauties of Derbyshire?'

Given such an attentive audience, Darcy waxed lyrical about his home county.

It was nearly an hour before Elizabeth recalled herself to the time.

'Mr Darcy, for a man as reticent as you purport to be, you are quite eloquent on subjects about which you are passionate. Derbyshire is obviously just such a passion.'

When Darcy looked into the smiling eyes of his companion, he realised that he had acquired a new passion. But now was not yet the time to speak of it.

Instead, he offered his arm to Elizabeth with a smile. 'Perhaps on the return to Longbourn, you would enlighten me about the subjects which rouse your passion?'

Elizabeth carefully schooled her features to suppress the blush which threatened, and spoke in loving terms about her family.

~~B~~

Mr Bingley maintained his new habit of rising early. He had discovered that the morning hours were conducive to study and quiet conversation, before his attention was diverted by the demands of the estate.

He was in the process of fixing a plate for himself, when his aunt joined him in the dining room.

After exchanging greetings, Aunt Mathilda, noticing the absence of the book, asked, 'do you not find the company of Plato congenial anymore?'

'It gives me a headache trying to understand it. I think I need Darcy or Mr Bennet to explain it to me.' He sighed. 'I am afraid that I was not made for scholastic endeavours.'

'Perhaps if Mr Darcy moved back to Netherfield, he could assist you.'

'Do you think it is safe for him to be under the same roof as Caroline? I would not wish for her to embarrass herself again. As much as I dislike her behaviour, she is still my sister, and I feel responsible for her.'

'I had a long conversation with her last night, and she now understands that there will be consequences for each of her actions. These consequences can be positive or negative.'

'How did you manage to do that? I have never known her to listen to anyone.'

'Did you ever set financial penalties for misbehaviour? Or even insist on anything?'

'No-o-o.'

'I gave her a list of expectations, or rules, if you prefer, and told her that for each infraction, I would deduct a fine from her allowance.'

'How can you know if she breaks any of those rules?'

'I will provide you with the list I gave to Caroline. I expect you to tell me if she ignores those rules. And of course, the staff will tell me, when neither of us is around. Especially, her new maid.'

Bingley took a sip of coffee, while he digested the information. 'I just wish I understood how Caroline turned out the way she did.'

'I suspect your father did Caroline no favours by sending her to the best seminary, where she would have been looked down upon, and possibly sneered at, by the titled students. A less distinguished school would have been better for her.'

'Father wanted the best for her and Louisa. The reports on the school were excellent.'

'Remember how you used to be set upon by your fellow students, until Darcy became your friend and protector?'

'I remember, but I would not have thought that gently bred young ladies would know how to throw a punch.'

'Those ladies tend to use words, rather than fists, which hurts even more.'

'But that still does not explain her manners.'

'That was how she was treated by the daughters of the first circles, and despite how much it upset her, she thought that was how ladies behaved towards inferiors. Since she is trying to appear superior, she uses those same manners to all except people with a title, or wealthy relations of those titled families. She did not understand that is how snobbish young women treat upstarts.'

Bingley thought about it for a few minutes, while he polished off the last of the ham. 'I can understand how she would have wanted a superior position, but it does not excuse her behaviour towards the people of Meryton.'

'No, it does not. She will now learn to modify her behaviour, or face the consequences.'

'No more new dresses for a year.' Bingley suddenly grinned. 'I will be able to afford that new horse I was hoping to buy.'

~~B~~

Since the advent of Aunt Mathilda, another change had taken place. Two more inhabitants of Netherfield were awake early.

Mr Hurst enjoyed the peace which reigned in the household for the first time since his marriage. As a consequence, he did not feel the need to numb his sensibilities with alcohol, like he had been doing more and more over the previous year.

This was a situation for which his wife was extremely grateful, since she was feeling decidedly unwell again on waking up.

This morning, as she cast up her accounts, her husband was awake and sober enough to notice. 'My dear Louisa, are you unwell? Did something disagree with you? It could not have been the wine, since you barely touched it last night.'

When her stomach was empty, and she could speak again, Mr Hurst handed her a damp cloth with which to wipe her face and hands. 'Shall I send for a doctor?' he asked with a worried expression.

Louisa Hurst smiled weakly, 'I think the services of a midwife would be more useful.'

'A midwife?' Mr Hurst exclaimed in startlement, before he broke into a delighted smile. 'Does that mean... are you... what I mean to say...'

Despite his incoherence, Mrs Hurst understood. 'Yes, Cedric, I believe we are to be parents,' she replied with a smile, relieved that her husband appeared to be pleased by her news.

She was certain of it, when Mr Hurst pulled her into a tight embrace. 'That is wonderful news, Louisa. I am so very happy that we are to have a child.'

'I am as well. I am also grateful that Aunt Mathilda is here.'

'You mean because she is keeping Caroline quiet?'

'That is part of the reason. But I was afraid that Caroline would convince Charles to return to London, and I find the country air much more agreeable, rather than the stink of Town.'

'In that case, I will encourage Charles to remain at Netherfield. I would not wish you to be discommoded in any way.' He gently brushed some stray hairs of his wife's face. 'Thank you, Louisa.'

Louisa was touched by her husband's concern. It had been a long time since they had been in such accord. She smiled up at him, and snuggled into his embrace.

~~B~~

Miss Caroline Bingley railed at the unfairness of it all.

First, her brother dragged her off to the wilds of Hertfordshire to this mouldy hulk of a house. The only saving grace was that Mr Darcy was to be a guest for several weeks, perhaps months, giving her an opportunity to prove to him that she was an excellent hostess, worthy to be Mistress of Pemberley.

But no. Within days, both her brother and Mr Darcy had become enamoured with a pair of sisters, country mushrooms with no sense of fashion and no sophistication.

While Jane was a pretty and sweet girl, she had no worthwhile connections to further Caroline's ambitions. Not only was she the daughter of a minor country gentleman, she had an uncle who was a solicitor, and another who was in trade and lived near Cheapside in London. Caroline dreaded to think what the other uncle was like, the one referred to by Eliza as Uncle Reggie.

No. Miss Jane Bennet would simply not do to have as a sister, and the idea that Mr Darcy could see any value in Miss Eliza was abhorrent.

Thinking about Eliza made Caroline's blood boil. After all the years she had spent being agreeable to Mr Darcy, in the hope that he would offer for her, the man had taken one look at the impertinent girl, and become smitten. Eliza had even refused to dance with Mr Darcy, preferring to do so with her father.

She had attempted to point out the failings of the Bennet sisters to her brother and Mr Darcy, in the hope to make them see reason.

But instead of agreeing with her, Mr Darcy set out to humiliate her by questioning her education, her manners and her sense of fashion. And to top it off, he categorically stated that he had no respect for her, and implied that he would not have her even if she compromised him.

All her attempts at separating the couples failed. And for once her brother stood firm. Instead of listening to her, and returning to London, he had written to their Aunt Mathilda, who had invited herself to Netherfield, and proceeded to make life a living hell for Caroline.

Now, if she did not want to be locked in her room like an unruly child, she had to follow Aunt Mathilda's rules.

Admittedly, the dress Aunt Mathilda had purchased for her. was much more comfortable than her London creations, but it was so very plain. The day after her arrival, the lady had taken her niece to the dressmaker, who had one day-dress ready to assemble, which was delivered within a day, giving Caroline something to wear, while a second dress was made up.

But being polite to everyone did not come easily to her, who had always been indulged, and who was used to throwing a fit, to bully her family into doing things the way she wanted them done.

She would have screamed in frustration, but did not want to reduce her allowance yet again.

~~B~~

Now she sat at her dressing table while Lucy, her new maid, brushed her hair and looked at the simple white dress with the pale blue ribbons hanging on the wardrobe, waiting for her to wear. 'I wish the dress looked just a little brighter,' she sighed.

'You could always change the ribbons on it, Miss,' Lucy suggested.

'What do you mean, change the ribbons?'

'You know, take off the ribbons that are on it, and replace them with different ones.'

'One can do that?' Caroline asked in astonishment.

Having grown up with wealth, Caroline had never learnt that a dress could easily be made to look different, by changing the ribbons which decorated the gown. When she wanted a gown that looked different, she had another dress made.

'Of course. Young ladies do that all the time. They save heaps of money that way, and that's why white dresses are so popular. They are easiest to change. Most any colour will go with it.'

'Can you do that for me?'

'Sorry, Miss. The Mistress said I was not to do that. But you can do it easily enough yourself.'

Caroline was about to throw a temper tantrum for being denied yet again, when she remembered the rules Aunt Mathilda had set for her, and the penalty if she broke the rule. Her allowance for the next quarter had been whittled in half in the first two days.

Since then, she had started to learn to curb her temper and her tongue. It was still difficult, since she never had to restrain herself other than during her time at the seminary.

Caroline considered the problem. 'Are you allowed to show me how to do it?'

'Yes, Miss, as long as you do most of the work.'

'Now the question is, where do I get some ribbons?'

'You could always use some from your ugly old dresses,' Lucy suggested innocently.

Caroline's temper flared briefly. 'Ugly?' she demanded.

'Well, the colour is horrible and looks really bad on you. I can't understand why you would have bought them.'

'They are fashionable.'

'Maybe so, but they still look horrible on you.'

'Everyone told me they looked wonderful.'

'Miss, if they said otherwise, would you have believed them, or would you have slapped them for telling you the truth?'

'Have I made a complete fool of myself?'

'That's not for me to say, Miss.'

'I think that you just answered my question.'

~~B~~

'You and Mr Darcy seem to get along rather well,' Jane commented to Elizabeth.

The sisters were sitting in the parlour, each engaged with needlework. They were alone, since their mother was resting, Mr Bennet was working in his library, Mary was practicing on the pianoforte, and their youngest sisters were at their lessons.

'Now that he knows that we are not fortune-hunters, he has relaxed and he is practicing the lessons I suggested to him.'

'I see. He is simply practicing the art of conversation with a lady, when he speaks to you.' Jane gave her sister a disbelieving look.

'Naturally. What else could it be?'

'I think that he has come to admire you greatly.'

'Nonsense, Jane, he is merely being polite and friendly. And while I admit that I enjoy his company, I do not believe that we can ever be anything other than friends.'

'Dear sister, I believe that you are denying what is obvious to everyone else. Mr Darcy always seeks you out when we are in company, and when you are engaged speaking to someone else, he is never far away and he watches you. I think it will not be long before he declares himself.'

'Jane, I am convinced that you must be mistaken. You know perfectly well that gentlemen in Mr Darcy's position are expected to make a match with a lady of wealth and position... and beauty,' Elizabeth added the last words in a whisper.

Mrs Bennet's comments on Elizabeth's beauty, or more precisely the lack thereof, as well as her mother's criticism of her interests and impertinence, had left an impression on Lizzy. While she might pretend unconcern, in unguarded moments, she admitted to herself that Mrs Bennet had a point. No man of consequence would be interested in someone such as she.

The more she came to know Mr Darcy, the more Elizabeth had come to admire the man. Yes, he was serious and somewhat inept in conversing with relative strangers, but he was intelligent and considerate, and in the right situation displayed a sly sense of humour. He was also the most handsome man of her acquaintance.

But such a man could never be interested in Miss Elizabeth Bennet, a lady of no consequence, no beauty and impertinent manners. As much as it hurt her, Elizabeth determined to guard her heart.

'Elizabeth, please do not take Mama's words to heart. Everyone else acknowledges that you are one of the loveliest ladies in the neighbourhood.'

'But Mr Darcy also said...'

'He also apologised for his ill-considered words. And even if you did not tempt him at the time, it is obvious to me that now nothing could be further from the truth.'

Mr Bennet leaves his study

Elizabeth shrugged, pretending unconcern. 'We shall see who has the right of it.'

Jane smiled mischievously. 'Very well, Lizzy, I shall attempt to live up to your opinion of me, being the most saintly of sisters, and not say *I told you so*.'

~~B~~

11 Changes

Darcy had just stepped out of the White hart, when he encountered Mr Bingley with his aunt and sister. Bingley performed the introduction.

Miss Mathilda Bingley was happy to make the acquaintance. 'Mr Darcy, it is good to meet you at last. Charles has spoken much about you over the years.'

'Miss Bingley, I am honoured to meet you. I too have heard much about you from your nephew. Will you be staying long?'

'Since I am now acting as hostess for Charles, I will stay as long as he needs me.' She smiled at Darcy in what he felt was a conspiratorial fashion.

'Indeed?'

'Yes, Mr Darcy. I am afraid that Charles was quite thoughtless putting such a burden on his sister's shoulders. I know that Caroline is grateful to be relieved of the responsibility. Is that not so, Caroline?'

'Yes, Aunt Mathilda,' her niece replied with a forced smile and through gritted teeth.

'Now, if you would excuse us, Mr Darcy, Caroline and I have an appointment with the dressmaker.'

'Of course, Miss Bingley. It has been a pleasure to make your acquaintance. Good day to you.' Darcy bowed politely, and then just as politely turned to Caroline. '*Goodbye*, Miss Caroline.'

The ladies returned his greeting and went towards the dressmaker for the fitting of Caroline's second dress, while Bingley remained behind with his friend.

'So, that was the redoubtable Aunt Mathilda.'

Bingley grinned at him. 'She certainly is all of that and more. She has taken charge of Caroline, and will not put up with any nonsense. It is now safe for you to return to Netherfield.'

Darcy looked doubtful.

'It is quite safe, Darcy. Caroline knows that if she tries to compromise you, Aunt Mathilda will assume that she is mentally unstable, and have her committed to Bedlam.'

'Would your aunt truly inflict such a fate on your sister?' Darcy was horrified.

'I suspect that she would find a place where Caroline would be treated with kindness, rather than Bedlam. But my sister believes that Aunt Mathilda is serious in her threat.'

'Remind me never to cross your aunt.' Darcy chuckled. 'Aunt Catherine blusters a lot, but compared to your aunt, she is a novice at getting her way.'

Bingley sighed. 'I have long suspected that Caroline is as stubborn as she is, because it runs in the family... Amongst the women.'

Darcy looked in the direction the ladies had departed and said thoughtfully, 'you could be right.'

'Well, now that you know it is safe, what say you? Will you return to Netherfield?'

'I would not want to inconvenience your aunt.'

'She knows that I planned to ask you to return, if she can control Caroline. It will be good practice for my sister to mind her manners.'

'Very well. I must admit to curiosity to see your aunt in her element.'

~~B~~

After instructing Parker to move his belongings back to Netherfield, Darcy, accompanied by Bingley started his interrupted walk to Longbourn.

They walked in companionable silence for a while.

'Do you think that Miss Bennet likes me?' Bingley asked suddenly.

'I have never known a lady who did not like you, although I cannot say how much Miss Bennet does.'

Bingley sighed. 'You are no help. I like her... quite a lot actually. I know we have only known each other, what is it, two weeks, but I feel like I have known her forever.'

'Three.'

'What do you mean by three?'

'Tomorrow it will be three weeks.'

Bingley laughed feebly. 'Of course, that makes all the difference.'

'Naturally. It means that you have known Miss Bennet fifty percent longer than you had thought.'

'Is three weeks long enough for you to know what you want?'

Darcy just smiled as he thought, *three days were enough for me*.

~~B~~

Jane and Elizabeth were upstairs keeping their mother company, when the lady spied the visitors walking down the driveway.

'Jane, Mr Bingley has come again to call on you. You must go down immediately. It would not do to waste such an excellent opportunity.'

When Jane agreed with perhaps more enthusiasm than was proper, Mrs Bennet turned to her second daughter. 'Lizzy, you must go with your sister, to distract Mr Darcy, so that Jane has an opportunity to converse with Mr Bingley privately.'

While Mrs Bennet had improved her relationship with her second daughter over the past year, old habits die hard, and it did not occur to her that a man of Mr Darcy's consequence could be interested in Lizzy.

Elizabeth, torn between amusement and exasperation for her mother's attitude, was happy to follow her instructions, although Jane could not help but defend her sister. 'Mama, you must know that Mr Darcy has been calling on Elizabeth. I believe that Mr Bingley might only accompany his friend, to keep *me* busy, while Mr Darcy speaks with Elizabeth.'

Mr Bennet leaves his study

'Mr Darcy is calling on Lizzy? Well, I never. Why is that man wasting his time with Lizzy, when he could be courting you?'

Elizabeth blushed at her mother's callous remark, but was rescued by an unexpected voice. 'Because Mr Darcy has enough sense to be interested in a woman with a lively mind,' Mr Bennet admonished his wife. 'Forgive me, Jane. I do not mean to say that you are not intelligent...'

'Do not fret yourself, Papa. I know that Lizzy and I are equally accomplished, simply in different ways, and her ways appeal to Mr Darcy. And while I think Mr Darcy is an estimable gentleman, I am thrilled that he appears interested in my sister and not myself.'

'Well, that gentleman and Mr Bingley are about to arrive at our door. I suggest the two of you go downstairs and chaperone each other. I will keep Mrs Bennet company until Mary has finished her lessons.'

The sisters hurried to follow his suggestion, while Mr Bennet took a chair near his wife. 'Fanny, I know this is a difficult time for you, but please remember your resolution to not criticise Lizzy.'

'I am sorry, Thomas. I have been getting exceedingly vexed lately...'

'I know, my dear, but it will not be long now.'

~~B~~

Their timing was perfect. The sisters and the gentlemen arrived in the foyer at the same time.

After the greetings, Darcy suggested a walk in the garden, to give him an opportunity to speak to Elizabeth privately. Bingley too, hoped to have a conversation with Miss Bennet without an audience. Both men were delighted when the ladies agreed to the plan.

Once they were in the garden, it did not take long for the two couples to drift apart. Although, ironically, now that he had the opportunity to speak to Elizabeth, Darcy suddenly found himself nervous and tongue-tied again.

~~B~~

For the last few days, Darcy had done a lot of soul-searching. When he had considered taking a wife, he had always assumed she would come from the first circles.

But he had never met a lady, with whom he had such a connection as he felt with Miss Elizabeth. Perhaps the lady was right, and he had driven away the best candidates, because he thought they were all the same... only interested in him for his wealth and position.

While that might or might not be true, the point was moot since he met Miss Elizabeth. Whenever they had met, she had treated him as a man, not a fount of jewels and carriages. Darcy admired her intelligence and wit, as well as the kindness with which she had pointed out his flaws, and made suggestions to help him improve.

Lately he could not help but picture her at Pemberley. How she would deal with the staff and the tenants. How gracious she would be to guests. How encouraging she would be to Georgiana. How delightful it would be to spend time with her... everywhere.

Darcy had come to realise that he could not imagine any other lady at his side. But would Elizabeth want to be with him? While she had been kind and friendly, she had not once given him any improper encouragement. Although... her blushes when she took his arm... did they indicate that she was just as affected as himself?

'Miss Elizabeth, would a courtship be agreeable to you?' Darcy suddenly blurted out, apropos of nothing.

'That would depend, Mr Darcy.'

'On what?' Darcy asked nervously, fearing some impossible condition.

'It would depend on who would want to court me.' Humour and impertinence sparkled in Elizabeth's challenging gaze, although they disguised a sudden nervousness. While she accepted that Mr Darcy seemed to enjoy her company and conversation, she had doubted that he would seriously consider the daughter of a minor gentleman as a suitable wife.

'Minx!' Darcy exclaimed with a laugh; his nervousness forgotten. 'Unless you have been keeping secrets, you know perfectly well that I propose myself as the candidate.'

'You should have said so in the first place, Mr Darcy.' Elizabeth continued to cover up her own excitement with impertinence.

'Now that I have said so, what is your answer?'

'I would be delighted to enter into a courtship with you, Mr Darcy. It will give you a chance to learn whether my impertinence is a quirk you can live with.' She did not say, that she was still concerned that his initial words might have some truth in it, and he would find a more beautiful lady to tempt him.

'It will also give *you* a chance to discover whether you can put up with someone as dour and reticent as myself.'

'Oh, I do not know. I must say that you do have your moments. I think all you need is a little encouragement, and you can be rather agreeable company.'

'In that case, I believe that I should speak to Mr Bennet.'

Elizabeth listened for the sound of the pianoforte, to determine if Mary was still at her practice. Since all was quiet, she suggested, 'I believe that my father is available now.'

~~B~~

'Mr Bennet, I would like your permission to court Miss Elizabeth.'

'While I appreciate the fact that you are short and to the point, I still have not forgotten that you insulted the very same daughter you now wish to court.'

Darcy sighed and sported a pained expression. While he abhorred to display his private affair, he felt that he must explain himself to Mr Bennet.

'Mr Bennet, the only explanation I have to offer for my abysmal behaviour that night was that I had a very bad experience with a fortune-hunter this last summer, and it had put me into a foul mood.'

When he hesitated, Mr Bennet looked at him searchingly, and prompted, 'go on.'

'My father was the godfather to our steward's son, who is the same age as I am. My father liked George Wickham and paid for his education. As a boy, George was a prankster, who usually managed to use his undeniable charm to put the blame on everyone else. During our time at school, his character deteriorated even further and he spent most of his time drinking, gambling and... ah... womanising. When I tried to warn my father about Wickham's dissolute character, he brushed it off as wild oats. Soon after we finished school, my father became ill and died.'

Darcy used those bland words to cover up the pain he still felt at the loss of his father, but Mr Bennet was more perceptive than he had given him credit for.

'I am sorry for your loss. I know what it is like to lose your father at an early age, and having to take on the responsibility of an estate, even though Longbourn is only a fraction of the size of Pemberley.'

'Thank you, Sir. But to get back to my story. My father wanted to see Wickham provided for, and bequeathed him one thousand pounds, and recommended him for the living at Kympton, when it became available. Since Vicar Johnson was an old man, it could not be too many years, and I dreaded having Wickham in charge of the parish.'

'Fortunately, Wickham decided that the church was not for him, and he resigned his claim in lieu of three thousand pounds, which I happily paid him. But when the vicar died a few years later, Wickham approached me, demanding the living since he had squandered all his money. Naturally, I refused him and he threatened to get even.'

'Last summer, my sister Georgiana, who is but fifteen years of age, needed to spend time at the seaside for her health. I had engaged a new companion for her, who came highly recommended. I later learnt that those letters had been forged, and that she was an accomplice of Wickham, who used her to get close to my sister while they were at Ramsgate. He courted Georgiana until she thought herself in love with the scoundrel and agreed to elope with him.'

'Did she...'

'No. As it happened, I finished the business, which had kept me in London, early, and arrived at Ramsgate two days before they planned to leave. On my arrival, my sister immediately confessed her plans, which she had hoped would reconcile me with my boyhood friend. When I confronted Wickham and told him that I would not release Georgiana's dowry until her majority, he became abusive, and made it quite clear to my sister that he had only been interested in the thirty-thousand pounds, and his revenge on me.'

'Your poor sister must have been devastated. Is she recovering?'

Darcy was grateful that Mr Bennet was more concerned with the wellbeing of Georgiana than with propriety. 'She is even more withdrawn now than she had been before this incident. I still blame myself for my sister's heartache, because I should have checked those references more thoroughly...'

'I only came to Netherfield because Georgiana urged me to come. I wanted to stay with her and try to help her. Instead, I was at that blasted assembly, trying to dodge Miss Bingley and all the other fortune-hunters.' He shrugged helplessly. 'What can I say. I am ashamed that I took my anger of Wickham out on Bingley and your daughter.'

Mr Bennet listened carefully to this tale of woe. He thought about how he would feel if someone targeted Lydia, or worse Kitty with such a scheme. He would want to take drastic actions.

'Have you done anything about that scoundrel?'

'I could not. I cannot risk him ruining Georgiana's reputation. You know how cruel society is, even the slightest hint of a scandal can ruin a young woman's life.'

Mr Bennet disagreed with Darcy on that subject, but that was an argument for another day.

'About your request... I will reserve judgement for the moment, until you have played and won a game of chess.' Mr Bennet smirked. He was curious to see how Darcy would deal with this challenge.

'A game of chess?' Darcy smiled. He loved the game and excelled at it. 'I would be happy to play against you, Mr Bennet.'

'No, Mr Darcy. That would be too easy. You will play against... Lizzy.'

'Miss Elizabeth plays chess?' Darcy was pleased to hear this. He was looking forward to help her improve her game on long winter evenings at Pemberley.

'Indeed.' Mr Bennet thought it would be interesting to see how Darcy reacted, losing against his daughter. It would give him a good indication of the man's character.

Half an hour later, Darcy was shocked to be check-mated.

He looked from the board at the smiling woman opposite him with a chagrined expression. 'I had hoped to help you improve your game, but it appears that you will be teaching me.'

He shook his head at his folly of thinking himself oh so superior.

Darcy glanced at Mr Bennet, who had watched the game with a satisfied grin. 'You expected this would happen, did you not?'

'Indeed.'

'I was a fool.'

'Indeed.'

'Even though I have lost, I would still like your permission to court Miss Elizabeth.'

'What say you, Lizzy? Should I give permission?'

'I wish you would. He is almost as good a chess player as Uncle Reggie, and he does not sulk when I win.'

'High praise indeed. Very well, you have my permission.'

Darcy had the grace to blush when he realised just how much of a fool he had been.

~~B~~

That evening, Mr Bennet reminded his family. 'Do you remember, we will receive a visitor tomorrow.'

Mrs Bennet sighed dramatically. 'Yes, I remember. That odious cousin of yours, who is to inherit Longbourn.'

'Who *may* inherit Longbourn,' Mr Bennet emphasised.

'I hope that I am dead, if he does,' huffed his wife.

'As I keep telling you, my dear, I have no plans to die any time soon, and I hope that you will be with me till the end,' Mr Bennet reassured his wife, and kissed her hand.

He did not mention that Elizabeth was being courted by Mr Darcy. While it might reassure his wife, he had no wish to raise her hopes, only to see them dashed, if the courtship came to nought. 'I also believe that he could not arrive at a more opportune time.'

'I certainly hope that you are correct, Mr Bennet.'

~~B~~

Later that evening Elizabeth confessed to Jane her exciting news.

Instead of getting excited and congratulating her sister, Jane folded her hands as if in prayer and looked heavenward.

As a reward for her efforts to appear saintly, Lizzy threw a feather pillow at her sister.

~~B~~

12 Expectations

Mr Darcy felt a certain amount of trepidation as he and Bingley approached Netherfield in his carriage. Parker, organised as ever, had sent it to Longbourn, after taking Darcy's trunks to Netherfield.

'Did you enjoy your conversation with Miss Elizabeth?' Bingley asked. 'I could not hear any raised voices, so you must have been in accord, rather than what you call debating.'

'We were very much in accord.' Darcy sported a relaxed and reflective smile.

'I noticed that both of you came out of Mr Bennet's library as we left. Did you discuss Plato again?'

'No, we did not. Instead, I was thoroughly trounced at chess.'

'That must have been a novelty for you. Mr Bennet must be as good as your godfather at the game, since I have not heard of anyone else to best you.'

Darcy shook his head with a wistful smile. 'I did not play Mr Bennet.'

Bingley looked at his friend in amazement. 'You mean to say that it was Miss Elizabeth...'

'Precisely.'

'What a blow that must have been,' Bingley sympathised.

'At least I am in good company. Apparently, she has won against my godfather as well.'

'The Duke would not have taken it well to be bested by a young woman.'

The comment raised a chuckle from Darcy. 'Seemingly he sulks when that happens.'

'But you seem to be none the worse for your defeat.'

'Since I took it in good grace, at least Mr Bennet gave his permission for me to court Miss Elizabeth.'

'You asked her for a courtship? Already?'

'Why not. I have had three weeks, to get to know the lady enough to know that I want to know her better.'

Bingley was about to ask if he should ask Miss Bennet for a courtship, when he remembered his aunt's words. That was a decision he had to make for himself.

~~B~~

When Darcy came down to dinner, after a bath and a change of clothes, Miss Bingley, Miss Caroline and the Hursts were already assembled in the drawing-room.

Aunt Mathilda, who had been warned by the housekeeper, who had been informed by Parker, of Mr Darcy's presence, greeted the gentleman cheerfully. 'Mr Darcy, I am exceedingly pleased that you have returned to Netherfield.'

Darcy bowed to her. 'I thank you for your gracious invitation. I am pleased to be with friends.'

Miss Caroline, who had not been warned of his presence, rose and started to rush to his side, to attach herself to him, when she heard a very pointed clearing of the throat by her aunt. She came to a stop after only two steps, and curtsied. 'Welcome back, Mr Darcy. I am delighted to see you again,' Caroline cooed, his insults from the previous week forgotten.

With this lady, Darcy was politely formal. 'Thank you, Miss Caroline.'

The Hursts were greeting Darcy more warmly, when Bingley rushed into the room. 'I am sorry that I am late. Smithers had a deuced hard time with my cravat tonight.'

Miss Bingley smiled indulgently. 'It might be easier for Smithers if you held still long enough for him to do his job.'

~~B~~

Dinner passed quite pleasantly for all. Miss Bingley had arranged the seating at the table, so that Darcy was next to herself, with Miss Caroline on the other side of the table, next to her brother.

Darcy's dinner companion on his right was Louisa Hurst. He was quite content with the company.

Miss Bingley chatted with him pleasantly about the Peaks District which she had visited a few years earlier.

Towards the end of the meal, Bingley tapped his glass for attention. 'I would like to announce a courtship,' he declared with a smile.

'Charles, you cannot be serious. You cannot court that Miss Bennet,' cried Caroline, forgetting her resolution not to squander her allowance on fines.

Before Miss Bingley had a chance to correct her niece, Mr Bingley asserted, 'whether or not I court Miss Bennet is my business, and not open to argument by you. But as it happens, I am not the one who has entered into a courtship.' He paused to raise the suspense. 'Miss Elizabeth Bennet is now officially being courted by... Darcy.'

Bingley raised his glass. 'Congratulations. I hope that you are successful.'

Darcy ignored the dismayed and venomous glance from Miss Caroline. While he had not planned to make his private affairs so public, at least everyone would know his intentions. He raised his own glass in response. 'Thank you, Bingley. That too is my hope.'

Miss Bingley sent a quelling glance at her niece, before she turned to her dinner companion. 'I would like to add my congratulations and good wishes as well, Mr Darcy. Miss Elizabeth is a charming young lady, Just like her sister.'

'Thank you, Miss Bingley.' Darcy smiled at his hostess.

Miss Caroline looked sullen.

~~B~~

Mr Collins arrived punctually at four o'clock, and found Mr Bennet and his five daughters waiting to greet him. Mrs Taylor was also present to ensure the two youngest girls would not disgrace themselves.

Mr Bennet leaves his study

Mr Collins was a young man of five and twenty, rather tall and heavy-set. By the looks of him, it was obvious that he enjoyed his food. In manner he was a curious mixture of self-important and obsequious.

He was gratified that he was being greeted not only by his cousin, but also by his cousin's five lovely daughters, and an older but still handsome lady.

'Welcome to Longbourn, Cousin Collins,' Mr Bennet greeted him. 'Allow me to introduce my family...'

'Thank you for your welcome, Cousin Bennet, but I am assured that no introductions are necessary.' He bowed to Mrs Taylor. 'Mrs Bennet, it is indeed a great pleasure to meet the lovely lady, who has gifted the world with five such enchanting daughters.'

Mr Bennet suppressed a smirk. 'As I said, allow me to make the introductions.' He indicated the governess. 'This is Mrs Taylor, the governess of my youngest daughters, Kitty and Lydia.' The named girls curtsied politely, although their smiles were just a touch on the impertinent side, since they thought Mr Collins' error to be highly amusing. 'And these are my oldest daughters, Jane, Elizabeth and Mary.'

'It is a pleasure to make your acquaintance at last,' Collins swallowed his chagrin, and addressed the family. 'I had heard that you had five beautiful daughters, Cousin Bennet, but I must say that the reports did not do them justice. I am certain that each of them will make excellent marriages in due time. One of them perhaps sooner than expected.' Although Collins managed to greet the assembled ladies politely, he was most put out to discover that the lady was the governess, and that his hostess was unavailable to welcome him.

The sisters were not as happy with his compliment as Collins had expected, since it was accompanied by a leering examination from the man.

Mr Bennet decided to ignore the comment for the moment and invited their guest inside. Mr Collins was pleased to enter the house and gave the contents his avaricious attention. He was pleased that the house was pleasantly decorated and well maintained.

As soon as he had refreshed himself, he joined the family for tea.

He soon waxed lyrical about his revered patroness. 'Lady Catherine de Bourgh is all that is gracious and condescending, and she takes great care to be the perfect hostess. She would never dream to stay abed when she had guests.'

Elizabeth could not resist to comment, 'I am certain that Lady Catherine is also not imposed upon by guests who invite themselves at an inconvenient time.'

Collins missed the reprimand, and expostulated, 'indeed not. No one would have the audacity to impose on such an important Lady.'

'She is fortunate indeed to be held in such great respect by all,' Mr Bennet commented blandly.

'As you say, Cousin Bennet. I am indeed fortunate that the gracious Lady has seen fit to bestow upon me the living at Hunsford. She is known far and wide for the excellence of her opinions and advice.' Collins smiled in a self-satisfied manner. 'It is on her advice that I have come hither to offer an olive branch.'

'What olive branch is that?' Lydia asked, curious and impatient as ever.

'Lady Catherine advised that as a clergyman I must set an example to my parishioners, and enjoined me to find a wife. Being aware that I am the heir to Longbourn, she recommended that I should choose a bride from amongst my cousins, to ensure the security of the ladies, at the sad time of Cousin Bennet's passing.'

'Heir presumptive,' corrected Mr Bennet.

'I beg your pardon?' Collins asked perplexed.

'I am not dead yet, and I might still have a son, who would be the heir apparent, superseding any presumption on your part,' Mr Bennet said repressively.

Collins deliberately let his gaze travel over each of the sisters in a proprietary manner, lingering on the exquisite beauty of Jane, before looking at Mr Bennet with a smirk. 'Of course, Cousin Bennet. I stand corrected.'

The smirk faded as the door opened and Mrs Bennet entered, her gravid condition eminently obvious. She smiled at the assembled family, letting her gaze come to rest on Mr Collins. 'Please forgive me for not being able to greet you when you arrived. I was feeling a little indisposed earlier and needed to rest, to be able to join you for dinner.'

Mr Bennet rose and rushed to her side to offer his arm. 'We managed well enough in your absence, Mrs Bennet. Will you allow me to introduce my cousin, Mr William Collins.' He turned to his cousin, who had reluctantly risen to his feet, staring at his hostess in consternation. 'Cousin Collins, I have the honour of introducing my wife, Mrs Bennet.'

'It is a pleasure to meet you, Mr Collins.' Mrs Bennet greeted the unwelcome visitor graciously, resting her free hand on her prominent midsection. 'We are fortunate to have you present at such an auspicious time for our family.'

'The pleasure is all mine, Mrs Bennet,' Collins managed to say politely. He was chagrined to see his cousin's wife in her present condition, until he consoled himself with the thought that after having had five daughters, the chances were greatly in his favour of the new addition also being female.

~~B~~

To spare his wife the aggravation of having to converse with Mr Collins, Mr Bennet insisted that his cousin should be seated at his right, with Lydia on the other side of Collins.

Elizabeth had the dubious pleasure of sitting at her father's left side, a position she would normally enjoy, but now she was seated opposite their cousin, whose eyes seemed to be drawn to her bosom. Mrs Bennet was being supported by Jane and Mary, while Kitty was seated opposite Lydia.

Mrs Taylor had requested a tray in her room to allow the family more privacy. At least that was the official reason. The governess had taken an instant dislike to the visitor, and felt that her absence would allow Lydia to speak more freely, if she needed to do so.

Very soon into the meal, Mr Bennet discovered that a question about Lady Catherine was enough encouragement to open the floodgates of Mr Collins' verbosity, giving everyone else time to eat.

Although Elizabeth was amazed how much their cousin was able to eat, in between singing the praises of his patroness.

Mr Collins regaled the family with stories about the graciousness and condescension of Lady Catherine, the delicate beauty of Miss de Bourgh, and the splendour of Rosings.

After dinner, the ladies adjourned to the drawing-room leaving Mr Bennet and Mr Collins to enjoy their port and conversation.

'As I said earlier,' Mr Collins broached the subject dearest to his heart, 'I have come to select a bride from your daughters. Having seen them I believe it only to be right and proper that I should choose by seniority. I believe Cousin Jane would make me an admirable wife, and future Mistress of Longbourn.'

While Collins might call it right and proper to select Jane, propriety had nothing to do with his choice. After taking one look at the most beautiful young woman he had ever seen, the stirring in his loins made the choice for him. He could already envision her in his home, being charmingly solicitous of his welfare, ready to do his bidding...

His pleasant daydream was rudely interrupted, when Mr Bennet told him bluntly, 'Jane is being courted by the Master of Netherfield.'

'Cousin Jane is being courted? I have had no such report. I was given to understand that all my cousins were available,' Collins was most put out.

'Your report was wrong.'

Collins digested the information for a minute and came to a decision. While Elizabeth was not a classical beauty as her older sister, she was still very pretty and had other, even more delightful, assets. 'In that case as the second eldest, Cousin Elizabeth shall have the honour of being my wife.'

'She is being courted by the Master of Pemberley.'

Collins opened his mouth to expostulate on the unfairness of such a situation, when Mr Bennet cut him off. 'I doubt any of my daughters would wish to marry you. They are determined to only marry for respect and affection. How can you expect one of them to marry you when they do not even know you? You have barely made their acquaintance.'

'But it would be an advantageous match for them, marrying the future Master of Longbourn.' Collins was outraged at being so casually dismissed.

'As I said before, I am not dead yet, and I may still have a son,' Mr Bennet pointed out. 'I see no reason to inflict on them the parson of some minor parish.'

Before Collins could protest further, Mr Bennet offered one small consolation. 'Although, if by some miracle one of my daughters finds you agreeable and wishes to marry you, I will not stand in the way of her happiness.'

Mr Collins had to be content with that.

~~B~~

13 The Heir of Longbourn

When the gentlemen re-joined the ladies, they found that Mrs Bennet had already retired, while the sisters were enjoying tea and quiet conversation. Mr Bennet immediately noticed the strategic seating arrangement. There were no seats available next to any of his daughters.

Mr Collins offered to entertain the sisters by reading to them from the book he was carrying. 'I found that Fordyce's Sermons are most uplifting and contain excellent advice for young ladies such as yourself.'

'I would prefer *The Mysteries of Udolpho* or even *Pamela*,' declared Lydia.

'How can you suggest such a thing? Mr Fordyce's sermons are much more appropriate for young ladies than frivolous novels.' Collins was aghast at being contradicted by the youngest daughter.

'Mr Collins, are you aware that *Pamela* was written by Mr Samuel Richardson, an author whom Mr Fordyce lauded in the strongest terms?' asked Mary.

'Miss Mary, I am afraid that you are mistaken. Although it is gratifying to hear that you have read and attempted to understand the inspired writings of Mr Fordyce.'

'May I borrow the book for a moment?' Collins was too perplexed to object, and handed the tome to Mary, who quickly flicked through the pages to find the passage she wanted.

She read aloud. '*Amongst the few works of this kind which I have seen, I cannot but look on those of Mr. Richardson as well entitled to the first rank; an author, of whom an indisputable judge has with equal truth and energy pronounced, "that he taught the passions to move at the command of reason:" I will venture to add, an author, to whom your sex are under singular obligations for his uncommon attention to their best interests; but particularly for presenting, in a character sustained throughout with inexpressible pathos and delicacy, the most exalted standard of female excellence that was ever held up to their imitation.'*

Collins stared at his cousins in consternation. He had counted on his position as the heir to Longbourn, which would give him the power to dispose of their lives. Therefore, he had expected the girls to be sweet and obliging, and eager to please him. Instead, they appeared to delight in contradicting him at every turn.

Mr Bennet accepted a cup of tea from Jane, as he settled back in his favourite chair. He smirked at Collins. 'I told you so.'

~~B~~

Being tired from his travels, and not having the congenial evening he had anticipated, Mr Collins was the second person to retire.

Although the bed was comfortable, he found it difficult to go to sleep, thinking about his cousins.

He had come on this visit with high expectations. His father, who had been an illiterate and miserly brute, had often spoken of the Bennets and Longbourn in unflattering terms. While Collins declared that he wished to heal the breach between the families, part of him had expected to be able to lord it over the Bennet ladies.

He had assumed that the olive branch he wished to extend would be eagerly accepted, and he would have first choice of his five cousins.

Instead, he discovered that the two oldest and most beautiful of the sisters were already being courted by wealthy gentlemen.

This would not have been too much of a problem while he was still assured of becoming the Master of Longbourn, which would give him the leverage of controlling the ladies' future. Potentially he could have insisted that one of those cousins should be released to him.

But Mrs Bennet was about to deliver a potential rival for his position as heir. This reduced his options. The two youngest girls were still in the schoolroom, and therefore too young to consider as potential brides.

That only left Cousin Mary.

When he thought about it, he realised that while not as beautiful as her older sisters, evaluated on her own merits, she was still an uncommonly pretty young woman. She also seemed to have studied scriptures and sermons, which would make her more suited to be the wife of a parson. Perhaps he should focus on this daughter.

He thoroughly suppressed remembrance of the incident after dinner, thinking it would be convenient to be able to ask his wife to research appropriate passages for him to use.

Having come to this decision, he prepared himself to go to sleep. As he was drifting off, he wondered why the name of Pemberley had seemed so familiar.

~~B~~

The following morning, Jane and Elizabeth were pleased to note that Mr Collins was a late riser. They were even more pleased when Mr Darcy and Mr Bingley came to call on them as early as was polite.

Elizabeth suggested a walk to avoid their cousin, a suggestion which was happily accepted by the other three.

When Jane, unwilling to leave Mary in peril of Mr Collins' company, proposed to her sister to accompany them, Mary declined. 'I believe that I shall go and join Kitty and Lydia in their lessons. I do not believe our cousin would invade the schoolroom.'

'Oh dear, that will place the burden of entertaining our cousin on Father's shoulders.'

Elizabeth chuckled. 'I believe he will be vastly entertained by his relative instead.'

Once they were out in the garden, Darcy asked, 'I gather that you too have a relative of whom you are not over fond?'

'Indeed, we do. Although you and he have something in common.' Elizabeth paused for effect. 'Lady Catherine de Bourgh. It appears that our cousin is her clergyman.'

'He is the parson at Hunsford?'

'Indeed.'

'You have my commiseration, Miss Elizabeth. Judging by your eagerness to leave the house, I believe that Lady Catherine has again chosen a grovelling sycophant.'

'Mr Darcy, how can you so insult... sycophants.'

'Is he that bad?'

'Worse. He came here planning on marrying one of us... on the advice of Lady Catherine.'

Darcy sighed. 'I am afraid that my aunt likes to order the lives of everyone she knows.' He hesitated before adding, 'it might be wise not to let Mr Collins know of our relationship, unless you wish to endure a visit by Lady Catherine.'

'Mr Darcy, you should know that *my courage always rises at every attempt to intimidate me.*'

'Miss Elizabeth, I am exceedingly glad to hear that, since you will need that courage to face the dragons of the *ton*.'

Meanwhile Jane had provided Mr Bingley with the same information with some trepidation. Mr Bennet had informed his daughters of the conversation he had had with Collins, and the answer he had given the man. Her father had finished with the comment, 'I hope Bingley gets up his courage soon, otherwise he might make a liar out of me.'

She was unsure how the gentleman would take the news, and whether he might be afraid that she was trying to get him to commit himself to something for which he was not ready.

'That arrogant...' Bingley spluttered, unable to find a word that would express his displeasure, but would be fit for the ears of a lady. 'He only arrived yesterday and does not even know you!'

'Mr Collins is following the instructions of his patroness, Lady Catherine de Bourgh.'

'Darcy's aunt? That explains much. But, Miss Bennet, please, I do not wish to pressure you, or have you think that I am only saying this because of Mr Collins, but would you do me the honour of allowing me to court you? Officially that is. I believe that you have realised that my attentions towards you have headed in this direction.'

'You wish to court me, Mr Bingley?'

'I would prefer to marry you today, but I will happily court you until you are ready to make such an important decision. I have come to realise that I need to grow up some more to be worthy of you.'

Jane smiled beatifically. 'I would be delighted to be courted by you, Mr Bingley. Take as much time as you need.' She took his arm again to continue their stroll.

'Should I not go and speak to your father?'

'I think it best if you did not encounter Mr Collins.'

~~B~~

Mr Collins eventually rose, and made his way to the dining room to break his fast. He was disconcerted to note that only one place setting remained on the dining table, and the eggs in the chafing dish had become congealed.

He rang the bell, and when Mrs Hill entered, he demanded a serving of eggs to be freshly cooked.

'Sorry, Sir. Those were the last of the eggs for today. We will have some more tomorrow.' Mrs Hill curtsied perfunctorily and went back to her proper duties.

Collins eyed the eggs with disfavour, but helped himself to a serving nonetheless, to complete the large plate of food he put together for himself.

When he had finished his repast, he enquired of the maid who had come to remove the dishes, 'where are my cousins?'

'Mr Bennet is at work in the library, Mrs Bennet is resting, Miss Bennet and Miss Elizabeth have gone for a walk with their beaus, and the rest of the young ladies are at their lessons in the schoolroom.'

Mr Collins considered his options. 'Is Miss Mary in the schoolroom as well?'

When the maid answered in the affirmative, he asked where he might find the room.

~~B~~

Mr Collins found the indicated room, and was assured he was in the correct place by the voices of his cousins coming through the door.

Having given a peremptory knock upon the door, he waited, but the only response was a burst of giggles. When no other response was forthcoming, he opened the door without waiting longer for an invitation.

He was confronted by Mrs Taylor, who informed him, 'you have no business in this room, Mr Collins. I would thank you to remove yourself instantly.'

'I have come to speak to Cousin Mary.'

'Miss Mary is busy and does not wish to be disturbed.'

'But...'

'Be off now.'

Before Collins could protest further, the door was shut in his face, and only narrowly missed hitting him. When he heard the sound of a bolt, Collins finally understood. There would be no bride for him from amongst the sisters.

At least not today. He cheered himself up with the thought that as soon as a sixth sister joined the family, he would be able to choose whomsoever he desired.

After all, as the future Master of Longbourn he would not be gainsaid.

~~B~~

Two days later, the early morning brought a considerable uproar to Longbourn, as the latest Bennet family member decided to make an entrance into the world.

The midwife was sent for, while Mr Bennet and his two oldest daughters remained with Mrs Bennet to support her.

Collins arrived in the dining room in a cantankerous mood, peeved with his inconsiderate hosts, who had woken him before he was ready to leave the arms of Morpheus.

He filled his plate and joined the three younger girls and Mrs Taylor at the table. 'Lady Catherine would never allow such a ruckus to disturb her guests' slumber,' he grumbled.

'Based on what you have told us about the lady, Lady Catherine would make even more of a ruckus, if she was about to give birth,' Lydia cut him off. 'She would have all at Rosings running hither and thither demanding all kinds of unreasonable things.'

Just then, Mr Bennet, Jane and Elizabeth entered the room. 'We have been given our marching orders by Mrs Jones and Mrs Hill,' he informed his family. 'We are to take a long walk as soon as we have eaten our breakfast.'

~~B~~

Mr Bennet could not contain his impatience, and he led the return to Longbourn at a brisk pace. His daughters were just as anxious, and easily kept up with their father. Collins, who was not used to this much exercise was soon left behind, panting as he followed his cousins.

As soon as they walked through the door, Mr Bennet demanded of Mr Hill, 'well?'

'I am sorry, Sir, but there is no news yet.'

'Very well. I will be in my library.' Mr Bennet rushed off to his refuge.

'Could we have some tea in the parlour?' Jane requested, before they all adjourned to that room to await the news of their new sister or, hopefully, brother.

Mr Collins, who was red-faced from his exertions, joined them just as refreshments arrived. For the next few hours, the sisters attempted to sew or read, to distract themselves during the wait, while they tried to ignore the muffled noises coming from their mother's rooms.

Suddenly those noises ceased, and were replaced by the cry of a baby. The sisters made a concerted rush to their mother's chambers, to arrive just behind their father. Collins, caught up in the excitement, brought up the rear.

They crowded into Mrs Bennet's sitting room, where they waited for a short period until the door opened and Mrs Hill stepped out, carrying a bundle of bedding. She smiled as she curtsied and announced, 'Mrs Bennet and the babe are well.'

Mr Bennet smiled and pushed past the housekeeper to see his wife and new child. The sisters followed him a little more slowly. When Collins again made as if to accompany the Bennets, Mrs Hill stepped before him. 'Have you no propriety, Sir? You may not enter the lady's bedchamber.'

Collins drew himself up to his full height. 'I am family and a clergyman.'

'You may be family, but it is a distant relationship, and you are not Mrs Bennet's clergyman. Therefore, out here you will remain.' Mrs Hill stood firm, refusing to be intimidated by this oaf.

'When I am Master of this estate, you had better look for a new position, I will not tolerate such insolent behaviour.'

'In your own home, you may do as you please. But in this house Mr Bennet is Master.'

~~B~~

The Master of Longbourn looked at his wife, who appeared tired from her ordeal, but she was beaming with pleasure as she held her youngest child to her breast.

That look of pleasure and pride as she looked up, provided a hint for Mr Bennet. 'Is it...'

'Mr Bennet, it gives me great pleasure to introduce to you your son and heir, Joshua Henry Bennet.'

Her husband gently took her free hand as he laid his other hand on the child's head. 'I am exceedingly pleased to meet you, Joshua. Thank you, Mrs Bennet, that was well done. I am inordinately proud of you.' There was a catch in Mr Bennet's voice, and a suspicious moistness in his eyes.

Mrs Bennet squeezed the hand which was holding hers, and returned the ecstatic smile, while their daughters looked on the scene with delight.

~~B~~

When Joshua Bennet finished his first meal and went to sleep, Mr Bennet picked up his heir. 'I believe that I should introduce our son to my cousin,' he said with a grin.

'I agree. I would also appreciate it if that odious man would remove himself from our home sooner rather than later.'

Mr Bennet entered his wife's sitting room, stepping around Mrs Hill, who was still guarding the door, to find his cousin pacing.

'Cousin Collins, you may congratulate me on the birth of my son and heir, Joshua Henry Bennet,' announced the proud, and admittedly extremely relieved, father. The majority of the relief was due to the fact that his wife had survived the birth quite well for a woman of her age, the rest was because he now had an heir apparent, and did not have to deal with the presumption of Mr Collins any longer.

Collins stopped in midstride and gaped. 'You have a son? After all this time and all those daughters?'

'Indeed.'

Collins looked suspiciously at the well wrapped babe in Mr Bennet's arms. 'You could just be saying that this is a boy. How can I be certain?'

'You wish proof? You insult me by mistrusting my word.'

'I wish to see for myself that this is truly a boy. Unless you have something to hide?'

'Very well, you shall see for yourself.' Mr Bennet loosened the wrappings and exposed his son to the cool air, which woke the child and he cried his displeasure.

Collins, who had approached, bent forward to see clearly, and received an eyeful, in more ways than one, as Joshua sent a stream of liquid into Collins' face. Collins jerked back, looking disgusted, at both the incontrovertible evidence that his nemesis was indeed male, as well as being the recipient of the child's displeasure.

'I guess you have seen enough.' Mr Bennet smirked as he covered the babe again. 'I had better take him back to his mother.' As he took his son back into Mrs Bennet's room, he gently patted Joshua, and murmured, 'well done, son, well done indeed.'

~~B~~

14 Recovery

The sisters were enchanted by the new addition to the family, not least because they would not have to endure Mr Collins at any time in the future. Their mother echoed their thoughts by commenting, 'now I know that my beloved daughters will be safe.'

Mr Collins, needless to say, was considerably less effusive, particularly since Joshua woke up at all hours demanding to be fed... loudly. In the process of alerting the household to his needs, Joshua managed to wake up Mr Collins on a regular basis.

After two nights of disturbed sleep, Mr Collins decided that his parishioners and Lady Catherine could not do without his services any longer, and he returned to Hunsford a sennight before his planned departure from Longbourn.

Although he arrived on Saturday afternoon, Collins let the curate conduct the service on Sunday, to take advantage of a quiet house, and catch up on much needed sleep.

~~B~~

Mr Collins' departure occasioned great joy and relief in the Bennet household, particularly with Mrs Bennet, who had refused to let her son out of her sight while *that man* was on the premises, although her fears had been completely unwarranted. While Mr Collins might be lacking in intelligence and social skills, he was not a vicious man.

But Mrs Bennet was able to relax at last. She had a son, who would grow up to be a wonderful Master for the estate, and if the worst should happen, and Mr Bennet predeceased her, she and any unmarried daughters would still have a home.

With the wet-nurse installed in the nursery, Mrs Bennet was able to get the first undisturbed sleep in several weeks. The sleep and the feeling of security contributed to a sense of wellbeing she had not known in years.

~~B~~

On Sunday morning, Mr Bennet and his daughters attended services at Meryton, where he officially shared the news that Longbourn had an heir.

After services, which had also been attended by the party from Netherfield, Mr Bingley approached Mr Bennet and requested an interview, which Mr Bennet was happy to grant, together with an invitation to tea at Longbourn.

When Bingley tried to protest that they did not wish to put any strain on Mrs Bennet at this time, Mr Bennet laughed. 'You obviously do not know my wife. She loves to entertain and has looked forward to being able to be in company again. She has been in conference with our housekeeper all day yesterday to ensure everything could be prepared to host your party.'

'In that case, I would not wish to waste all that preparation. I shall look forward to seeing you this afternoon.'

With the exception of Miss Caroline, all the residents of Netherfield were delighted at the prospect.

~~B~~

Mrs Bennet, although still weak, was eagerly looking forward to entertaining guests again. She had dressed with care in a dress that fitted her again, and Mr Bennet had solicitously assisted her into the drawing-room, where she was pleased to greet the visitors.

Miss Bingley congratulated Mrs Bennet on the birth of their heir, and commented with a smile, 'looking at you I wonder if I missed something, remaining single. You are positively glowing.'

The other guests added their congratulations, before most of them found their favourite partners for conversation. Miss Bingley and Mrs Hurst remained with their hostess. Due to her condition, Mrs Hurst in particular, was hoping for a word with Mrs Bennet, who with six healthy children, must be considered an expert.

Caroline, was still clinging to her prejudices regarding the inhabitants of Meryton in general, and the Bennets in particular. Knowing that Mrs Bennet was the daughter of a rural tradesman, she expected a vulgar display by their hostess, but she was disappointed. While the lady was not refined, the relaxation brought on by having a son and heir, had calmed the lady significantly.

When Caroline was at a loss where to sit, Mary took pity on her and invited her to share a sofa. 'I understand from your brother that you are very skilled on the pianoforte,' she offered as a conversation starter.

Since Mrs Hurst had been rather preoccupied lately, as well as no longer inclined to support her sister, Caroline was starved for conversation with someone of similar age. So, instead of superciliously trying to put the younger girl in her place, she surprised herself by heatedly discussing the relative merits of Mozart versus Beethoven.

The youngest girls were sitting with Mrs Taylor, who was using the opportunity to reinforce their lessons about manners at tea time.

Once everyone had been served and became engrossed in their own discussions, Mr Bennet quietly asked Jane, 'please keep an eye on your mother, while I have a brief word with Mr Bingley.'

Mr Bennet kept his word, much to Bingley's relief. Instead of a lengthy period of teasing, Mr Bennet approved Bingley's courtship of Jane.

'I will be along in a minute,' Mr Bennet added and sent Bingley back to his daughter.

~~B~~

Mr Darcy had sought out Elizabeth as soon as the greetings were done with, and now enjoyed a conversation with the lady.

'I must confess that I am greatly relieved to have a brother. While I expect that my sisters will all marry, and will have comfortable homes of their own, I am pleased that Longbourn will have a more reliable steward than Mr Collins.'

'In what way do you think he would be deficient?'

'I should not say so, but I believe he would simply be incapable of understanding the interdependent relationship between the Master of the estate and the tenants. He believes that as a landowner, all he has to do is sit back, collect the money from the estate and spend as he pleases.'

'I am afraid that my aunt has some responsibility for his attitude. That is exactly how Lady Catherine thinks of Rosings. She seems incapable of understanding that without the tenants, she would have no income, because if there is no one to work the land, it will lie fallow and not produce any profit.'

'Is that why you are so very careful with your own tenants?'

'Indeed, it is. My father taught me that when tenants have good working conditions, they can be more productive and they are more loyal. After all, if a landlord does not make repairs and provide the resources they need, tenants can leave and find a better situation.'

'That is precisely why I feared for our own tenants, if Mr Collins was to be in charge. He would ride roughshod over them and then wonder why no one wants to work Longbourn lands. This is my home, after all, and I would hate to see it go to wrack and ruin.'

~~B~~

When Bingley returned to the drawing-room, Mr Bennet looked sadly around the shelves of his library. 'I expect I will not be able to spend as much time with you, my friends,' he murmured. 'But I do not have the excuse of Collins inheriting any longer. I suppose I had better take a greater interest in the estate, now that it will remain in the family.'

Suddenly his mien and posture changed as the realisation finally sank in. His spine straightened. 'I have a son. I HAVE A SON!' Gone was the gloom. Instead, Mr Bennet felt a sense of purpose which he had not realised had been missing from his life.

He had a son to raise and train, and to whom he could pass on everything that he had learnt.

Admittedly, he loved all his daughters, and he had enjoyed teaching Lizzy, but as a woman she was restricted in the use she could make of his teaching. Joshua would be able to make full use of everything his father had to teach. It was a heady feeling.

Now he was doubly glad about the epiphany he had experienced, when he took steps to improve himself and his family. Becoming closer to his family had also brought him closer to his wife. Much closer than he had been in years. And now he reaped the rewards.

Mr Bennet leaves his study

For a moment, Mr Bennet considered selling his books, but then decided that Joshua might enjoy reading them when he got older, and if not, he could sell them later and add the proceeds to his daughters' dowries. And in the meantime, there was sure to be the occasional evening when he could indulge himself with his old friends.

That settled, Mr Bennet left the library to join his family. For the rest of the visit, the Master of Longbourn sat in quiet contentment, watching his glowing wife enjoying the company.

~~B~~

Towards the end of the visit, Mr Bingley managed to quietly have a brief conversation with his aunt, informing her of Mr Bennet's approval of his courtship with Jane, and asked if she would be able to arrange a ball at Netherfield.

When his aunt agreed, Bingley announced, 'I have considered hosting a ball at Netherfield, to repay the kindness of our neighbours being so welcoming to us. I hope that you will all do us the honour of joining us.'

When Mrs Bennet looked hesitant, Miss Bingley reassured her. 'It will take me at least three weeks to make the arrangements. I hope that by then you will be well enough to enjoy the festivities.'

She smiled at the lady in a conspiratorial fashion. 'Perhaps the week after your son's christening would be convenient for you?'

'You are most kind, Miss Bingley. My family and I will be delighted to accept.'

'In that case, I will send out the official invitation in the next day or two.' Bingley offered with enthusiasm.

'I will write the invitations, dear nephew. After all, we want our guest to be able to decipher the date and time of the ball,' Aunt Mathilda teased.

Bingley heaved an exaggerated sigh of relief. 'Thank you, Aunt. I would hate to give a ball, and nobody came.' Once this was established, both Bingley and Darcy requested the first and the supper sets from their respective ladies.

~~B~~

The guests had departed and Mrs Bennet retired to her rooms with her son.

'How are you feeling, my dear?' asked Mr Bennet, who joined her soon afterwards.

'Truth be told, I am tired, but I am well content. Ever since Joshua's arrival, I have felt more relaxed. It is good to know that I will never have to leave my home.'

She smiled at her husband. 'I feel that at last I have achieved something that has eluded me for decades.'

'You know, I never held the lack of a son against you.' Mr Bennet took her free hand and gave it a gentle squeeze.

'But I did. Remember, when we were first married, I promised to give you the best possible heir. I always keep my promises, and it upset me that this was one promise which I would break.'

'Now you have an unblemished record, my dear. But since you say that you always keep your promises, I would like you to promise me something else.' Mr Bennet gave his wife a mischievous smile.

'What would you like me to promise?' Mrs Bennet asked cautiously.

'The first set of dances at Bingley's ball. It has been much too long since we stood up together.'

Mrs Bennet's eyes lit up. 'It will be my pleasure. I will be the envy of all the matrons,' she declared with an appreciative glance at her husband.

~~B~~

It was getting late, when Bingley and Darcy retreated to the library for a nightcap. Bingley poured them both some of his excellent brandy, which they took to seats by the fire.

'I noticed that you and Mr Bennet had a private conversation today.' Darcy commented after his first sip.

'I thought you too engrossed with Miss Elizabeth to notice anything,' his friend prevaricated. What he felt at present seemed quite fragile in its perfection, and he was loath to expose it to potential criticism. At last he admitted, 'Mr Bennet gave permission for me to court Jane, I mean Miss Bennet.'

'So, you are serious about a lady at last. Despite what your sister thinks of the match.'

'No matter what anyone thinks of the match.' Bingley confirmed, giving Darcy a challenging look. 'I realised that I am the one who will have to live with the lady for the rest of my life. I need someone whose company I find congenial. I cannot hug a title, or find comfort in a connection.'

Bingley took another sip of his brandy, and chuckled. 'Caroline should be pleased about my choice. She will get her wish, if Miss Bennet is agreeable. We will have family ties to the Darcys.'

Darcy joined Bingley in his laughter. 'Yes, she hoped that we would be brothers. That is now a distinct possibility.'

'Does it bother you to have a brother whose family came from trade?' Bingley asked almost shyly.

'Bingley, apart from Richard, you have been my best friend for years. Considering the number of titled rakes I know, I will be delighted to have you as family.'

Darcy raised his glass in salute. 'To family.'

'To family,' Bingley echoed with a relieved smile.

~~B~~

15 Aunt Catherine

On Monday, Mr Collins presented himself at Rosings, to pour his woes into the receptive ear of his esteemed patroness.

'Mr Collins, I must congratulate you on your speedy return. I had not expected such decisive action from you, to select and secure a bride within only a few short days.'

'Alas, gracious lady, I will not be marrying any of my cousins. I was most sorely abused by them.'

'They dared to abuse the future Master of Longbourn? Are those women mad?'

'I am afraid that is the problem. Not that my cousins are mad, but that I am no longer the heir. Last week, Mrs Bennet was delivered of a healthy son.'

'While I congratulate the woman on doing her duty to her husband at last, I can understand that you have suffered a disappointment. But infants have been known to die. They should have taken the opportunity to secure their future. After all, five unmarried daughters are a trial to any woman.'

'There too I have been misinformed. The two oldest daughters are being courted by two apparently very eligible gentlemen.'

'Who are these men that they should dare to usurp your precedence.'

'Due to the uproar caused by my replacement's arrival, the house was in such a state that visitors were not received, and I did not have a chance to meet my rivals.'

'Do you have no idea who they are?'

'Cousin Bennet only referred to them as the master of Netherfield and the Master of Pemberley.'

'Did you say Pemberley? In Derbyshire?'

'I did say Pemberley, but I do not know in which county the estate is located. Cousin Bennet did not specify.'

'Did you ever see the man?'

'I did see Cousin Jane and Cousin Elizabeth walking with two gentlemen, but I did not have a chance for an introduction.'

The reason that there had not been a chance for an introduction was that Elizabeth had spotted their cousin, and hurried her sister and the gentlemen in the opposite direction.

'Describe the men.'

'The one with Cousin Jane was a young man a little above medium height, fair haired and boyishly handsome. The gentleman with Cousin Elizabeth, was exceedingly tall and well built, with dark hair and a noble mien.'

'The tall, darkhaired man must be Mr Fitzwilliam Darcy, of Pemberley in Derbyshire. There cannot be another Pemberley, and the description fits my nephew.'

'Your nephew, Lady Catherine?'

'My nephew, who is supposed to marry my daughter.' Lady Catherine scowled. 'It cannot be. There must be some mistake. Darcy would not dare to ignore my wishes and court some other woman. He must marry Anne and combine the great estates of Pemberley and Rosings.'

She considered a moment. 'Tell me of this Cousin Elizabeth of yours,' she demanded.

'Miss Elizabeth is the second of the sisters, while she is quite pretty, she does not have the classical beauty of her older sister. She is also quite outspoken and impertinent.'

'She does not sound like the sort of woman for whom my nephew would forget family duty. What else can you tell me.'

Lady Catherine's musing had given Collins an idea. 'I suppose that some men might find Cousin Elizabeth's rather... ah... womanly figure to be appealing...' He certainly had found it so.

'That must be it. She is attempting to draw my nephew with her vile arts and allurements.'

Lady Catherine decided on her course of action. 'Yes, I must put a stop to this.'

Mr Collins was a very unchristian clergyman, when he gleefully contemplated what his revered patroness was about to do to that ungrateful family.

~~B~~

The ladies of Longbourn were thrown into excitement, when a large and unfamiliar equipage drove up to the house. Although she was out of bed and fully dressed, Mrs Bennet was still mostly keeping to her rooms. Not only was she still recovering from her ordeal only a week gone past, her sitting room was closer to the nursery.

Her oldest daughters were visiting with her, and taking turns holding their little brother.

'I wonder who could be visiting us at this early hour?' speculated Mrs Bennet. 'Whoever it is, you must go and greet them and convey my apologies.'

~~B~~

Mr Bennet too, had been informed of the arrival of the visitor. He met Jane and Elizabeth coming down the stairs, and accompanied them into the drawing-room to greet the lady.

Upon entering the room, they saw an imposing middle-aged woman with a haughty mien.

'I am Lady Catherine de Bourgh and you must be Mr Bennet,' she declared.

'I am indeed, Lady Catherine. To what do we owe the honour of your *unexpected* visit?'

'I presume these are your daughters?' Lady Catherine, ignoring the question, asked with a sniff, indicating Jane and Elizabeth.

'You surmise correctly. It is my pleasure to introduce Miss Jane Bennet and Miss Elizabeth Bennet.'

The lady dismissed Jane with a glance. 'You may leave, I have no business with you.'

Mr Bennet bristled. 'You do not order my daughters about in my house.'

Lady Catherine waved a negligent hand at the comment, and examined Elizabeth from head to foot, before turning her attention back to Mr Bennet. 'I would speak to Miss Elizabeth privately.'

Mr Bennet, who suspected the topic of the conversation, was not about to allow this arrogant woman the opportunity to upset his daughter without his protection. 'You may speak to my daughter in my presence or not at all.'

The lady glared at him, but saw a steely determination which she had not expected. 'Very well. I am certain that you can be in no doubt about the reason for my presence.'

'I can see no reason at all why you would have journeyed here all the way from Kent,' Mr Bennet stated. 'But please have a seat.' He gestured towards a chair.

'I will stand.'

'Suit yourself,' Mr Bennet replied casually and strolled to a settee, and seated himself, lounging back and crossing his legs. He was starting to enjoy himself. While he had done his utmost to curb his penchant for teasing and ridiculing his family and friends for the past year, he felt that Lady Catherine, with her superior attitude, was fair game.

'How dare you sit in my presence.'

'You are in my house. I offered you a seat... which you refused. I see no reason why I should be uncomfortable, because you choose to be so.'

Lady Catherine huffed, but opted to seat herself, since her ploy had failed. Once the lady was seated, Jane and Elizabeth joined their father on the settee.

'Now, pray tell, why have you come all this way to speak to us?' Mr Bennet asked ingeniously.

'Do not attempt to toy with me. I am known far and wide for my sincerity and frankness, and I will most certainly not deviate from this. I have been reliably informed that Miss Elizabeth has used her arts and allurements to seduce my very own nephew away from his duty to his family.'

'Who is your nephew, and how dare you suggest that my daughter would seduce anyone?' Mr Bennet asked, after all, Lady Catherine had several nephews.

'Mr Fitzwilliam Darcy is my nephew, and he is engaged to my daughter. Mr Collins has reported that Miss Elizabeth is attempting to snare him and his fortune.'

'If Mr Darcy is truly engaged to your daughter, you cannot suppose he would be so dishonourable as to court another lady.'

Lady Catherine grudgingly admitted, 'it is a peculiar kind of engagement. They have been intended for each other since they were in the cradle, because it was the dearest wish of his mother and myself that, on reaching their majority, our children should marry. It is insupportable to think that when that happy union is about to take place, my nephew should be diverted from this plan by a young woman of inferior birth, of no importance whatsoever.'

'They were supposed to marry on reaching their majority, you say? I happen to know that Mr Darcy reached his majority six years ago. If in all this time he has not been tempted to fulfill your wish, why do you suppose he would ever do so in the future.'

'Because as his nearest relation, I expect him to bow to my wishes.'

'But I understand that Miss de Bourgh is sickly and unable to provide Mr Darcy with an heir. Would you condemn the two great estates of Pemberley and Rosings to go to some distant relative, due to the lack of an heir? That is not a sensible proposition.'

Mr Bennet smirked. 'Or are you keen to have your daughter marry and move to a distant county, to allow you to rule unchallenged at Rosing?'

'A wife always lives with her husband.'

'True, but if your daughter chooses a husband without an estate, the husband would by right take control of Rosings.'

'That is irrelevant. Darcy will marry my daughter. Not some chit of no consequence and no fortune. While you may be a gentleman, I am familiar with the antecedents of your wife. No member of my family shall be connected in any way whatsoever with trade.'

'But if Mr Darcy is not by honour or inclination bound to his cousin, I see no reason why he should not make another choice. If I am that choice, why should I not accept him?' Elizabeth interjected before they went too far afield.

'Because you are an upstart, who should not quit the sphere in which you were brought up.'

'I would not be quitting my sphere. Mr Darcy is a gentleman, and I am a gentleman's daughter. Our stations are equal. There can be no objections.'

'I object, because it is my wish for him to marry Anne, and I am not accustomed to being gainsaid.'

'Your wishes are irrelevant. Mr Darcy is his own man, and the head of his own family.'

'But if you were to marry him, do not expect to be acknowledged by his family or his friends. Society will shun you. You will never be received in the drawing-rooms of the ton and most certainly you will never be welcome at Rosings.'

'Promise?' Elizabeth beamed at Lady Catherine.

The question completely confounded the lady.

'You impertinent chit. How dare you insult me like this?'

'Since you have been insulting me and my family for the past ten minutes, I believed that was the established mode of address in the *ton* these days. After all, I would expect a lady with such a noble ancestry as yourself to be exquisitely familiar with the current manners of society.'

This time it was Mr Bennet, who thought it time to intervene. 'Lady Catherine, while you have made it quite clear that you object, your objections are irrelevant. Was there anything else you have to say?'

'I have barely started. I will not allow for the Shades of Pemberley to be polluted by this harlot, who throws herself at my nephew…'

'How dare you call my daughter a harlot,' shouted Mr Bennet, rising to his feet and confronting his unwelcome guest. 'You will leave my house this instant, and if I ever hear even a whisper of such an accusation, I will ruin you.'

The first part of the shout was echoed from the door, which Mrs Hill had opened to announce Mr Darcy. 'How dare you call the woman I love a harlot. You forget yourself, Madam.' Darcy was just as angry as Mr Bennet as he strode into the room and stood next to the gentleman.

'Just because you compromised Sir Lewis de Bourgh into marriage, it does not follow that other women will sink to your level. Certainly not a woman *I* would marry.'

Lady Catherine looked dumbfounded. 'How...'

'My mother told me that no sensible man wanted to marry you, and the only way you could get a husband, was to get an honourable man drunk and getting him into your bed. Mother inform me so as to ensure I would never fall into such a trap, especially one of your making. There is only one harlot in this room and that is you. For the final time, no, I will not marry your daughter. It is bad enough to be connected to you by blood, but I would not wish you as a mother-in-law on my worst enemy, not even Wickham.'

Darcy glowered at his aunt, who had turned white. She had thought her past to be buried and forgotten, not to be aired in public. Especially in front of these Bennets.

To make matters worse, no one had ever stood up to her like this, and she did not know how to respond.

Since Lady Catherine was mute, Mr Bennet turned to Mrs Hill. 'Lady Catherine is leaving and will never be allowed into my house again.'

'One moment, please, Mr Bennet,' Darcy requested. 'Lady Catherine, I will add my warning to Mr Bennet's. You will keep your opinions to yourself, otherwise your whole history will become public knowledge. In future, you will not be welcome in any of my homes. As long as you do not speak to me, I will ignore you, otherwise I will give you the cut direct and publicly cut all ties. Do I make myself clear?'

Darcy did not bother to demand an apology, as he was certain none would be forthcoming.

Lady Catherine rose to her feet and gave both men venomous looks. 'I take no leave of you.' She declared before she stalked out of the room.

Once the door was closed behind her, Darcy turned to Mr Bennet. 'Sir, I must apologise for my aunt.'

Mr Bennet chuckled. 'There is no need. You are not responsible for the actions of your relatives. Apart from that, I have not had such fun in a long time. What say you, Elizabeth?'

'This was certainly an unusual experience.' The lady chuckled. 'But I am afraid that she has upset Jane.'

Jane looked at each person in the room, before smiling weakly. 'Lady Catherine has certainly provided me with a new experience... She made me so angry that I wanted to slap her.'

Mr Bennet took her hand and kissed her on the forehead. 'There is hope for you yet, my dear,' he said with a smile.

The door opened again and Mr Bingley carefully stuck his head into the room. 'Is it safe to come in?'

'Perfectly safe, as long as you do not insult my daughters.'

Bingley smiled in relief. 'I would not dream of it.'

~~B~~

16 Confessions

Mrs Bennet could hear raised voices in the parlour, and was concerned about the cause. She noted the arrival of Mr Darcy and Mr Bingley, and soon after, the departure of the large carriage.

She had just decided to go downstairs to discover the cause of the disturbance, when her husband arrived.

'Who was that loud visitor?'

'Cousin Collins' patroness.'

'Lady Catherine de Bourgh? Why could she want to visit us?'

'It seems that Mr Darcy is her nephew and it had been her wish for him to marry her daughter. While Mr Darcy and Miss de Bourgh do not agree with her, Lady Catherine would not be swayed.'

'That still does not explain her presence in our house.'

'I may have let it slip to Collins that Mr Darcy is courting Lizzy, and she came to put a stop to it. She was quite insulting about it.'

'How dare that woman come into my home and insult my daughter. I do hope that you showed her the door.'

'I did indeed, with a little assistance from Mr Darcy.'

'Good. The nerve of that woman. Thinking she could prevent Lizzy from being courted by Mr Darcy.' Mrs Bennet suddenly realised what she was saying. 'Wait... did you just say that Mr Darcy is *courting* Lizzy? As in, he is officially courting our daughter?'

'I did and he is.'

'Why did you not tell me before?'

'I am sorry, my dear. With all that has been going on in the last few days, it slipped my mind.'

'Mr Bennet, how could such a thing, like a gentleman of Mr Darcy's consequence paying court to our Lizzy, slip your mind?'

Mr Bennet looked chagrined, not wanting to admit he had been holding off until he was more certain of that relationship. 'Between trying to distract that fool Collins from our daughters, and your wonderful contribution to our family... what can I say? I was preoccupied.'

'Mr Darcy is courting Elizabeth? Who would have thought?' Mrs Bennet looked dreamily out the window. 'Just think, little Lizzy will be the Mistress of a large estate. I think she will do wonderfully well.'

Mrs Bennet noticed the sceptical look on her husband's face. 'I know I complained about you teaching her, but I could not see how that would be useful to Lizzy. It seems that I was wrong.'

'Since we are speaking of courtships, I have to confess that Mr Bingley has asked Jane for a courtship.'

'Oh that. I have known about *that* courtship for the past week. Jane is less reticent about telling me her news than some other members of my family.'

'You knew? But why did you not tell me?'

'I was busy presenting you with an heir. What can I say... I was preoccupied.'

Mr Bennet thought his eyes must be playing tricks. Mrs Bennet could not possibly look so very mischievous, like Lizzy at her best... or worst.

~~B~~

The couples under discussion remained in the drawing-room. Mrs Hill had provided them with tea, and after everyone was served, the two couples took seats at opposite ends of the room.

Although Elizabeth had claimed that she was well, Darcy was still concerned about the effect his aunt's vitriol had caused to her.

'Miss Elizabeth, are you truly well? While I did not hear much of what she said, I know that Lady Catherine can be rather overbearing, to put it mildly.'

'I must admit that I was grateful that you had mentioned the lady's mistaken determination to see her daughter married to you. Otherwise, I might have been greatly affected by her words.'

'You could have thought me so dishonourable as to court you, while engaged to another?'

'Never dishonourable, but I might have been concerned that there was some truth in her opinions…'

Darcy suddenly smiled. 'There was a great deal of truth in what I suspect my aunt said. You have indeed drawn me in with your allurements, although they are not what Lady Catherine propounded. I love your character; I am enchanted by your intelligence and wit, and you have completely captivated me with your charm and compassion.'

Elizabeth still sensitive to the subject, noticed an omission. 'But not my looks or accomplishments,' she said softly, dropping her gaze.

Darcy took hold of one of her hands and squeezed gently. 'On the contrary. Once I truly looked at you, I realised that you are one of the most handsome women of my acquaintance. It is simply that your looks are eclipsed by all your other attributes. As for your accomplishments, I think your performance on the pianoforte is exquisite. But for me your most important accomplishment is your understanding of, and compassion towards, the needs of your tenants.'

Lizzy could not help it. At those words she raised her eyes and saw admiration and sincerity. A slight blush rose to her cheeks and she caught her breath. She too had come to admire the gentleman, and for similar reasons. The care he displayed for his sister and his friend, as well as tenants of Netherfield. His intelligence and education, which challenged her own.

But even more appealing was the fact that he listened to her opinions, and gave them his full consideration. Even when he disagreed with her, he did so with a well-reasoned argument. He never demanded that she accept his opinion simply because he was a man and supposedly her intellectual superior. On the contrary, he seemed to enjoy that she would disagree with him, rather than defer to his opinions.

He had also accepted his defeat at chess with grace and good humour. And when he directed a smile, on that incredibly handsome face, at her, it caused swarms of butterflies to take wing in her stomach.

She suddenly remembered his word to lady Catherine as he had entered the room. The woman I love. Could it really be true? Did he...

It seemed that Darcy was remembering the same words, as he coloured slightly. 'Miss Elizabeth, what I said to Lady Catherine was nothing but the truth. I had not meant to speak so soon, but I have come to ardently admire and love you. I would count it an honour if you agreed to become my wife.'

Elizabeth could hardly believe her ears. This declaration, so soon after the confrontation with Lady Catherine, left her momentarily speechless.

When she did not immediately answer, Darcy suggested carefully, 'if you need more time to give me an answer, I will wait. I have no wish to rush you...'

'Yes, Mr Darcy,' Elizabeth interrupted him.

Darcy tried not to show his disappointment. 'I understand. I was too impatient.'

'No, Mr Darcy. You misunderstand. I answered your first question.' Elizabeth smiled at him happily.

His eyes widened and he needed to clarify. 'You mean you will marry me?'

'Yes, Mr Darcy, I will marry you. As it happens, I love and admire you too.'

Elizabeth would never forget the look in Darcy's eyes, as he raised her hand to his lips and simply said, 'thank you.'

They sat in silence, drinking their tea for a few moments, both relishing the knowledge of the other's love. Eventually, Darcy spoke. 'I suppose that I had better speak to your father.'

Other considerations occurred to Elizabeth. 'Mr Darcy, would you mind if we could wait a little longer to make our understanding official?'

Darcy cautiously asked, 'may I ask why? Are you having second thoughts already?'

'Not at all. But at present I would like my mother to have the attention she deserves. Having a child so late in life, has been a great ordeal to her. I would hate for her accomplishment of producing an heir for Longbourn to be eclipsed by other news.'

The tension Darcy felt, dropped away. 'Again, you confirm my opinion of your compassion. I will wait... albeit reluctantly.'

~~B~~

A week passed and at Longbourn life settled down, after a fashion. At least as much as was possible with a new baby in the house. Joshua continued to loudly demand being fed. At least during the night that duty was taken on by the wet-nurse, allowing Mrs Bennet the rest she so desperately needed.

The first few days had been difficult for the new mother. Although she had gone through this process five times before, it had been fifteen years since the birth of Lydia. At the age of forty, it took Mrs Bennet longer to recover, but the relief of having a son and heir for Longbourn, gave her an impetus to leave her chambers as soon as possible.

She spent brief periods every day in the drawing-room or at least having dinner with her family. Although she still refused to leave the house, since she did not wish to be parted from her son, and was uncomfortable about exposing him to the weather, which she felt was becoming too inclement for a newborn.

~~B~~

Since Mr Bingley and Mr Darcy were busy with estate matters at Netherfield, all the sisters decided to take the opportunity to spend an afternoon in Meryton, to do some shopping and to visit their Aunt Phillips. Kitty and Lydia were invited to the outing, and Mrs Taylor accompanied the young ladies.

As they passed Lucas Lodge, they were joined by Charlotte and Maria Lucas, who were going into Meryton to run some errands for Lady Lucas.

Maria joined the youngest girls, as Charlotte took Elizabeth's arm to gently pull her away from her sisters for a private conversation.

'Elizabeth, you should know that I am seriously considering taking a position as a companion. I do not have enough accomplishments to be a governess, but I cannot bear the idea of being a useless burden to my family any longer.'

'Charlotte, please, wait just a little longer. If Mr Darcy and I should get married, I will make a point of inviting you to spend time with us, and to introduce you to eligible gentlemen. There must be gentlemen out there who are more interested in intelligence and good sense, rather than beauty and money.' While Elizabeth trusted her friend, she wanted to keep her understanding with Darcy private for a little longer.

'You are a good friend, Eliza, but you know perfectly well that I am seven and twenty years old and gentlemen prefer someone younger and prettier. Or at least someone with a large dowry. I cannot provide them with any of these.'

'There must be at least a few gentlemen who are more interested in an intelligent and practical wife, and while in comparison to Jane, hardly anyone can match her in beauty, you are not as plain as you make yourself out to be.'

'But around here, Jane is always present as the one woman with whom all others are compared.'

'In that case, I shall invite you when Jane is not around.'

Charlotte laughed. 'Very well, Eliza. You have convinced me. I will wait a little longer, and perhaps you shall be the one to employ me to teach your children.'

~~B~~

On reaching Meryton, the Lucas sisters parted from the Bennets, who continued on to the haberdasher's, where they planned to purchase materials for Joshua's Christening gown.

They were just passing their Aunt Phillips' house, when they were hailed by three gentlemen in uniform, the most senior of whom was Captain Carter.

After greeting them politely, he said, 'Ladies, I believe you already know Lieutenant Denny, but allow me to introduce to you the newest member of our company, Lieutenant Wickham.'

Greetings were exchanged, during which Lt. Wickham favourably impressed the ladies with his handsome looks and gentlemanly speech. Lydia and Kitty were particularly taken with the officer, but were disappointed when he singled out Elizabeth for special attention. 'My friend, Lieutenant Denny, extolled the beauty of the local ladies, but to my shame I must admit I did not believe him. But now I must own that he was incorrect after all, since his words did not do justice to the true beauty I see before me.'

Elizabeth, who was accustomed to Jane getting the lion's share of attention when it came to beauty, was flattered, but also a little uncomfortable. Mr Darcy had worked hard to convince her that her looks were much more than just tolerable, but there was something about the effusive praise that did not ring true.

She smiled self-consciously. 'I admit to a bias, but I have to agree that my sister is indeed the most beautiful creature of my acquaintance.'

'Beauty certainly runs in your family, Miss Elizabeth. Now I regret that I did not join the militia earlier, since I have missed the additional time which I could have spent in your delightful company.'

Elizabeth was saved having to respond to the excessive flattery, when Mrs Phillips bustled out of her house to greet her nieces and their companions.

'My dear nieces, how good it is to see you again. I have so looked forward to your company at tea.'

'Thank you, Aunt Phillips, we too have missed you. We were about to make some few purchases, before coming to take tea with you.'

'Splendid. But I am also giving a small card-party tomorrow. Say that you will attend, and of course you gentlemen will also be most welcome.'

'Mrs Phillips, you are most gracious. We would be delighted to accept your most generous invitation.'

'Splendid, splendid. But I will not keep you any longer from your shopping, and shall look forward to your company soon.' Mrs Phillips returned to her house to order her nieces' favourite cakes to be prepared.

Mrs Taylor thought it best to remove her charges from the company of the officers. 'Since Mrs Phillips has reminded us of our purpose, we had better be on our way. If you would excuse us, gentlemen?' she said in her best governess' voice, which informed the officers that their presence was no longer... required.

Since Colonel Forster had given strict instruction that the men had to be on their best behaviour, if they wanted an opportunity to mingle with the inhabitants of Meryton, they said their farewells graciously.

'I shall look forward to seeing you at your aunt's card-party tomorrow,' Lieutenant Wickham added to Elizabeth, as he bowed and walked away with his fellow officers.

Once they were out of earshot, Lydia huffed. 'I cannot understand what that gorgeous Lieutenant saw in you, Lizzy.'

'He saw a lady with impeccable manners,' Mrs Taylor pointed out to Lydia who just rolled her eyes.

~~B~~

17 Aunt Phillips

The sisters had completed their purchases, and were ensconced in their aunt's front parlour, where they could see all the passing traffic of the High Street of Meryton.

Mrs Phillips loved the fact that her husband's business required him to be in the centre of town, giving her the opportunity to see all the comings and goings of the inhabitants of Meryton. The location and her observational skills, gave the lady access to all the gossip available, although she was in the habit of calling it information. The word gossip had such unpleasant connotations.

'I hope your mother, my dear sister is not upset with me not calling on her the last few days, but I had such a dreadful cold, I could barely stir from my bed. And of course I thought it best not to risk the health of your baby brother. Now tell me, how is Joshua?'

The sisters answered enthusiastically.

'He is adorable.'

'He is rather loud when he is hungry.'

'Yes, I agree, he can be rather noisy, particularly in the middle of the night, when I am trying to sleep.'

'He has the most adorable face.'

Lydia could not help but comment, 'He is rather smelly.' When she saw the disapproving expressions of her sisters, she added, 'but he is very sweet.'

'Your mother must be so relieved that that awful Mr Collins will not inherit Longbourn.'

'To be honest, we all are.' Jane admitted.

'I have to confess that I prayed that mother would give us a brother,' Mary added.

'But he is doing well. I believe you can almost watch him grow day by day. Although I hope that he will soon sleep through the night.'

Their aunt laughed. 'Well, I suppose that if you do need a good night's sleep, you could always come and spend a night here.'

'Please, Aunt, do not tempt us.'

They chatted pleasantly for an hour, before the sisters decided that they had to return home, and make a start on Joshua's gown.

~~B~~

The whole family and Mrs Taylor enjoyed dinner together. Mr Bennet was pleased how well his wife looked, and how much calmer she appeared.

He only half listened to the girls' chatter about their outing in Meryton, when a name caught his attention.

'Who were the officers you met today?' he asked Lydia who had waxed lyrical about the handsome officer.

'Captain Carter, Lieutenant Denny and the most handsome Lieutenant Wickham.'

'And they will attend tomorrow's card party at your aunt's?'

'Indeed. I can hardly wait to see him again.'

'Mrs Taylor, what was your impression of the officers?' Bennet asked the governess.

'I thought that Captain Carter was the epitome of an officer and a gentleman. Lieutenant Denny is quite young, but I believe he is perfectly harmless.' She paused to consider how to describe the final officer.

Elizabeth voiced her opinion. 'Lieutenant Wickham is exceedingly handsome, as Lydia says, but he made me uncomfortable. He paid a great deal of attention to me, despite Jane being present. I found it disconcerting.'

Mrs Taylor smiled at Lizzy's words. 'Miss Elizabeth is quite correct. Please forgive me for saying so, but I thought he was insincere. There was something predatory about him.'

'You mean he was deliberately focusing on the less beautiful sister, and by praising her, he had hoped to achieve... what?' Elizabeth asked.

'It is a successful tactic if a man is planning a seduction.' Mr Bennet answered her question.

Lydia objected. 'Papa, a man as handsome as that could not possibly be dishonourable. Such an open and friendly countenance can only belong to a man full of goodness.'

'Or a practiced deceiver.' Mr Bennet cast his eyes over all his daughters. 'I have heard of a man by the name of Wickham, which you must agree is an uncommon name, and the man described to me is indeed a practiced seducer.'

Mr Bennet addressed his wife. 'My dear, if you are agreeable, I shall attend the card party with our daughters, to ascertain what kind of man he is, and to ensure the girls do not succumb to a rake.'

Mrs Bennet beamed at her husband. 'It is good of you to take such an interest. I shall be well enough at home, although I hope that Mrs Taylor might keep me company.'

Mrs Taylor was happy to agree to the plan, and Mr Bennet advised his daughters, 'until I can ascertain his intentions, I wish you to stay away from that man, particularly you, Kitty and Lydia.'

'If he is the man of whom you have heard, perhaps he has taken the commission to make a new start?' Jane suggested.

'I sincerely doubt it, although it is remotely possible.' Mr Bennet thought about the matter. 'Lizzy, you said he was particularly focused on you?'

'Yes, he was excessively fulsome in his praise of my beauty. It made me quite uncomfortable.'

'If he is going to be at the card-party, chances are that he will attempt to speak with you. Grant him some conversation, and perhaps you will get an indication of his intent.'

'I shall do so, since you will be there.'

'Most certainly. I would not risk any of my daughters to the company of a potential rake without my presence and protection.'

Mr Bennet leaves his study

Elizabeth smiled fondly at her father. She delighted in the change he had wrought on himself over the past year. A year ago, he would have shrugged off any concerns and laughed at everyone's folly. While he was still imperfect, Lizzy was pleased that Mr Bennet was now determined to protect his daughters.

~~B~~

In the morning, when Mr Bingley and Mr Darcy came to Longbourn for a brief call, before attending to the business of Netherfield, Mr Bennet intercepted Darcy. he also invited Elizabeth into his library.

'Darcy, yesterday my daughters met a man by the name of Wickham. Would you please describe him.'

Darcy had stiffened at the mention of the name and his face took on a cold demeanour. He obliged Mr Bennet and his description matched the officer whom the sisters had met.

'Do you trust Lizzy?' Bennet asked when Elizabeth confirmed the identity of the man. At Darcy's nod, he requested, 'please tell her everything that you told me.'

'It is not a pretty tale, Miss Elizabeth,' Darcy warned her before he laid the whole of his interactions with Wickham before her.

Elizabeth's first reaction was to enquire about Georgiana. 'Your poor sister, I hope that she is getting over the hurt that *mumble* has inflicted.'

'Yes, she is getting better. But I am more concerned that Wickham has turned up in Meryton at this time. I wonder if that is happenstance or if there is a more sinister reason.'

'I suppose we might find out tonight.'

'I too will attend.'

'No, you will not.' Both Mr Bennet and Elizabeth objected.

Mr Bennet explained further. 'If you are there, he will be on his guard, and we will not be able to discover if he has a purpose. And I can assure you that I am quite capable of protecting my daughters.'

Darcy had to be content with that for the moment.

~~B~~

While Darcy agreed to stay away from the card party at the Phillips house, he decided that there was some action which he could take, since his nature demanded to protect those whom he loved.

On his return to Netherfield, he had Bingley meet with his steward, while he wrote a letter to his favourite cousin, requesting Colonel Richard Fitzwilliam to run an errand for him.

Once he had sent the letter off with his groom, he joined Bingley in his meeting.

~~B~~

George Wickham, the newly commissioned Lieutenant in the militia, was feeling optimistic.

His new employer, who had arranged for the commission, and supplied him with ample funds, had set him a task which he relished. He had been encouraged to indulge in his carnal desires, although no reason was given. Wickham wondered why his employer wanted Miss Elizabeth Bennet to be ruined.

He still smarted from his failure to secure Georgiana Darcy. Or to be more precise, her dowry. But, while his current job would not gain him as much remuneration, still, five thousand pounds without the burden of a wife, was much more to his liking.

A week ago, he had been in London loitering about a neighbourhood where he had no business to be, namely near Matlock House. He was trying to find out if Georgiana was in residence, when he had spotted Lady Catherine storming into her brother's house followed a minute later, by the colourless form of Miss de Bourgh.

He had waited a while longer, thinking that if Georgiana was at Matlock House, she would probably sneak out to avoid her aunt. When no one exited for two hours, he gave up and went in search of other entertainment.

The following afternoon, he was approached by a rough looking man, who made him an offer he could not refuse. Especially since he was down to his last few pennies, having lost yet again at the gaming tables.

Mr Bennet leaves his study

Within days Wickham had arrived at the camp at Meryton in high spirits, and proceeded to make himself popular.

He could not believe his luck, when on the second day, while exploring the local town with Carter and Denny, Carter introduced him to his target.

Now he had an introduction, and this evening they would attend the same function, giving him the opportunity to begin his campaign for the lady's favours. He had been pleased to see that Miss Elizabeth was exceedingly pretty, making his job much easier on himself. He would not have to pretend to be interested in her. It had been some time since he looked forward as much to a seduction.

He had been right, things were looking up.

~~B~~

Mr Bennet escorted his daughters to the card party. While the girls were busy greeting their aunt and several other guests, Mr Bennet had a quiet word with Mr Phillips, informing the wily solicitor of the potential problem, although leaving out the more sensitive details.

Soon after, the officers arrived and Lieutenant Wickham made a concerted effort to charm Elizabeth.

'How delightful to see you again, Miss Elizabeth. I must admit I have eagerly awaited tonight, in the anticipation of seeing you again.'

'Have you indeed?' Elizabeth replied with a smile, which she did her best to make pleasant rather than mocking.

'Upon my word, I have never encountered a more enchanting lady.'

'You are quite the flatterer, Lieutenant Wickham.'

'It is not flattery when I speak nought but the truth.'

Elizabeth wanted to make certain that Lieutenant Wickham was the same George Wickham of Darcy's acquaintance. 'Please, Lieutenant, my vanity can take no more compliments. Tell me instead about yourself. From where do you hail?'

'I was born and raised in Derbyshire. While it is an excellent county, it does not have the beauties of Hertfordshire.'

'Derbyshire, you say? What a coincidence. We have another visitor from that county in our neighbourhood at present. A Mr Darcy, who I am given to understand is well known in that county.'

'Indeed, he is. It may surprise you, but I happen to know Mr Darcy better than most.' Wickham was pleased that Darcy was in the area. Knowing the gentleman's reluctance to engage with society, he felt that he could ingratiate himself with the populace of Meryton even better.

'Do tell. I cannot imagine that a man with your character would be intimately acquainted with Mr Darcy.' Elizabeth stated truthfully, although her statement was designed to be misinterpreted by Wickham.

The Lieutenant was pleased to hear this, as it agreed with his plans. 'As it happens, my father was the steward at Pemberley and the previous Mr Darcy was my godfather. His son and I grew up together. What kind of impression has he made in this town?'

'The first impression we had was that he was exceedingly arrogant and disdainful...'

'I am sorry to say that does not surprise me,' Lieutenant Wickham interjected in the slight pause, before Elizabeth could go on to say that opinions had since changed. 'He has always been thus. His father was the best of men, but it pains me that this cannot be said of the son. Two years ago, he denied me a living, which my godfather had intended for me.'

Since he had often been able to garner sympathy with a distorted version of the events regarding the living, he poured the tale into Elizabeth's ear.

Before Wickham could push his perceived advantage, he was interrupted. 'Lieutenant Wickham, I am sorry, but I could not help but overhear your sad story. It really is most dreadful, but if you wait but a minute, I will fetch my husband, and I am certain that he can help you to get justice. Everyone hereabouts says that he is an excellent solicitor.'

'Please, Mrs Phillips, do not trouble yourself. I am afraid that even your husband could not help.'

'Sir, my husband may be only a country solicitor, but he is very clever, and I am certain that he can help you.'

'No, Mrs Phillips. It is very good of you to suggest this, but I could not afford to pay for your husband's services.'

'That does not matter at all. Mr Phillips is always prepared to help a friend, and he does so enjoy a good battle of wits.'

'I am afraid even the best wits would be unsuccessful. You see, *there was just such an informality in the terms of the bequest as to give me no hope from law.*'

'That is too bad. And there was no one else who could have given you a living? I happen to know that some clergymen look after several parishes. Since that is the case, I am sure that there must be such a scarcity of clergyman that surely some parish could have been in need of an ordained minister of the church,' gushed Mrs Phillips. 'Pray tell, how long ago were you ordained?'

'I am sad to say that when the living was denied to me, I did not have the heart to obtain my ordination.'

'But did you not say that your godfather left you the living in his will, and it was only years later that the son denied you the living? Perhaps if you had become ordained and then worked as a curate, the gentleman would have seen your sincere desire to serve the parish.'

'Unfortunately, the death of my godfather also left me too short on funds to finish my education.'

A male voice behind Wickham taunted him. 'I suppose it must have become excessively expensive to spend a year at Cambridge, if one thousand pounds was not enough to feed and shelter you, and pay your school-fees. In my days, two hundred pounds was quite sufficient for that purpose. Unless of course you are a bad gambler. Then no amount of money is enough.'

Wickham's face drained of colour. He turned around and saw a middle aged, somewhat corpulent gentleman regarding him with extremely intelligent eyes.

'Mr Phillips, how you jest at times. I am sure it is not as expensive as all that. But never mind, this young man was telling me that he was denied a living by the son of his godfather, who had recommended him in his will. I wondered if perhaps you could help him get justice.'

'I am sorry to disappoint you, Mrs Phillips, but I am afraid that this is a lost cause. Do you not agree, Lieutenant Wickham?'

The Lieutenant swallowed convulsively, before he could answer. 'I quite agree, Mr Phillips. I would not wish to trouble you on my behalf.'

'But, Mr Phillips, do you not always tell me that you enjoy lost causes. And I know for a fact that you have always won.' Mrs Phillips was very proud of her husband's ability, and would not be gainsaid.

'You heard the Lieutenant. He does not wish for me to pursue the subject. Is that not correct, Lieutenant?'

'Quite correct, Sir. But if you will excuse me, I find that my duties today fatigued me more than I expected. I think I had better return to camp.'

'That is probably for the best. Good night, Lieutenant Wickham.'

~~B~~

As soon as Wickham removed himself, Mr Bennet, who had also listened in on the conversation from nearby, addressed Mrs Phillips. 'My dear sister, you displayed an unexpected turn of mind.'

'I have not been married to a solicitor for nothing for nigh on twenty years. I may be silly and enjoy gossip, but I am not stupid when it comes to people. That young man's story had too many holes in it. What did he mean to gain by it?'

Elizabeth, who had listened to the earlier exchanges with a bland smile, answered. 'We suspect, sympathy from impressionable young ladies. Myself in particular it seems. Although we cannot fathom the reason.'

'Well, I say. He certainly picked the wrong lady.' Aunt Phillips smiled and patted Elizabeth's hand.

~~B~~

18 Wickham

George Wickham left the party in a cold fury. He could not understand what had happened. His charm and glib tongue should have won the support of all. Instead that old biddy had asked him some very uncomfortable questions.

How Miss Elizabeth felt remained a mystery. She had appeared sympathetic to him, but had not intervened when her aunt asked all those clever and awkward questions, choosing instead to listen.

The even bigger surprise was that Darcy must have spoken about him to someone, since that solicitor knew about the thousand pounds legacy from old Mr Darcy. And even though Mr Phillips had not mentioned the three thousand pounds which Wickham had received in lieu of the living outright, the hint had been strong enough.

Wickham decided that he must discover what was happening in this town. Generally, Darcy was disliked for his disdain and haughty demeanour, which Miss Elizabeth had confirmed was their first impression of his old acquaintance. Wickham now cursed himself for his eagerness to agree with Miss Elizabeth. Was she going to say that after the initial dislike, Darcy had shown his true colours, which were that he was honourable to a fault, compassionate and, once he was in congenial company, Darcy displayed a sly sense of humour?

What in Hades had made his old enemy act like the perfect gentleman that he was? All Wickham could do at present was to keep quiet and make enquiries, before he found a way to complete his mission.

Darcy might be a thorn in his side, but that man was not going to stop him from earning his bounty.

~~B~~

The following morning, a council of war was convened at Longbourn, as soon as Mr Darcy and Mr Bingley arrived. Mr and Mrs Phillips had joined the family for breakfast.

Since Mr Bennet was concerned about all his daughters, he included them, as well as his wife and Mrs Taylor.

While everyone assembled, Mr Bennet quickly filled Darcy in on the events of the previous evening. Darcy shook his head in amazement. 'This must be the first time that anyone questioned Wickham's veracity. And, forgive me for saying so, I would not have expected Mrs Phillips to be the one to do so.'

Mr Bennet chuckled. 'She surprised me as well. Now that I started paying attention, I find that the world is full of delightful surprises.'

'Papa, what is going on? Not that I mind missing comportment lessons, but you look all too serious and it is too early for a party,' Lydia, predictably, was impatient and curious.

Darcy cleared his throat, and said, 'you have met Lieutenant Wickham...'

'He is ever so handsome, but Papa said that he was a scoundrel.'

'He is indeed, and since I have known him all my life, I thought I had better tell you all that I know about him.' He gave Lydia and Kitty a hard look. 'There are some details in this story which I need you to keep quiet, but I decided to tell you all, so that you can be on your proper guard.'

Kitty and Lydia exchanged glances. Normally, the adults in the house did not tell them anything confidential, in fear that the girls would gossip about it without considering consequences. For Mr Darcy to trust them, it must be important. Both suddenly felt quite grown up and resolved to keep that trust. 'We will not say anything, Mr Darcy,' declared Lydia for both of them.

Darcy proceeded to tell his story yet again.

'Mr Darcy, you do know that you have just told this story to the two biggest gossips in town,' Mrs Phillips teased.

'I trust that you would not reveal information that could harm a member of your family.'

'No, I would not, but you are not family.'

'Not yet, but I hope to be,' Darcy smiled at the lady. 'Unfortunately, Wickham too appears to be interested in Miss Elizabeth.'

Mr Bennet asked. 'Now, while I think Elizabeth is very beautiful, like all her sisters, she has nothing to recommend herself to a penniless man. Why would Mr Wickham focus on her?'

'If he knew that I was interested in Miss Elizabeth, that would be enough incentive on its own. He is bent on revenge against me, because I will not fund the kind of lifestyle to which he thinks he is entitled, due to his upbringing.'

'I have to ask an indelicate question. You know the man better than anyone else here. Do you think he would use force?'

Darcy looked thoughtful as he considered the question. 'I have never known him to be violent in the past, since his charm usually gets him what he wants.' He sighed. 'But in the past five years, I have seen him a total of three times. He may have changed. But I still cannot understand why he would focus on Miss Elizabeth.'

'I have a suspicion, but I would not wish to slander your aunt, Darcy.'

'You think that she hired Wickham to turn Miss Elizabeth's head?'

'Perhaps that, or perhaps she wanted him to take more direct action.'

Darcy paled at the thought. Even Lady Catherine would not sink so low as to put a young woman in harm's way, simply to further her own interests. Or could she? 'I do not know,' he admitted at last.

'Neither do I. As it is only a suspicion, but I have no proof, I will not make any claims.'

'If Lady Catherine is as determined as you describe her, it would make a horrible kind of sense.' Elizabeth looked stricken. 'Mr Darcy, I have no wish to be such a bone of contention in your family...'

'Miss Elizabeth, I do not care what my aunt's wishes are, they will never change what I feel. But it means that until my cousin gets here with the receipts to throw Wickham into debtor's prison, you need to be vigilant. I beg you, do not go out unattended under any circumstances. I do not wish you to be hurt in any way.'

Darcy stopped, as another thought occurred to him. 'I just realised that I am being exceedingly selfish. My wish for you to be mine, is putting you in danger. I should not do that, Miss Elizabeth. I can completely understand if you...'

This time it was Elizabeth, who interrupted. 'Mr Darcy, stop. I will not be frightened off by anyone. Certainly not by a rude bully.' She looked at her father, who looked to be torn between pride and worry. 'Might I borrow your stablemaster, if I need to go out?'

Mr Bennet's face cleared as he smiled in relief. 'You are a genius, my dear. That is an excellent idea.'

Darcy on the other hand looked puzzled and doubtful. 'What could your stablemaster do, other than act as a deterrent?'

'Kill that scoundrel either with his bare hands, or any other weapon on which he can lay his hands. And I have yet to see him go anywhere unarmed.' Since Darcy still looked unconvinced, he added, 'he used to be a sergeant in the Regulars.'

Darcy subsided and looked at Elizabeth with a small smile. 'According to what my cousin has told me about his sergeants, you should be in no physical danger. Although their language can be rather colourful.'

Elizabeth smiled impishly. 'I know, I have heard Mr Dowling when he had to deal with recalcitrant horses or grooms.'

~~B~~

Several uneventful days went past. Mr Phillips warned the local shopkeepers about extending credit to the militia, particularly Lt Wickham. Mrs Phillips warned the mothers of nubile daughters about the dangers of smooth talking soldiers.

Elizabeth gave up her solitary early morning rambles. Whenever she ventured out of the house, she was always accompanied by at least one of her sisters, as well as her father or Mr Dowling. The younger sisters never went anywhere without Mrs Taylor and a footman.

Mr Darcy made a point never to be seen with Miss Elizabeth outside her home, to minimise the risk of her becoming a target for Wickham's revenge. Whenever he visited, it was always in company of Mr Bingley, who made it quite obvious that he was courting Jane.

To compensate for these restrictions, Mr and Mrs Bennet, as well as the sisters gave Darcy and Elizabeth as much privacy as possible, to converse and get to know each other. The two of them usually sat in a corner of the drawing-room, as far as possible from everyone else.

'Your family is very understanding,' Darcy commented one day.

'Since you are officially courting me, they want me to have the opportunity to get to know you. While they may not have the refined manners of some of your acquaintances, they all love me and want me to be happy.'

'Are you happy?'

'Deliriously.'

~~B~~

Lieutenant Wickham was getting frustrated.

He rarely saw Miss Elizabeth in public, and when he did, he never had an opportunity to engage her in conversation. While she nodded politely at him, when they encountered each other, she never stopped to speak, and the looks he received from either Mr Bennet or that scarred hulk of a man accompanying the ladies, clearly told him not to approach.

But that was not all. Wickham was used to purchasing whatever he wanted on credit, and when he could no longer put off the merchants demanding payment, he would depart for greener pastures. Or at least an area where he was unknown.

Since the card-party that stopped being an option. The merchants of Meryton had become more cautious. They were willing to forgo a sale, unless the buyer could pay cash for their purchases. Credit was not extended to anyone wearing regimentals.

That meant that Wickham had to use the funds provided by his employer, if he wanted to have a drink or anything else in Meryton.

To make matters worse, he could not even find a merchant's daughter to commiserate with him and console him. When he tried to tell his tale of woe, how he had been victimised by Darcy, he received no sympathy.

The blacksmith's daughter went so far as to laugh at him, and tell him that he should try to come up with some new lies, since no one in Meryton would believe that that nice Mr Darcy was anything other than honourable.

The only woman in the neighbourhood, who would give him what he wanted, was the barmaid of the Red Bull, and she expected payment... in cash.

If it were not for the lure of five thousand pounds, Wickham would have packed up and tried his luck elsewhere.

~~B~~

The Christening of Joshua was only a few days away, when Mr Bennet escorted his daughters into Meryton, to collect a present for his wife.

The girls wanted an opportunity to purchase a few items for themselves, and eagerly invaded the haberdasher's. Deciding that the girls would be busy for some time, and quite safe as a group, Mr Bennet went to the goldsmith to pick up a locket he had commissioned.

Elizabeth quickly made her choices, and wondered how to pass the time until her sisters would come to their decisions. She remembered that a book which she had ordered from Mr Browning, the owner of the bookshop next door, should have arrived, and decided that she would be perfectly safe to walk the few yards on her own.

'If my sisters look for me, please tell them that I have gone to pick up a book from next door,' she requested of the proprietor of the haberdashery, before stepping out of the shop.

~~B~~

19 Confluence

Elizabeth had collected her new book, and was on her way back to the haberdasher's, when she heard an unwelcome voice. 'Miss Elizabeth, what a delightful surprise to run into you.' Wickham bowed and smiled winningly at his target.

Elizabeth, who immediately regretted leaving the security of the rest of her party, tried to sidestep the man with a murmured, 'good morning, Lieutenant.'

Wickham blocked her path. 'Miss Elizabeth, it is most unkind of you to toy with me and make me suffer. Have you not realised that I have fallen madly in love with you?'

'In love you say? We are barely acquainted, Lieutenant.'

'It is true. Have you not heard of love at first sight? I felt it when I first beheld your lovely countenance. Please, let me accompany you to your destination.'

'No, thank you, Lieutenant. I can walk five yards quite well on my own.' Elizabeth again tried to get around Wickham, this time on his other side.

Wickham realised that Elizabeth would never willingly go anywhere with him, and since this was the first time in days when she was unaccompanied, he relied on any lady's reluctance to create a scene. He grasped her arm in a firm grip, and murmured, 'I will not take no for an answer, Miss Elizabeth. You will come with me.'

As he pulled her arm, Elizabeth was thrown off-balance. She flailed her free arm trying to regain her equilibrium, still holding onto her purchase. By good luck, rather than good management, the trajectory of her flailing hand brought the parcel into close vicinity of her attacker's head. While the spine of the heavy book missed Wickham's cheekbone, his nose was not so lucky. There was a crunch, followed by a scream, as blood started to pour out of the injured proboscis. As Wickham doubled over in pain, his grip on Elizabeth's arm loosened, and she tore herself away.

Wickham's scream attracted the attention of passers-by.

'I believe that Mr Wickham was stung by a bee,' declared Elizabeth loudly with fake concern.

'That must have been some bee, Miss Elizabeth. But do not concern yourself, I will take care of Mr Wickham,' came the friendly and amused voice of Mr Baker, the blacksmith, who had noticed Wickham blocking her path, and had come to offer his assistance to Elizabeth. He grabbed hold of the injured man's arm.

'No, I will,' came a coldly angry voice. 'I will not tolerate some scoundrel in a uniform believing that he can lay a hand on my daughter and get away with it... with his life.' Mr Bennet had caught sight of Elizabeth being importuned by Wickham from the shop across the street and had rushed to her side.

'I am sorry, Sir, but I have a prior claim,' a new voice cut in.

When Mr Bennet angrily turned to face the man, he was confronted by a tall Colonel of the Regulars, who was in the process of dismounting. 'Who are you? And what is your claim?'

'Allow me to introduce myself. I am Colonel Fitzwilliam, cousin to Mr Darcy, and this scoundrel has been a thorn in my side for years. Unfortunately, he has a habit of disappearing before I have a chance to catch up with him. He is a liar and a cheat, and those are his good points. He usually leaves behind debts and ruined women.'

'I know Mr Darcy. Can you prove your claims?'

The Colonel grinned. 'As a matter of fact, I can. That is why I was late arriving. I had to stop off at Pemberley to collect the receipts of Wickham's debts which Darcy paid. They are enough to let him rot at Marshalsea for the rest of his miserable life.'

Wickham was slowly straightening up. 'I want to speak to Darcy,' he mumbled indistinctly through a groan.

'Not this time, Wickham. I will not let Darcy's soft heart get in the way of making you pay for your sins.'

'I think he would not want any rumours about his sister coming out, and neither will you,' Wickham spat in desperation.

'Oh dear, Wickham. Did you just try to blackmail a Colonel in his Majesty's armed forces and my cousin with your lies? In front of witnesses, no less. Oh dear, dear, dear. That was most unwise of you.'

Wickham, realising that he let himself get carried away, looked around desperately to find a way out of this situation. To his chagrin, not only were there too many of Meryton's inhabitants gathering around them, but amongst the crowd he spotted Colonel Forster. Judging by the angry expression of the Colonel, he must have seen or heard enough.

Wickham cursed confluence of circumstances that had brought all these people to this location at the same time. It seemed his luck had run out, and everyone was baying for his blood.

Wickham's fear proved to be correct. Colonel Forster stepped forward, and said, 'Colonel Fitzwilliam, it is an honour to meet you. I am Colonel Forster, the commanding officer of this... ah... man. Having witnessed this incident, I would be most happy to bring Lieutenant Wickham up on charges. I suspect a court martial will find him guilty, and we can simply hang him.'

Colonel Fitzwilliam looked thoughtful, when Mr Bennet suggested, 'Colonel, what do you think is the more appropriate punishment? A quick merciful death, or rotting in Marshalsea?'

A malicious grin spread over Colonel Fitzwilliam's countenance. 'What say you, Wickham. Do you prefer a quick death or a long miserable life?'

Wickham looked in horror from one man to the other. He could not detect even a shred of mercy in the demeanour of any of them. While he expected no less from Colonel Fitzwilliam, or even Colonel Forster, Mr Bennet was a civilian, not used to the almost casual bloodshed of war.

Then he noticed how the gentleman had stepped protectively in front of his daughter. He obviously realised what Wickham had planned to do. No, Wickham would find no mercy in that quarter. 'I do not want to die,' he wailed as he futilely tried to wipe the blood off his lips.

'What do you say, Colonel? Instead of the bother of a court martial, you could simply cashier him for conduct unbecoming, and then hand him over to me, to take him to Marshalsea?'

'I suppose that would be a better use of my time, and it will reduce my paperwork. Although, I believe that I will file a report on this attack, that way you can have him hanged if he does not behave.' Forster turned to Mr Bennet. 'Is this an acceptable solution to you, Mr Bennet?'

'As long as you can guarantee that this scoundrel will never again be in a position to harm anyone.' Mr Bennet turned to Colonel Fitzwilliam. 'Although we have not been introduced, your cousin has spoken of you highly. I will trust you to take care of Wickham.'

The name Bennet did not ring any bells for Colonel Fitzwilliam, since the news that the man had stood up to Lady Catherine, and won, had not made its way to Derbyshire. 'Mr Bennet, it is an honour to meet you. Could I trouble you to inform my cousin of what has transpired, and that I will return as soon as I can.'

When Mr Bennet agreed, Fitzwilliam addressed the other Colonel, 'Thank you, Colonel Forster. That is an excellent suggestion. Shall I accompany you, and we can take care of the formalities?'

Fitzwilliam turned to Mr Bennet. 'Would you care to accompany us?'

'No, thank you all the same. I believe I shall take my daughters home. Goodbye, gentlemen. Good riddance, Wickham.'

~~B~~

Colonel Fitzwilliam was well satisfied. Darcy's letter had caught up with him only four days before, while he was recuperating at Matlock, from wounds he had received in Spain.

As soon as he received the note, the Colonel had made his way to Pemberley, where he was well known to the staff. Mrs Reynolds was most helpful when he showed her the request, but insisted that he spend the night, before setting off in one of Darcy's carriages, accompanied by two footmen and a groom.

'If you need to ensure that that scoundrel gets to Marshalsea, you had better have some help,' the housekeeper reasoned.

Mr Bennet leaves his study

The following day he was unsure whether to be amused or irritated with the officiousness of Mrs Reynolds. He discovered that she had given strict instructions to the coachman that he was to provide the Colonel with the least strenuous journey possible.

Instead of rushing from Pemberley to Hertfordshire in two days, it had taken nearer three days. But he had to admit that he was feeling better for the relatively easy journey. He had even felt well enough that at the last stop he had decided to ride the rest of the way, and have the carriage follow.

As it turned out, without a passenger who needed coddling, the coachman had made good time, and arrived just as the Colonels were ready to take Wickham to the militia camp.

Since the transport was available, Colonel Forster was agreeable to save himself the walk.

The coachman handed a rag to Wickham. 'Don't bleed all over the upholstery.'

~~B~~

Once the officers had quit the scene, and the onlookers had dispersed, Mr Bennet turned to Elizabeth.

Before he could berate her for her stupidity of walking alone, and putting herself in danger, Elizabeth spoke up. 'I am sorry, Father. I know that I was not supposed to walk anywhere on my own. I just thought that it was but a few steps from one shop to the next.'

'You nearly gave me an apoplexy, when I saw that Wickham had gotten hold of you. You could have ruined not only yourself, but all your sisters along with you. I thought you to be smarter than that.'

'But at least I had a book in my hand, rather than a few lengths of ribbons.'

'It was sheer luck that brought you safely through your escapade. Have you no consideration for my nerves?' cried Mr Bennet. He was about to continue his harangue, when he realised what he had said. He gave a weak chuckle and calmed down a little. 'Remind me to apologise to your mother. I can suddenly understand her plaints about your actions.'

'All's well that ends well?' quipped Elizabeth hopefully, with a return of her impertinence, now that the shock of the encounter was wearing off.

'Do not ever do something that stupid again,' insisted Mr Bennet forcefully, even though he was beginning to think that Elizabeth had the right of it. If only she had not put herself in such danger.

~~B~~

'Do not ever do something that stupid again.' Those same words were echoed by Mr Darcy, when he was informed of the incident, after arriving at Longbourn in response to an urgent note.

'It worked out perfectly. The scoundrel will not be a danger to anyone any longer.' Elizabeth defended herself.

'I shudder to think what could have happened to you.' Darcy glared at Elizabeth, angry that she had put herself in danger.

'I do not understand why you are angry. As you can see, nothing did happen to me. Apart from a brief fright.' Elizabeth defended herself. She worried that if she allowed Darcy to see how frightened she had been, he would attempt to wrap her in lambswool and curtail her freedom after they married.

'Something could have happened. I could not bear to see you hurt.' Darcy at last admitted the cause for his irritation.

'As I keep saying. Nothing did happen to me. Wickham is being taken care of, and we can get on with our lives, without looking over our shoulders.'

'You do show a remarkable streak of conceited independence.'

'I suppose that comes from having a mind and opinions of my own.'

Darcy shook his head in frustration, although it was leavened by a grudging respect. He loved the fact that Elizabeth had a mind of her own, even though at times it was most inconvenient.

'At least try to consider your actions in future,' he grudgingly compromised.

Elizabeth, who in truth had been concerned about Darcy's reaction to her folly, smiled in relief as she agreed, 'I will try.'

Mr Bennet leaves his study

~~B~~

'What possessed you to attack a gentlewoman in broad daylight on the High Street.' Colonel Fitzwilliam asked the rhetorical question.

'Would you believe that I fell in love with Miss Elizabeth?' Wickham tried to put his actions in a better light.

'No.'

'You should get to know her, then you will understand.'

'From the brief glimpse I had of the lady, and seeing how she dealt with you, I can believe that it is possible to fall in love with her. I simply do not believe that you can love anyone but yourself.'

Wickham realised that Colonel Fitzwilliam knew him too well, and he had lost his last chance. He shrugged and seemed to shrink into himself. He presented a picture of abject misery, and barely roused himself when Colonel Forster confiscated the balance of his funds, which almost covered his debts of honour amongst the militia.

~~B~~

Colonel Fitzwilliam watched as Wickham changed out of his uniform into civilian clothing. When Wickham pulled the tunic over his head, the Colonel noticed a piece of paper fluttering to the ground.

He picked it up out of simple curiosity. The message was short and cryptic. It contained a name and an address, followed by the words, *'Love or Lust?'*.

It was written in a feminine hand, which seemed hauntingly familiar to Colonel Fitzwilliam.

~~B~~

20 Questions

Darcy, having been informed of his cousin's presence in Meryton, tracked him down at the militia camp, where he was finalising Wickham's transfer into his custody.

Colonel Forster had sent for Sir William Lucas, who, as the magistrate of Meryton, was needed to sign off on Wickham's arrest, and removal to Marshalsea. Having been warned by Mr Bennet about Wickham, he had been waiting for proof of the man's debts, which were now before him.

'How the devil did this man manage to squander this much money in only five years?' Sir William exclaimed.

'And not to forget the thousand which was left to him by Darcy's father, as well as the three thousand Darcy paid him in lieu of the living, which Wickham did not want. The living, that is, he certainly wanted the money.'

Sir William looked from the pile of papers before him at Colonel Fitzwilliam and back at the receipts, shaking his head in disbelief. 'If I had not known it beforehand, this proves that Mr Darcy is a good man. He could easily have ignored these bills, and a lot of small tradesmen would have lost their businesses. It is greatly to his credit that he saved them.' Sir William had been a merchant before he was given his knighthood, and could understand the difference which a few pounds could make to a man's livelihood.

He happily signed the papers consigning George Wickham to debtor's prison.

Sir William was leaving Colonel Forster's office as Darcy arrived. He bowed to Darcy and declared, 'thank you, Mr Darcy. You are a true gentleman,' before leaving without giving Darcy a chance to respond.

Darcy looked after the retreating back in puzzlement. 'What did I do?'

'He appreciates that you reduced the number of lives ruined by Wickham. Hullo, Cousin.'

'Richard,' Darcy acknowledged. 'I am happy that you arrived in an almost timely fashion.'

'Well, since you sent your groom to London instead of to Matlock, you are lucky that I arrived at all. Especially since your officious housekeeper slowed me down by being a mother-hen.'

Darcy looked carefully at his cousin, detecting a certain stiffness in his movements and silently thanked Mrs Reynolds. 'How are your wounds?'

The Colonel shrugged. 'Well enough, although they still hurt in cold weather.'

'Well, I still need someone to take over that horse-stud near Newmarket...' Darcy suggested tentatively, expecting Colonel Fitzwilliam to bite his head off... again.

To his surprise, the Colonel answered, 'I am considering it. It is certainly warmer than Derbyshire.'

'Or the mud in Spain.'

'That too.' Fitzwilliam looked as if he was going to say more, but instead straightened and told Darcy. 'As much as I would like to catch up with you, I think I will take Wickham to Marshalsea immediately. I have just enough time to get to London before dark.'

'I am staying at Netherfield Park with Bingley. Why not join us when you are free. I am certain that he would love to put you up.'

'That sounds like an excellent idea. And if you do not mind, I will stay at Darcy House. Mother fusses too much.'

'Certainly. Georgiana will be pleased to have your company. Come to think of it, when you return, bring Georgiana with you. There is someone I want her to meet.'

~~B~~

Darcy returned to Netherfield, where he related the happenings to the other residents.

Mr Bingley and Aunt Mathilda were shocked to hear of Elizabeth's narrow escape. Bingley was pleased to hear that Wickham was on his way to Marshalsea.

There was only one person who was not so pleased that Elizabeth had escaped being compromised... or worse. While she had learnt to behave in a manner acceptable to her aunt, since she had not been fined for a whole week, Miss Caroline was still not reconciled to the idea of Mr Darcy making Elizabeth his wife. Since there had been no announcement of an engagement, she still held out a small hope that he would tire of the hoyden.

While thinking that it was a pity that Miss Eliza was unscathed, she almost missed Darcy's next comment.

'Miss Bingley, Bingley, I must apologise but I have imposed on your hospitality, by inviting my cousin Colonel Richard Fitzwilliam and my sister to join me here at Netherfield. If this is inconvenient, I can send a note for them to stay in London.'

Miss Bingley smiled and reassured him. 'Not at all, Mr Darcy, I would love to meet your sister, and Charles has often spoken of your cousin as well. There are plenty of empty guestrooms. Feel free to invite anyone you like. I always say, the more the merrier. And based on the descriptions of your cousin, it should be very merry indeed.'

~~B~~

Colonel Fitzwilliam was not very merry at all at present, since he did not enjoy the company of his travel companion.

'Who put you up to compromise Miss Elizabeth?

'What is worth to you to find out?'

'Nothing. But you will save yourself some more bruises.'

Wickham gave him a sour look. 'As it happens, I think it was Lady Catherine. I recognised the bloke who approached me as one of her footmen.'

'What did he tell you?'

'Just that his employer wanted someone compromised. He did not know who, but he gave me an envelope with that paper and told me that his employer would pay me five thousand pounds if I succeeded. He also gave me a purse with two hundred pounds in it. I figured that five thousand pounds and a bit of fun was a good deal.'

'But why Miss Elizabeth?'

'Maybe she was trying to eliminate potential competition? Not that I heard anything of that kind, although Miss Elizabeth was not impressed by my charm, which made me wonder... Darcy did tell her family about me.'

Richard too wondered. He had only briefly seen the lady, most notably when she broke Wickham's nose. She seemed to be quite a fiery young woman, and he suspected that Darcy could be attracted to her. Which would explain Lady Catherine's interest. But how would his aunt have heard anything, if Wickham, who was in the same area, did not know anything for certain.

'Why did you keep the paper?'

'I thought that if the old bat reneged on the deal, I had a hold over her, to make sure she paid up.'

The Colonel could not get any further information from his prisoner.

~~B~~

Reports of Darcy's infatuation had found their way to London, to Matlock House via Lady Catherine.

Even though she did not wish to admit it to her irate sister-in-law, Lady Eleanor was concerned about the report. Unlike Lady Catherine, she had never expected Darcy to marry his cousin Anne, but she did expect him to marry a lady from the first circles.

Regrettably, her husband, the Earl of Matlock, was absent from London and not available to deal with his sister. At last, after days of listening to Lady Catherine ranting, and Anne de Bourgh whining, she managed to convince the harridan to take her ailing daughter, whose health was severely affected by the London air, back to Rosings Park.

Although this outcome required her to promise to investigate the matter as soon as her husband returned.

~~B~~

Meanwhile, at Darcy House, Miss Georgiana Darcy was delighted with the letters she received from her brother from Hertfordshire.

He wrote in such glowing terms about Miss Elizabeth Bennet, that Miss Darcy wished to meet the lady. She was even prepared to tolerate Miss Bingley for the opportunity to become acquainted with her potential future sister.

When she raised the subject with her brother, he was initially in favour of the idea, but suddenly changed his mind. Apparently, a situation had arisen which made it inadvisable for her to join him at present.

Fitzwilliam Darcy promised to send for her as soon as the problem was resolved.

The arrival of Colonel Fitzwilliam put Miss Darcy into high spirits. Especially when he informed her of the reason for his arrival.

'You mean that George Wickham is out of our lives forever? And I can go to Hertfordshire to meet Miss Elizabeth?'

'You know about Miss Elizabeth Bennet?'

'I do indeed. William's letters have been full of praise for the lady. I am hoping the he wishes to marry her. She sounds quite wonderful. She even stood up to Aunt Catherine.'

This information made it clear to Richard why Lady Catherine might have hired George Wickham, but it worried him that the note had not been in her handwriting.

~~B~~

Colonel Fitzwilliam decided that he had procrastinated for long enough. Speculations did not give him answers. He needed to speak to his mother.

'Where did you get that?' his mother asked in surprise when he showed her the note he had confiscated from Wickham.

'Is that your handwriting?'

'Yes, of course it is. You should know it by now. I have written enough letters to you.'

'Why did you write this?

Lady Matlock frowned at her son. 'Why this inquisition?'

'Please, Mother, just tell me.'

The pained expression on Richard's face softened the lady's irritation. 'Catherine came here recently with a bee in her bonnet about a Miss Elizabeth Bennet luring Darcy away from his duty to Anne. She wanted your father to put on his *Head of the Family* hat and talk your cousin out of his supposed infatuation. Since my husband was unavailable, she insisted that I should note the name and address of the young woman, to ensure that I would not forget it or get it muddled.'

Lady Matlock shrugged. 'You know your aunt. Sometimes it is easier to go along with her ideas, rather than argue. Especially, since it was not worth arguing about. Does that answer your question?'

'Why did you write Love or Lust?'

'Because I wondered which it was,' his mother chuckled. 'You know your cousin better than I do. Would a pretty girl be able to turn his head because of her *arts and allurements*? Those were Cathy's words, not mine.'

'No, Darcy would not fall for a pretty face, unless it was attached to an intelligent mind.'

'Will you now answer my questions? Where did you get that note, and why is it important to you?'

'The note was in the possession of George Wickham, and he had been hired to compromise the lady.'

'What! Did he succeed?' cried Lady Matlock, horrified.

'No, he did not, but it was a near thing. Luckily Miss Elizabeth is fond of heavy literature. She broke his nose with a book.'

Seeing the honest puzzlement, followed by concern and then relief, put Richard's fears to rest. He had not thought his mother capable of such a dastardly scheme, but the note in her handwriting had raised some uncomfortable question. He now related his part in the happenings at Meryton.

'So, Wickham is rotting at Marshalsea and Miss Elizabeth is safe?'

'Yes, to both, but the question remains. Who had access to that note?' Richard had his suspicions, but he needed Lady Matlock to confirm them.

'Apart from my staff, whom I trust implicitly, only Cathy and Anne could have taken it. But why would either of them do so?'

'To shift the blame to you, if the note was discovered. Aunt Catherine's footman knew that his employer wanted a woman to be compromised. But he did not know who. That information was in a sealed envelope, in your handwriting. I guess she thought that the plan could not be traced back to her.'

'You said the footman claimed that his employer wanted Miss Elizabeth compromised. He did not actually name your aunt.'

'No, but who else would have reason to send him.'

'I suggest you go to Rosings and find out. On the way, you might consider the Mistress of Rosings.'

'Aunt Catherine...' Lady Matlock stopped him with a peremptory eyebrow.

~~B~~

Richard had no wish to spend more time than absolutely necessary at Rosings, and definitely not overnight. Therefore, he left London early the following morning, yet again in the Darcy coach.

He considered what his mother had implied, but decided to approach the problem with an open mind. Instead of worrying, he used the journey to good purpose. He went to sleep.

'Do you recognise this note?' Colonel Fitzwilliam asked Lady Catherine, as soon as the obligatory greetings were done.

'Yes, of course I do. I am not yet in my dotage after all. This is the name and address of the young woman who is trying to lure Darcy to forget the duty he owes his family. But there is no question in my mind. What he feels is lust, not love. But why do you have this note? Your mother was supposed to give it to your father, to put a stop to this infamy.'

This was not the reaction which Richard had expected from his aunt. 'You have not seen it since my mother wrote it?'

'Of course not. Why should I? That information is seared in my mind; I have no need of a note to remind me.'

'You did not by chance give it to anyone?'

'No, I did not. Stop these foolish questions.'

'I have only one more question. Remind me if you will, how old is Anne?'

'She is five and twenty. Which is why it is high time that Darcy stopped procrastinating and marry her.'

'I quite agree, Mother. But I expect it will not be long now, before he sees the error of his ways.' Anne de Bourgh declared languidly as she entered the room, having heard the last statement.

'And what makes you think that Darcy will came to you?'

'He will come as soon as he realises that his lady love is but a lady-bird. Which should be any day now.' Miss de Bourgh smiled dreamily.

'You were the one who hired George Wickham to compromise Miss Elizabeth Bennet?'

'Of course. You heard Mother. It is insupportable for Darcy to lose his head over a lightskirt. Since no one in our family will do anything to bring him into line, I had to do something.'

'But, Anne, did you not claim that you had no interest in marrying Darcy?'

'That was ten years ago. I did not want to marry such a stuffed shirt. But Mother has kept me prisoner at Rosings, and since I was tired of her telling me what to do, I decided that I needed a husband. Darcy might be boring, but at least he is handsome, and mother will not prevent me marrying him. And once we are married, not only can I leave Rosings, Rosings will no longer belong to mother. Then I will be the Mistress of Rosings, and can throw Mother into the hedgerows.'

'But you already are the Mistress of Rosings. You have been since your twenty-fifth birthday, although your mother is entitled to live in the Dower House.'

'What? Mother always told me that Rosings will only be mine when I marry. You mean that I do not have to marry Darcy to take control of Rosings?'

'Now, not so fast,' cried Lady Catherine. She had been shocked to hear that her daughter had plotted to ruin a young woman, but to her that was acceptable to separate Darcy from that impertinent chit. To hear that her daughter only wanted to marry Darcy to become the Mistress of Rosings, so that she could usurp Lady Catherine's place was too much. 'You are not capable of running my estate.'

'Neither are you and it is my estate,' Anne shouted back at her mother.

'You ungrateful child, after everything that I have done for you...'

Since Colonel Fitzwilliam had the answers to his questions, he decided to leave. Although it was unsatisfactory that he could not do anything else, he considered that Miss Elizabeth had not been hurt, while his cousin had had a lifetime under her mother's tyranny. He reasoned that Anne had had her punishment in advance.

For the nonce, he would leave them be, to let them fight out ownership of Rosings amongst themselves.

He quietly exited, and returned to London and sanity.

~~B~~

21 Answers

Now that the threat of Mr Wickham had been removed, everyone heaved a sigh of relief. None more so than Elizabeth Bennet.

The morning after Wickham's removal, Elizabeth woke at her usual time and smiled as she realised that she could again go for her solitary rambles. With that idea in mind, she hurried out of bed, dressed and, after picking up a fresh muffin and an apple from the kitchen, rushed out of the house.

She breathed deeply of the fresh morning air, as she walked briskly towards her favourite place.

Elizabeth reached the top of Oakham Mount, just as the sun crested the horizon, illuminating a figure seated on her favoured rock.

Darcy rose when he heard her approach, and bowed politely. 'Good morning, Miss Elizabeth. What a delightful surprise to encounter you on this beautiful morning,' Darcy greeted her with a mischievous smile.

'Good morning, Mr Darcy. A surprise you say? Did you truly not expect me to take the opportunity to resume my morning walks to Oakham Mount?' Elizabeth responded in the same tone of voice.

'If I had any such expectations, it would be most improper of me to venture to the same spot which you favour, in the hopes of meeting you. Would it not?'

'As you say, it would be most improper, and knowing you to be the perfect gentleman, I could never countenance such an idea.'

'I am pleased that you know me so well. But since by pure chance we are both here, shall we enjoy the view together?'

They took a seat on the rock, although perhaps the distance between them was less than strictly proper. Elizabeth and Darcy did indeed enjoy the view, both of the landscape and the person sitting next to them.

'Miss Elizabeth, do you still feel as you did after my aunt's visit?'

'Why do you ask? Have you changed your mind after what happened yesterday?'

'Not at all. On the contrary, I would like our engagement to be official, so as to be allowed to protect you.'

'Even from myself?'

'No man will ever be able to do that. Although I hope that you would try to consider my feelings on the subject, and be prepared to compromise.' Elizabeth raised a questioning eyebrow, waiting for Darcy to continue. 'I will try to respect your independence, if you will try not to give me an apoplexy.'

'I suppose that is a fair request.' Elizabeth sighed. 'I am afraid that we are both the product of our upbringing. I was raised to think for myself and make my own decisions, and you were raised to be protective of ladies.'

'And by inclination I will protect the ones I love, irrespective of sex.'

'Very well, Mr Darcy. I will endeavour to consider your feelings and only put myself in danger while you are present to protect me,' Elizabeth teased.

Darcy huffed in good humoured exasperation. 'If that is the best you can do, I expect that I have no choice but to accept.' He took her hand and raised it to his lips. 'But to return to the question I asked earlier. Are you still willing to marry me?'

'Yes, it would give me the greatest pleasure.'

'Do you think that your mother had enough time to bask in her achievement? As I indicated, I would dearly love to make our engagement official, by speaking to your father, and asking his permission to marry you.'

Elizabeth considered the question. Mrs Bennet had fully recovered and was looking forward to the christening. Her mother was also aware that Darcy had been courting her, and although she had not said so, appeared hopeful that an engagement was not too far off.

'Yes, I believe now would be the appropriate time to speak to my father.'

She did not mention that the sensations caused by the kiss on her hand made her eager to marry sooner rather than later.

Darcy beamed. 'Excellent, in that case, might I accompany you back to your home? I would like to speak to Mr Bennet as soon as possible.'

He stood up and extended his hand to Elizabeth. She took it and rose to her feet, looking up at him with a happy smile. Darcy could resist no longer. He slowly bent forward, giving Elizabeth time to realise what he meant to do, and brushed those enticing lips with his own.

The effect was electric. Elizabeth's grip on his hand tightened and pulled him closer. Darcy did not need more of an invitation. Their second kiss was no light brush of lips, but released their pent-up passions. But before too long, Darcy pulled back slightly and took a shuddering breath.

'I think I would prefer a short engagement, what do you think?' Darcy suggested huskily.

Elizabeth was still trying to regain her composure, and swallowed convulsively. 'Very short,' she agreed.

~~B~~

'What took you so long?' asked Mr Bennet when Darcy asked him for permission to marry Elizabeth.

'Miss Elizabeth did not wish to detract from her mother's news.'

Mr Bennet was taken aback that he could not tease Darcy over the delay. 'Silly girl,' he muttered, although his eyes moistened due to his daughter's consideration.

He cleared his throat. 'How soon are you planning to marry?'

'We have considered getting a common licence. That would allow us to marry as soon as we wish, and we would not have to worry about Lady Catherine's interference when the banns are being read.'

'You think she would cause trouble despite the fact that you could ruin her?'

'After her performance the other week, I simply do not know what she might do, and I have no wish to take a chance.'

'Do not rush too much. At least give my wife some time to prepare.'

'As long as we can be married by Christmas. Although I would prefer next week.'

'Eager, are you?'

'Very.'

'I cannot say that I blame you.'

~~B~~

Mr Bennet escorted Darcy back to the dining room, where the ladies were having breakfast.

'Mrs Bennet, I have some wonderful news for you. Mr Darcy has just offered to take your most troublesome daughter off your hands.'

'Mr Bennet, I thought that you had stopped teasing me,' pouted Mrs Bennet.

'It is quite true, Mrs Bennet. Although I would say that Mr Bennet has kindly given permission for me to marry your wonderful daughter, Elizabeth,' Darcy replied before the conversation could get out of hand.

Mrs Bennet looked pleased at the prospect of seeing Lizzy so well married, but then she raised a concern. 'You do know that Lizzy is impertinent?'

'Yes, I do. It is one of her more endearing attributes.'

'She will never be an obedient wife.'

'If I wanted obedience, I would buy myself a dog.'

'You must truly love her, Mr Darcy.'

'Yes, Mrs Bennet, you are correct. I love Elizabeth very much.'

Lydia and Kitty started to giggle at that statement, only to be quelled by a disapproving look from Mrs Taylor.

Mrs Bennet turned her attention to Elizabeth. 'I just hope that you love this dear man just as much. I cannot think of anyone else who could match you so well.'

'I do, Mother.' Elizabeth answered with a big smile. Much of her pleasure was for the restraint Mrs Bennet had shown. Not fearing for the loss of her home seemed to have caused a minor miracle.

'When are you planning to get married?' Mrs Bennet asked, wondering if she had enough time to arrange for a proper wedding by April.

'Next week?' suggested Darcy.

'Next week?' shrieked Mrs Bennet, making Elizabeth cringe. 'I cannot possibly arrange a wedding at such short notice. We need a dress, a trousseau, flowers for the church, the wedding breakfast...'

'I do not need a dress,' protested Elizabeth, and blushed as Darcy smiled and said, 'I agree'.

'I mean I do not need a *new* dress.' Elizabeth corrected her statement, trying to avoid looking at her intended. Although when she cast a brief glance in his direction, she saw him mouth 'pity'.

The argument went on for a while. At one point Darcy murmured into Elizabeth's ear, 'we could always elope...'

'No, we could not. I would not want to give Lydia ideas.'

Eventually Mr Bennet intervened. 'Mrs Bennet, Lizzy and Darcy want a simple wedding, and I quite agree with them. I would wish you to conserve your energy for looking after Joshua.'

When Mrs Bennet reluctantly agreed, her husband surreptitiously winked at Elizabeth.

~~B~~

On his return from Rosings, Colonel Fitzwilliam stopped off at Matlock House to see his mother.

'Did you get your answers?' asked the Countess after greeting her son and ordering refreshments for him.

'You were correct in your assumption. Anne was the one who arranged to hire Wickham. She did it so that she could marry Darcy, since her mother would not allow her to marry anyone else.'

'Why was she so desperate to get married? I remember her saying that she did not want to marry Darcy.'

'I gather that Aunt Catherine told her that she would only get control of Rosings if she married.' Richard shook his head in frustration. 'How did it come about that Anne did not know that she was the Mistress of Rosings on her twenty-fifth birthday?'

'She did not know?' The Countess was stunned, but considered the information. 'Anne was only ten when her father died, and of course as a child, she was not present at the reading of the will. I guess we all assumed that Cathy would tell her when she came of age.'

'You trusted Aunt Catty to voluntarily give up control of Rosings?' asked Richard in disbelief, using his derogatory childhood nickname for his aunt.

The Countess sighed. 'I suppose we should have known better, but in recent years we have all avoided contact with her. It simply did not occur to me to think that she would be so determined to remain in control.'

'Anne said that her mother had held her prisoner at Rosings. I suppose Aunt Catherine wanted Anne to marry Darcy, so she would go and live at Pemberley, while Aunt reigned at Rosings unchecked.'

'Oh dear. I suppose it is too late to fix the situation now?'

'Considering that Anne hates her mother and wants to throw her into the hedgerows, I would say that it is too late. Although legally Aunt Catherine is entitled to live in the Dower House. I wonder if we will hear anything from either of them?'

'When he returns, I will speak to your father. Perhaps he will have an idea how to deal with the situation.'

'My guess is that he will say Aunt Catty has reaped what she has sown.'

~~B~~

By the time Colonel Fitzwilliam returned to Darcy House, it was quite late and he felt exhausted.

When Georgiana asked about the events of the day, he begged off, wanting nothing more than a good night's rest in a warm bed. By the time he rose the following morning, the Colonel was feeling better and joined his ward for breakfast.

Georgiana observed him carefully as he explained the situation at Rosings, noting his lingering exhaustion. 'Poor Anne. I had never realised that Aunt Catherine was effectively holding her prisoner. I always thought that since Anne has been unwell and frail most of her life, she preferred to be in her own home. At least that was what she used to say in her letters.'

'You correspond with Anne?'

'I used to, but lately she has not responded.'

'Perhaps Aunt Catty censored her mail.' Richard wondered aloud. He shook off his pensive mood. 'That still does not give her the right to ruin a young woman who has done her no harm.'

'How would she have learnt what is right or wrong? I was taught about what is proper, and I still agreed to elope with a man who made me think that I was quite grown up and in love.'

'But you did tell your brother about your plan, when you had a chance to do so. Yes, it was stupid that you ignored propriety, but in the end, you did the right thing.'

Georgiana smiled at her cousin. 'Thank you, Richard. You are the first person who does not completely absolve me of my actions. William kept telling me that it was all Wickham's fault, as well as his own for not warning me about the scoundrel, and he would not countenance that I had any culpability. That never felt right.'

Richard smiled and, to Georgiana's disgust, ruffled her hair. 'You are growing up, since you can take responsibility for your own actions. But as I said, while you were stupid, you did try to fix it. That counts for quite a lot in my eyes.'

Georgiana looked thoughtful as she smoothed her hair. 'I can live with that,' she said, as she felt a weight lifting off her shoulders. She graced her cousin with an impish grin. 'Leave it to a soldier to be blunt and not to make excuses.'

'I am glad to have been of service. But as a reward I request you to be patient for another day. I have spent too many days on the road, and I need to recover before I let another carriage rattle my bones.'

'By all means, Richard. Rest for as long as you need. It will give me more time to pack.'

Her plan was derailed later in the day, when Georgiana received a letter from her brother.

'Darcy is getting married? To Miss Elizabeth? Good for him.' Richard studied his excited ward. 'I suppose we could leave tomorrow,' he offered.

'Perfect. I will inform Mrs Annesley.'

Colonel Fitzwilliam sent a note to his mother, informing her of Darcy's engagement. He was unaware that Lady Matlock had decided to discover more about Miss Elizabeth, by the simple expedient of meeting her.

The note arrived while she was on her way to Netherfield.

~~B~~

22 Aunts

The unexpected arrival did not cause Miss Bingley any problems, and she invited the Countess to remain as long as she liked. An unfortunate consequence of the surprise visit was that Darcy and Bingley were absent, having accepted an invitation to dine at Longbourn.

Lady Matlock thought to use the opportunity to gather information about Miss Elizabeth from independent sources, without Darcy interfering. Her son had not been able to provide much information, having met Miss Elizabeth briefly and only once, other than to say that she was very pretty.

When Miss Bingley was called away to deal with a household issue, Lady Matlock was interested that Miss Caroline raised the subject of Miss Elizabeth. 'I gather that you have heard of Mr Darcy's infatuation with one of the daughters of our neighbour.'

While she knew Miss Caroline's penchant for vicious gossip, she was also aware that such gossip was usually based on a kernel of truth.

'What do you think of Miss Elizabeth? I will not credit Lady Catherine's opinion of the young lady, as she has always held the futile notion that Darcy would marry her daughter. I would rather hear from an independent source.'

Caroline very carefully considered her wording. She would not say one word that was untrue, to avoid being penalised yet again, but much could be said by not saying anything.

'I believe Mr Darcy must be greatly in love with her... charms.'

'Are you saying that my nephew and that young lady... ah?'

Caroline pretended embarrassment before she answered. 'That is the only reason I can account for the attachment. They do seem rather... ah... cosy together. While I would not want to cast aspersions, but as you are Mr Darcy's family...'

'Go on...'

'She is the daughter of a... gentleman. But I was given to understand that the estate is perhaps not as productive as it could be. Otherwise, the daughters, all five of them, would not have to rely on a share in their mother's portion... after her death. And even then, it is merely one thousand pounds.' Caroline conveniently forgot to mention the word *each*.

'You think that the girl is only interested in my nephew for his wealth.'

'I really could not say. It would be merely speculation.'

'I see.' Lady Matlock considered the implications. 'What about the rest of her family?'

'Mrs Bennet is the daughter of a country solicitor. I believe Miss Eliza has three uncles. One is a solicitor here in Meryton, the second is a tradesman and lives in or at least near Cheapside. I have not heard any details about the third uncle, but Miss Eliza customarily refers to him as Uncle Reggie. I dread to think what such a man could be like, when he allows Miss Eliza to address him so casually.'

The more she heard about Miss Elizabeth and her family, the more convinced Lady Matlock became that she needed to have a serious word with her nephew, to find out how much of Caroline's insinuations were true.

Although Miss Caroline presented the solicitor uncle as a tradesman because he had to earn a living, she seemed to forget that solicitor, clergyman and soldier were considered occupations suitable to a gentleman. The merchant uncle could be a problem, but she had a few friends from that sphere, and they were intelligent and sophisticated people. Any potential objections would depend on the people.

Lady Matlock wondered who Uncle Reggie could be. Miss Caroline obviously had no uncles who loved her well enough to allow her to address them so informally. Considering her personality, that was no great surprise.

There were only two concerns. The family's finances and the implied intimacy. Could Darcy have been ensnared by an unscrupulous hussy?

The Countess thought it unlikely, but there was only one way to find out. Ask her nephew.

Unfortunately, Darcy did not oblige her by returning to Netherfield before the rigours of the journey caught up with her, and she went to bed, determined to speak with Darcy in the morning.

~~B~~

The Gardiners arrived late on Friday afternoon, to attend the christening of their nephew on Sunday.

They were met at the door by a beaming Mrs Bennet. 'Edward, Madeline, I am so very happy that you could join us. Come inside and meet your nephew.'

The Gardiners were carried off to the nursery by an exceedingly enthusiastic Mrs Bennet. After dutifully admiring the latest addition to the family, the couple were allowed to refresh themselves, before joining the family for dinner.

Madeline Gardiner was surprised when she was introduced to the other guests. She greeted Bingley pleasantly, before turning to Darcy. 'Mr Darcy, please allow me to say that you have grown considerably since the last time I saw you.'

Darcy was startled and looked at her more closely. 'Please forgive me, although your face seems vaguely familiar, I cannot recall where we have met.'

'I would have been surprised if you had remembered. I grew up in Lambton. My father was the vicar, but I left twelve years ago to marry Mr Gardiner, and only returned once, for my father's funeral.'

'Miss Brooks. Of course. I was sorry to hear of your father's passing. He was a good man.'

They spoke briefly about Derbyshire until they were called in to dinner. Mrs Gardiner was surprised when Darcy escorted Elizabeth to the table and sat next to her.

Mr Bennet noticed the look, and informed the Gardiners. 'You do not yet know the most recent developments. Elizabeth is to marry Darcy.'

Madeline Gardiner was delighted to hear the news. She still corresponded with friends from her home town, and had heard only good reports about the Master of Pemberley.

'That must be a very recent development.' She turned to Darcy. 'I saw your aunt, Lady Matlock earlier this week, and she did not mention that you were engaged. And to my niece.'

'Miss Elizabeth only officially agreed to become my wife yesterday. I have not yet had a chance to inform anyone but my sister, although I suspect she will have told my cousin. Hopefully he will inform his mother.'

Much of the following discussion revolved around their wedding plans, and it was quite late by the time Darcy and Bingley excused themselves to return to Netherfield.

They both sought their beds, since Darcy had promised to return to Longbourn early. None of the servants thought to mention Lady Matlock's presence.

~~B~~

Lady Matlock missed her nephew again in the morning, since, as promised, he had gone to attend Mrs Bennet to discuss more plans for the wedding. She therefore decided to visit Meryton to see the environment in which Miss Elizabeth had grown up.

She had just turned from perusing the wares in the haberdasher's window, when she spied a familiar face.

'Madeline, it is such a surprise to see you. What are you doing here?' she greeted Mrs Gardiner, who had become a good friend, as they worked together for various charities.

'Eleanor, I am delighted to see you too. I am here for my nephew's christening and to visit my nieces.'

'Your nieces live in this area? I never knew.'

'They do. I gather that you are staying at Netherfield Park.'

'Indeed, I do, but how did you know? I only arrived yesterday, and have told no one of my arrival. Not even my nephew, who has been conspicuous by his absence.' This absence was a concern to the

Countess, as she had no explanation for it other than the one she preferred not to consider.

'As it happens, I met your nephew at dinner last night, and know that he is staying at Netherfield. Which is why I assumed you would be at the same house. I had better tell my sister that there will be another two for dinner. You and Andrew are coming to dinner? Are you not?'

'I am here on my own. Mrs Bennet is your sister?'

'Yes, she is. I could have sworn that I mentioned her to you.'

'I remember you mentioned a sister, but I must confess I did not remember her name. And Miss Elizabeth Bennet is your niece?'

'Indeed, she is.'

'Well, that changes everything. I was going to warn Darcy off the match in the strongest terms, but if she is your niece, I shall be delighted to welcome her into the family.'

'You did not think that her intelligence, character and beauty were sufficient reasons to do so?' Mrs Gardiner realised that Lady Matlock was unaware of the engagement, and decided she would let Darcy break the news.

'I thought she was after Darcy for his money, like all the other women we know. Especially since I was told that all the girls are penniless and have only unsuitable connections in trade.' Lady Matlock grinned as she gave her friend a pointed look.

'Nothing could be further from the truth, unless you consider me an unsuitable connection.'

'Of course, I have no objections to you and your delightful husband, but which other part is untrue?'

'I have known those girls for years, and they have always expressed a desire to marry for love and respect. It does not matter to them whether they are to live in a castle or a cottage, as long as they are part of a loving family.'

'But still, there is an inequality in wealth.'

'Eleanor, how many single women of marriageable age are Mr Darcy's equal in wealth?'

'When you put it that way... none.'

'Therefore, no matter whom he marries, he will be wealthier than his bride. And while my nieces might not be wealthy, they are far from penniless.'

'But I was told they only would receive a share of their mother's portion, which is only one thousand pounds, and only after their mother's death.' Since Mrs Gardiner was a reliable source of information about Miss Elizabeth, Lady Matlock was only too happy to avail herself of the opportunity.

'You should know better than to listen to servant's gossip.'

'Madeline, you ought to know me better than that. If I had heard this from a servant, I would have instantly dismissed the idea. My source was much closer to the Bennet family.'

'Did you hear this at Netherfield?'

'Yes.'

'Let me guess. Your source is a strawberry blonde young woman.'

'Perhaps. What makes you think so?'

'I do not know all the details, but I suggest that you speak to your nephew, and inform him of any allegations made against Lizzy.'

'I did not wish to broach such a delicate subject...'

'Delicate?'

'Ah... it was intimated that the young lady had become rather... ah... close to Darcy.'

'In that case, I must insist that you do speak to your nephew. I suspect that you have been deliberately misinformed.'

'Actually, I was not informed of anything, although much was implied.'

'As I said, ask your nephew, and then tell him the source of your information. I believe his reaction should be... interesting.'

Lady Matlock agreed, and after briefly chatting about their respective families, the ladies parted company.

Mr Bennet leaves his study

~~B~~

'Darcy, could I have a word with you in private?' Lady Matlock quietly asked her nephew as soon as she returned to Netherfield.

Mr Darcy had returned early, since he had been informed about his aunt's presence. He saw the pensive expression on his aunt's face and was immediately on his guard, but decided that it would be better to get the potentially uncomfortable discussion over with. 'I think the library is unoccupied at present.'

Once they were sitting in front of the fire, Lady Matlock immediately came to the point. 'William, I have been told a number of things about Miss Elizabeth, which I would like you to confirm or deny.'

Darcy was relieved that his aunt was prepared to listen, and prompted, 'go on.'

'I have been given to understand that Miss Elizabeth has used her considerable charms to lure you in and that you and she have become very... ah... close.'

Her nephew's expression turned from expectant to thunderous, and he drew himself up to his full height. 'Aunt Eleanor, if anyone but you made such an allegation, I would be forced to call them out. Whoever laid this charge, insulted not only Miss Elizabeth's honour but also mine.'

'There is no truth in this claim?'

'None whatsoever. Who told you this barefaced lie? No, wait. Let me guess. Aunt Catherine or Miss Caroline.'

'Both actually.'

'I suppose Miss Caroline wanted to ensure that if she could not be Mrs Darcy, then Miss Elizabeth should not have that privilege either.'

'Privilege?'

'Her words, not mine. Personally, I consider it a privilege that Miss Elizabeth has allowed me to court her.'

'That would explain her attitude. But she also mentioned relations of Miss Elizabeth's. Her uncles...'

'One of them, Mr Phillips, is the solicitor here in Meryton. A highly intelligent and pleasant man. The other, Mr Gardiner, is a tradesman in London, who, Elizabeth assures me, is a most honourable and sophisticated man. I met him and his wife, who is from Lambton, last night, and I thoroughly enjoyed their company.'

'I know the Gardiners. As it happens, Mrs Gardiner is one of my friends.'

'Then you know that there is no cause for concern.'

'Not with those uncles, but Miss Caroline mentioned a disreputable Uncle Reggie.'

'She mentioned an Uncle Reggie who is disreputable?'

'Not directly, but she implied it.'

This time, Darcy's reaction was unexpected by his aunt. He broke into unrestrained laughter.

'What is so funny?'

'The disreputable Uncle Reggie. As it happens, I know him… and so do you.' Darcy grinned at the puzzled expression on his aunt's face.

'Well… go on. Stop keeping me in suspense. Who is this uncle?'

'My godfather, the Duke of Barrington.'

'The Duke? Oh dear. Poor Miss Caroline…' Now it was the Countess' turn to chuckle. 'I should not laugh at someone's misfortune, but Miss Caroline certainly put her foot in it this time.'

Darcy's expression turned speculative. 'I believe that we should not disabuse the lady about the identity of Uncle Reggie.

'I thought disguise of any sort was your abhorrence.'

'I am simply minding my own business,' Darcy replied with an assumed air of innocence.

~~B~~

23 Engagement

Once Darcy had cleared up his aunt's concerns, he told her the good news.

'I am pleased that you do not have any further objections to my match with Miss Elizabeth, since we are now officially engaged.'

'Engaged? When did that happen?'

Darcy grinned. 'Unofficially the day of Aunt Catherine's visit. I was so very concerned about that woman's abuse of Elizabeth, that I wanted to reassure her that my aunt has no control over my life. In the heat of the moment, I blurted out a proposal, and Elizabeth accepted.'

'But that was weeks ago!' exclaimed Lady Matlock.

'Elizabeth asked me to keep quiet, since she did not wish to detract attention from her mother, who had just given birth to a son.'

'What is so special about a woman giving birth to a son? It happens every day.'

'The Bennet's next oldest child is fifteen. They have five daughters, and the estate is entailed to the male line.'

'I see. I suppose that makes a big difference.' Lady Matlock shook her head. 'I could never understand why men must be such misogynists. Women are perfectly capable of running an estate. Catherine excluded, of course. She may consider herself to be a proficient at everything, but if it were not for you, Rosings would be bankrupt.'

'It may come to that. After Aunt Catherine's performance at Longbourn, I have no intention of ever helping her again.'

'Normally I would ask if you would be prepared to help Anne, since she is now Mistress of Rosings, but I suspect you will have issues on that account.'

Before Darcy could ask any further questions, Mrs Nicholls announced, 'Miss Darcy and Colonel Fitzwilliam are here to see you.

~~B~~

Mrs Nicholls was an excellent housekeeper, and able to deal with unexpected situations. While she had not been thrilled with the hostess Mr Bingley had brought to the estate, she had been quite content since the change in leadership.

On the advice of Miss Mathilda Bingley, who informed her of her nephew's habit of spur of the moment invitations, Mrs Nicholls had ensured that all the guestrooms received a proper cleaning and could be made ready for occupancy within minutes.

Therefore, when the Countess had arrived the evening before, while the lady had not been expected, it had not caused a major problem.

Today, the arrival of Colonel Fitzwilliam and Miss Darcy was mostly expected, although there had been a question about the date. Mrs Annesley was a surprise, but she was not averse to waiting until her room could be made up.

Miss Bingley and Miss Caroline were on hand to greet the newest visitors, with Caroline making the introductions.

'This is turning into quite a family affair,' joked Miss Bingley. 'Soon your family will quite outnumber my own.'

When Richard and Georgiana looked puzzled, the lady added. 'I believe that Lady Matlock is your mother?' At Richard's nod, Miss Bingley informed them, 'she arrived yesterday and is even now in conference with Mr Darcy.'

Colonel Fitzwilliam grinned. 'I should have known that Mother would not be able to resist getting information first-hand.'

When he looked torn between being polite and spending time with their hostess, and his desire to see his cousin, Miss Bingley took the decision from him. 'There is no need to stand on ceremony, Colonel, Miss Darcy. Please feel free to join your relations. In the meantime, I shall be delighted to become acquainted with Mrs Annesley.'

That lady was pleased to have tea with her hostess, while her charge and the Colonel attended to family matters.

Mr Bennet leaves his study

~~B~~

Darcy was delighted to greet his sister and cousin. 'I gather that you received my news?' he asked with a smile.

Georgiana rushed to her brother and gave him a hug. 'We did indeed, and I am so happy for you.'

Meanwhile Richard greeted Lady Matlock. 'Good afternoon, Mother. I see that you would not take my word on the suitability of Miss Elizabeth.'

'What can I say. In my experience men are not particularly reliable when it comes to judging the character of a pretty young woman. If Darcy was determined to go ahead with this attachment, I wanted to know what I had to work with.'

'You can find out at dinner tonight,' interjected Darcy. 'We have all been invited to dine at Longbourn. Mrs Gardiner informed Mrs Bennet of your presence, and I was informed that you and all other late arrivals will be welcome.'

He grinned at his cousin and sister. 'I had hoped that news of my engagement would hurry your arrival, and Elizabeth's family are all eager to meet you.'

When they had settled down with tea supplied by Mrs Nicholls, Darcy returned to the question he had been distracted from, earlier.

'Aunt, why do you think that I would not assist Anne?'

'Because we discovered the reason why Wickham was so persistent about pursuing Miss Elizabeth...' Colonel Fitzwilliam answered the question instead with a sigh. 'Anne had hired him to compromise the lady, to ensure that you would not marry her.'

'Anne? Why the devil would she do such a thing?' Darcy was so shocked by the revelation that he forgot to watch his language.

The ladies chose to ignore the slip, understanding the devastation caused by the blunt statement.

'It seems that your aunt did not tell her that Rosings was to be hers on her twenty-fifth birthday, and since she was not allowed to meet anyone, she had decided that marrying you was the only escape she had.'

'But to do such a thing…'

Lady Matlock sighed. 'While I do not condone her actions, I can understand her desperation.'

'If she had the means to hire Wickham, she could have asked for help from the family…'

'I do not believe she was thinking clearly, but considering who her mother is, that is no great surprise.'

Darcy thought about the revelations for a few minutes. 'I think we should ask Elizabeth how she would like the situation to be dealt with. After all, she was the intended victim,' he decided in the end.

~~B~~

Darcy was getting ready for dinner at Longbourn, when there was a soft knock on his door. His call to enter was followed by his sister coming shyly into the room, carrying a parcel wrapped in a cloth.

'William, when I received your note, I thought you might want to have this.' She extended the parcel to her brother.

Darcy unwrapped the parcel and discovered several small boxes. 'This is some of the jewellery mother had put aside for your bride. I think these things were in London because you had them cleaned some time ago,' Georgiana explained.

'Thank you, Georgie.' Darcy smiled in gratitude and gave his sister a hug. 'I had completely forgotten that some of the jewellery was in town. That was exceedingly thoughtful of you.'

Georgiana returned the hug enthusiastically, pleased with the praise.

~~B~~

Longbourn was filled with light, warmth and happy chatter. Mrs Bennet had been thrilled to welcome Lady Matlock and her son, as well as Miss Darcy.

Lady Matlock had to agree with Darcy, when he proudly introduced Elizabeth. The young lady was lovely and had impeccable manners.

'Lady Matlock, it is an honour to meet you at last. Mr Darcy has often spoken of you with great respect and affection.'

'Did he not also mention all those times that I was cross with him for participating in the scrapes that Richard led him into?'

'This, I believe, was the cause for his respect and affection. I have discovered that he dislikes people who always agree with him, especially when he is wrong.'

'Darcy wrong?' Richard disclaimed in mock horror. 'I had thought that to be an impossibility.'

'I have not come across many instances of this miracle, but it has been known to happen.'

Georgiana watched the interchange with uncertainty. While she had never seen her brother smile as much in company, the way Miss Elizabeth spoke to and about him seemed disrespectful to her.

Lizzy noticed the discomfort of the young woman, and strove to reassure her. 'Please forgive our teasing, Miss Darcy. Your brother claims that my teasing makes him laugh, and when he does, he displays the most devastating dimples. How can I resist such encouragement?'

Georgiana glanced at Darcy, who nodded with a smile, which did indeed display his dimples.

'I suppose that I am not used to seeing my brother so greatly relaxed unless he is at Pemberley. It has quite astonished me. But would you call me Georgiana, since we are to be sisters?' she asked shyly.

'I should be delighted to do so, if you in return call me Elizabeth or Lizzy, as my sisters do.'

Lady Matlock watched the interchange and decided that no matter what the *ton* might think, Elizabeth was good for Darcy, and would be good for Georgiana as well.

Miss Caroline also watched the group with considerable chagrin. It seemed that all her carefully placed barbs against Elizabeth had failed. Lady Matlock seemed to be as charmed as the rest of her relations with that irritatingly affable chit.

Miss Bingley noticed her niece's pensive stare. 'You could be just as well liked as these ladies, if only you could get off your high horse,' she murmured quietly. 'Not that it would change *this* situation of course, but there are other good men out there.'

Caroline looked startled at the first comment, and then simply nodded her acceptance of the advice. For the rest of the evening she spoke politely whenever someone addressed her, but spent most of her time watching the various Bennet sisters.

~~B~~

Since there was time before dinner, Darcy quietly asked Mr Bennet for an interview, and included Elizabeth, Lady Matlock and Colonel Fitzwilliam.

The Colonel laid out his findings of the investigation into Wickham's attack on Elizabeth. When he finished, Lady Matlock addressed Elizabeth. 'Darcy suggested that since you were the target of the attack, you should have a say in what is to be done about Anne.'

Elizabeth had listened with horror to Anne's plan, but also her plight, and gave the matter some thought, before she answered. 'Miss de Bourgh's punishment is that she failed. William and I will be married, while she is still stuck at Rosings.'

'But she will be rewarded by control of the estate.'

'Does it truly matter? Like the Colonel explained. She was desperate to get out from under the control of Lady Catherine. Having achieved that end, albeit in a different fashion, I do not believe that she will ever attempt such a thing again. She is welcome to whatever life she makes for herself.'

'I suppose that if she runs the estate into the ground, I can always buy it and keep it for our second son,' suggested Darcy.

'I suggest you do not count your sons until you have them. Lizzy might follow in her mother's footsteps and produce a gaggle of daughters,' admonished Mr Bennet with twinkling eyes.

'If that is the case, it is fortunate that Pemberley is not entailed to the male line,' Darcy declared, sanguine at the thought of a gaggle of daughters just like his beloved Elizabeth.

~~B~~

Dinner was a sumptuous affair of three full courses. Mrs Bennet and the cook had outdone themselves. Even Lady Matlock was impressed by the quality of the meal.

During the separation of the sexes, the ladies were pleased to become better acquainted.

Georgiana in particular treasured the opportunity to chat with Elizabeth. She had watched the couple during dinner and had been impressed by the easy camaraderie between them. She confessed to Elizabeth, 'I believe that you are the first woman to treat my brother as a person, rather than a commodity.'

'I may have been the first woman, other than family, to whom he showed his true character. The mask he used to wear, would put off anyone but the most determined fortune-hunter.'

'But he always complained that even his scowling did not deter them. I cannot understand how you managed to get him to stop.'

'Did he not tell you about our first meeting?' When Georgiana admitted that her brother had only mentioned meeting an interesting lady, Elizabeth related the episode.

'I suppose that explains why he wanted to prove that he is a true gentleman, and that you were able to see what a good man he truly is. I have been hoping he would find a lady who would appreciate him.'

Elizabeth noticed that despite those encouraging words, Georgiana was twisting a handkerchief. She said gently, 'but something is troubling you. Will you not tell me what it is?'

Georgiana blushed and lowered her eyes. 'I just wondered... after you are married... will you be sending me back to school?'

'Do you wish to go back to school?'

'No,' came the whispered answer, as Georgiana kept her eyes on her hands.

'In that case, you shall not go back to school. You will remain in your... our home until you wish to leave,' Elizabeth said with a smile and squeezed the girl's hands.

'I will not be in your way?' Georgiana met Elizabeth's eyes at last.

'Of course not. Since I have to leave behind four sisters, I will need at least one to take their place.' Elizabeth gave her future sister her most impish grin, which caused a delighted response.

'I always wanted to have a sister.'

'And now you shall have one in residence, as well as four others to call on.'

~~B~~

Lady Matlock watched the interaction between her niece and Elizabeth, and was well satisfied with the way Georgiana was coming out of her shell.

She took the opportunity of some of the ladies moving about, to have a quiet word with Caroline.

'Although I could hardly credit it, you were quite correct, Miss Caroline. My nephew and Miss Elizabeth do seem quite cosy together. I have rarely seen a couple so well suited to each other.'

Caroline had the grace to blush. The evening before she had seen the presence of Lady Matlock as an opportunity to drive a wedge between the couple. But she had not considered the personalities involved. Instead of accepting the gossip at face-value and spreading it, the way Caroline's friends would have done, the Countess had gone to the people involved and asked direct questions to determine the truth behind the gossip.

Earlier in the day, when she realised that Lady Matlock was discussing the situation with Mr Darcy, Caroline realised that she had made a mistake. Since then, she had tried to discover a way she could get out of the hole she had dug for herself.

Now that the time had come, all she could do was to tell the truth. 'My apologies, Lady Matlock. I let my jealousy run away with me,' she blurted out.

The lady was startled by the honest admission, and searched Caroline's face for any evidence of sincerity. The chagrin displayed gave her a cautious hope that the young woman might have learnt a lesson. 'Very well, Miss Caroline. I understand. But I would hate for anyone to get the wrong impression. Do I make myself clear?'

'Quite clear, My Lady.'

~~B~~

24 Uncles

Lord Matlock arrived in London, only to find that his family appeared to have deserted him. His wife had left a letter for him explaining the latest happenings in the family.

He was horrified when he read about the actions of Lady Catherine and Anne de Bourgh. He was more amused about his wife's concern regarding Miss Elizabeth. The Earl knew his nephew well enough to trust him not to fall for some over-endowed fortune-hunter. After all, Darcy had been avoiding them for years. And the ladies of the *ton* were the most mercenary creatures he knew. A simple country Miss was a refreshing change by comparison.

Since his wife had gone to Meryton to inspect their prospective future niece, the Earl decided that he had better attend to the mess at Rosings.

He sent a note to the family solicitor, requesting him to accompany the Earl to Rosings the following morning, with a copy of the will.

He also thought it wise to take along half a dozen of his best trained footmen.

~~B~~

There was a hushed atmosphere settled over Rosings Park, when the Earl and the solicitor arrived.

They were immediately escorted into what the family described as Lady Catherine's throne room. The lady herself was sitting in her customary chair, but today her strength seemed to have deserted her.

Instead of sitting erect and imperious, she appeared shrunken as she huddled in her seat.

'Fitzwilliam,' she said listlessly.

'Good afternoon, Catherine. Where is Anne?'

'She is in her chambers.' This reply too was given without true attention.

'I would see her now.'

Lady Catherine waved a negligent hand. 'Perkins will show you the way.'

The Earl of Matlock was getting more concerned by the minute. He nodded at the butler, who had remained to await orders.

'Take me to my niece.'

'Certainly, My Lord. Please follow me.'

The Earl followed Perkins, gesturing for the solicitor to accompany them.

'What is happening?' he asked the butler, as they ascended the stairs to the family wing.

Perkins sighed. 'Miss de Bourgh is unwell. She has been so for the last couple of days. Doctor White is with her at the moment.'

'Do you know what ails her?'

'I could not say, My Lord. The doctor will be able to tell you.' He softly knocked on a door, which was opened by a maid. 'The Earl of Matlock and his solicitor, Mr Thompson are here to see Miss de Bourgh.'

~~B~~

The Earl was shocked to see the pale young woman propped up in her bed, struggling to breathe.

A middle-aged man stood up from where he had been sitting by the side of the bed. 'I am Doctor White.'

The Earl introduced himself and the solicitor.

Anne de Bourgh, although weak, was conscious. 'Just the men I want to see. Hello, Uncle. Mr Thompson.'

'Anne, what happened to you?'

'It seems that I have a weak heart, and the argument I had with mother strained it to breaking point. Apparently, I am dying,' came the careless reply.

Lord Matlock looked at the doctor for confirmation. 'Miss de Bourgh is quite correct.'

'I am glad you brought the solicitor with you. I need to make my will.'

'Certainly, Miss de Bourgh. If you will allow, I will make some notes, and can draw up the document for you to sign,' Mr Thompson agreed.

'There is no need to take notes. I leave all my worldly possessions to my cousin... Colonel Richard Fitzwilliam. I trust him to take care of all else.'

'Everything?'

'I do not have time for a lengthy document. Write it up now, so that I can sign it.'

Although flustered at the speed with which he was supposed to do this, Mr Thompson took but a few minutes to write two clean copies of the will. 'Perhaps Your Lordship, and you, Doctor, would be good enough to witness Miss de Bourgh's signature...'

Anne de Bourgh signed the documents, which were duly witnessed by the gentlemen.

'Thank you, Uncle. You may leave now, and let me die in peace.'

'Do you not wish me to stay?'

'Why? You were never here while I lived. You all just left me here to rot with mother. At least Richard tried to make me laugh when he visited. Goodbye.'

Anne closed her eyes. Whether it was because her energy was exhausted and she fell asleep, or because she did not wish to argue, the Earl never discovered. He respected his niece's wish and quit her chambers.

~~B~~

The Earl and Mr Thompson returned to the throne-room, where they found Lady Catherine in exactly the position in which they left her.

'Anne is dying,' the Earl said without preamble.

'I know.'

'She made a will, leaving everything to Richard.'

'I thought she might.'

'What will you do now?'

'I will stay, in case Anne wishes to see me.'

'And then?'

'I do not know and care even less.'

'Why, Cathy?'

'I made mistakes, and now I am paying for them.' Lady Catherine shrugged listlessly. 'You have your answers. You might as well go.'

The Earl took a last look at his sister. 'As you wish, Cathy. Goodbye.'

'Goodbye, Fitzwilliam.' Lady Catherine did not even bother to look up, but kept staring out the window, where the trees were shedding their leaves.

On their way out of the house, Lord Matlock requested of the butler, 'keep me informed of happenings.'

'Of course, Sir.'

The Earl returned to London, relieved that there had been no need for his footmen.

~~B~~

In Meryton, the Sunday service was drawing to a close, when there was a slight disturbance at the entrance to the church.

A distinguished looking gentleman quietly slipped into the church, and made his way to the Bennet family pew. As he sat down, he gave Mr Bennet an apologetic look, which the gentleman acknowledged with a nod, before turning his attention back to the vicar, to whom he nodded in turn.

The vicar, alerted to the fact that all necessary godparents were now present and accounted for, went on to the christening service for Joshua Bennet.

Mr Bennet leaves his study

Mr and Mrs Gardiner, as well as the gentleman, who identified himself as the Duke of Barrington, stood as the godparents for Joshua Henry Reginald Bennet.

Due to the temperature, the vicar confined himself to sprinkling water on the infant, to prevent the child catching a chill.

Mrs Bennet smiling countenance exuded pride in her son... and the fact that he had a Duke as a godfather. Mr Bennet was simply proud of his whole family, and could not help the moisture gathering in his eyes.

The vicar concluded the service with a minimum of fuss, to allow Mrs Bennet to take her precious son back to their warm home.

~~B~~

The extended family, and soon to be family, gathered at Longbourn for yet another celebratory meal.

Even Miss Caroline attended at the last minute, having recovered from her indisposition that morning, and wanting to make a good impression on Lady Matlock. She arrived just in time for her brother to escort her and Jane to the table.

Since it was a family celebration, even Kitty and Lydia were allowed to join the adults. Apart from Mr and Mrs Bennet, at the head and the foot of the table, the Duke at Mrs Bennet's right, and Lady Matlock to the right of Mr Bennet, the rest of the family took whichever seats were most congenial to them.

Due to this, all the youngest girls and Miss Caroline, sat in the middle of the table, and soon there was a lively discussion about fashion taking place.

Towards the end of the meal, Mr Bennet stood up and tapped his glass to silence the table.

'I would like to propose a toast. To my dear wife, who has not only gifted me with five wonderful daughters, but also my son and heir. I thank you from the bottom of my heart.' He raised his glass to salute Mrs Bennet, who blushed at the sincere praise.

The rest of the diners joined in the congratulations, making the lady feel giddy with delight.

~~B~~

Darcy leaned towards Elizabeth and whispered, 'a year from now that could be us.'

Elizabeth blushed at the reminder what would be happening in just a few days' time. 'Perhaps, or perhaps not. I have heard of couples who had to wait for years to be blessed with children.'

'Perhaps it is merely a matter of practice. If you wish to be a mother, I am willing to practice most assiduously.'

Colonel Fitzwilliam, who was sitting nearby and had heard the quiet exchange, muttered under his breath, 'I bet you are.'

~~B~~

Bingley and Jane were also discussing potential families. Each was trying to discover how many children the other hoped to have.

Although Jane was pleased to hear, 'I do not care how many children I have, or what sex they might be, as long as you are their mother,' she blushed and gently chided Bingley. 'How could you say such a thing, Mr Bingley. After all, we are only courting, and we have not yet agreed to anything.'

'Please forgive me, Miss Bennet. I was carried away, since I cannot imagine any other lady in my life. I am afraid that patience has never been my greatest virtue.'

'If it is not patience, what is your greatest virtue?'

'An honest heart, and once my heart is truly given, loyalty.'

The look in Mr Bingley's eyes pushed Jane ever closer to a point of no return.

~~B~~

After the meal, Lady Matlock took Caroline to meet the Duke, since they had not yet been introduced. 'Your Grace, would you allow me to introduce to you, Miss Caroline Bingley. Miss Caroline, I have the honour of introducing the Duke of Barrington.'

Miss Caroline curtsied deeply.

'A pleasure to make your acquaintance, Miss Caroline. Am I right in assuming that you are the sister of Darcy's friend from Cambridge?'

'Yes, Your Grace, indeed I am. And may I say what an honour it is to meet you at last. Mr Darcy has often spoken about you. But I must say, I am astounded that you would deign to visit such a place as Meryton.'

'There is no great mystery about my presence. I am here for my godson.'

'I am certain that Mr Darcy is delighted that you would take the trouble to visit him here. Although I feel convinced that he would have been thrilled to visit you in London, and saved you the journey.'

'While I am happy to see Darcy, he is not the godson I have come to see. I am here for Joshua Henry Reginald Bennet.'

'You are the godfather of Miss Eliza's new brother?'

'Indeed. It has taken twenty years, but Bennet has at last taken me up on my offer... to be the godfather of his heir.'

'I was not aware that you are acquainted with the Bennets. Considering some of their relatives, I am astounded that you would associate with that family.'

'And which relatives would that be, Miss Caroline? I have met the Gardiners and the Phillips', and I find them intelligent and charming company.'

'I quite agree. Although I have only met them briefly, they are, as you say, charming company. I was referring to an uncle whom Miss Eliza has mentioned, and the impression I received was... unfavourable. I shudder to think what kind of man would permit his niece to address him as Uncle Reggie.'

'Do you know Miss Elizabeth well?'

'Not all that well. We have only recently come into the area from London.'

'I have to admit that Miss Elizabeth has been known to humiliate me on a regular basis,' sighed the Duke theatrically.

Caroline took the bait. 'That is insupportable. I am afraid that Miss Eliza has no respect for rank,' she cooed.

'Quite the contrary, I get tired of those sycophants who are always flattering me. With most of them I never know whether I won at chess, or whether they let me win. At least with Lizzy I know.'

'You play chess against Miss Eliza, Your Grace? That is most gracious of you, although if I understand correctly, she does not comprehend the honour you bestow upon her, allowing her to practice her mediocre skills with you. It must be humiliating wasting your skill against such an inferior opponent.'

'You misunderstood, Miss Caro. It is humiliating being trounced by a mere slip of a girl, but at least I do not have to wonder about the outcome of the game. With Elizabeth I know that I lost.'

'She wins?' Caroline was horrified. Not only had Elizabeth such skill, but that the Duke seemed to appreciate losing to her.

Just then the lady under discussion joined them. 'I hope that you will be here long enough to have a game, Your Grace. It has been much too long.'

'I have time now. Shall we join battle, my lady?' The Duke bowed gracefully and offered Elizabeth his arm.

'I would be delighted, Uncle Reggie,' replied Elizabeth with a mischievous grin as the Duke led her away, but not before he glanced over his shoulder to see the effect the appellation had on Caroline.

The Countess, who had kept quietly in the background during their exchange, delighted in seeing the colour drain from Caroline's face as she gaped at the backs of the pair.

'I know it must be a tribulation to someone of your exalted rank having to spend time with such low relations as Elizabeth's Uncle Reggie, is it not?' Lady Matlock asked with a bland smile.

Those quiet words reminded Caroline of her company, and her pallor was replaced by a hot scarlet flush. 'A word of advice, Miss Caro. Never, ever try to denigrate a member of my family again. You will be the one to suffer.'

Caroline wished the ground would open up and swallow her.

~~B~~

Mr Bennet leaves his study

Darcy watched in fascination the battle royal which ensued between his beloved Elizabeth and his godfather. He was amazed that Elizabeth could focus on the game, while entertaining the Duke with snippets of their courtship.

It was not until he noticed the Duke becoming engrossed in her account of Lady Catherine's visit, and moving one of his chess pieces without properly paying attention, that he suspected Lizzy's strategy.

It was confirmed four moves later, when she moved her queen into position and declared, 'check mate.'

The Duke looked at the board in consternation, and huffed in mock anger, 'I cannot understand how you always manage to get the better of me.'

Darcy suppressed the laugh which threatened to bubble up, when Elizabeth suggested with an innocent expression, 'perhaps I am the better player?'

Barrington looked doubtful, but then shifted his attention to Darcy. 'Well, my boy, are you ready to give me a game? I need to salvage my pride after that imp has beaten me yet again.'

Darcy accepted the challenge by his godfather, and attempted the same strategy employed by Elizabeth. Occasionally he glanced at Elizabeth, who was watching the game he played with suppressed amusement. While he was not as proficient at the art of distraction, he managed well enough, and succeeded in winning the game.

'Drat. You have improved, William. Have you been playing against Lizzy?'

'I have indeed.' Darcy grinned at his godfather, and then turned to wink at Elizabeth. 'And she has been an excellent teacher.' '

Although she blushed at the compliment, Elizabeth returned his smile in full measure. There was a lot to be said to marry a man who showed such a marked respect... as well as dimples.

She could hardly wait for them to be married.

~~B~~

25 Caroline

Since the ground refused to cooperate, Caroline Bingley did the next best thing. She quietly and unobtrusively left the room and asked for her carriage to be brought.

On the way back to Netherfield, she huddled miserably in her seat, battling with conflicting emotions.

She was furious that she had been humiliated yet again, and tried to find someone to blame.

Why could Eliza Bennet not have told her that the man she called Uncle Reggie was a Duke, instead of letting her believe that he was some uncouth tradesman?

Had Lady Matlock discovered the identity of the Duke, and was just waiting for her to make a fool of herself?

Or worse, could Mr Darcy have known all along who the mysterious Uncle Reggie was?

Had everyone known that the Duke enjoyed being called Uncle Reggie by Eliza?

Why could they not have told her? Caroline would never have made any disparaging comments, if she had known the gentleman's identity.

The carriage was nearly at Netherfield, when Caroline remembered her aunt's rule about vicious gossip.

If she had obeyed that rule, she would not have made a fool of herself.

That realisation cooled her temper as if she had been doused with a large bucket of iced water. Caroline was so caught up in her epiphany, that the footman had to call her name several times, before she noticed that they had arrived at Netherfield.

She exited the carriage and rushed to her room, where she paced between the window and the fireplace, while she considered the last few weeks.

When her aunt had given her that list of rules, Caroline had eventually memorised them to ensure that she would not lose any more of her allowance, by accidentally breaking those rules.

Since then, she had given lip service to the behaviour Aunt Mathilda insisted upon, but she had never truly thought about those rules. As long as she did not act blatantly against the rules, she had considered that was tantamount to obeying them.

Some of her behaviours had become so ingrained that Caroline had not even realised what she was doing. Like her need to prove to everyone that she was better than the other untitled members of her company, so that no one would remember that her father had been a tradesman. She automatically flattered anyone of the peerage, and highlighted to them the perceived faults of anyone else.

All her friends in London had done the same.

She reviewed the women of her own circle, all of whom acted like she had. Caroline could only think of two who had married relatively well, but each of them to men who had an unsavoury reputation.

At last, it was driven home to her that she would never be accepted by members of the first circles, perhaps not even the second circle. Some of the younger sons would consider a wife from her background, but only for her dowry, and only if they were in desperate need of money.

It seemed that Louisa had been lucky. Her more easy-going nature had prevented her from becoming obsessed with the need to climb the social ladder. As a result, she had attracted Cedric Hurst, the heir to his parents' estate.

While Louisa had pandered to her sister's foibles, Caroline realised that by being more agreeable and not reaching as high, Louisa had found a better husband than Caroline could hope for, with her continued belittling of others.

In her current situation, even after the set-down by Mr Darcy, and the rules imposed by Aunt Mathilda, Caroline had not been willing to accept their verdict. While she had been more careful about what she said, she had continued with her old habits.

And everyone had given her enough rope to hang herself.

The comprehension of her foolishness at last came crashing down on Caroline. She had been given a chance to prove that she could change, and she had pigheadedly wasted it.

She collapsed onto her bed and cried out her misery.

~~B~~

Caroline woke up and discovered that someone had covered her with a blanket. She assumed that Lucy had been her benefactress, and mentally thanked her for the kindness.

Judging by the sun coming into her room, she realised that it must be morning. After tidying herself up, she went in search of her aunt, whom she found seated by a fire in her sitting room.

'Good morning, Caroline. Would you care for some tea?'

'Thank you, Aunt. I would dearly love a cup.' Caroline gingerly sat down opposite Aunt Mathilda.

The lady prepared the tea just as Caroline liked it, and then sat back and carefully studied her niece. It had indeed been Lucy who had found Caroline the evening before and provided the blanket. Lucy had then informed Miss Bingley about the state her niece was in. Seeing Caroline's still puffy eyes, and her now subdued demeanour, Aunt Mathilda had hopes that Caroline had had a change of heart at last.

'Aunt Mathilda, I have been a fool, and worse, I have made a complete fool of myself.'

'True.'

Caroline looked as if she had bitten into a lemon at the short reply. 'I do not know what to do now,' she admitted helplessly.

Aunt Mathilda gave her a small smile to soften the impact of her words. 'You now have a choice to make. Slink away into obscurity and lick your wounds, or the more difficult option is to face up to your mistakes and apologise.'

'Apologise to whom?'

'Everyone you have harmed or tried to harm.'

Caroline nearly choked on the sip of tea she was in the process of swallowing. 'Everyone? There are so many,' she exclaimed in despair.

'I did say it was the more difficult choice, but in the long run you will find it more rewarding. If you have the courage.'

Miss Bingley waited patiently while Caroline considered what she would have to do. It felt like she was being forced to make a fool of herself again. But since she had already made a fool of herself, perhaps a double negative could make a positive.

If she went ahead with this, she would be in for a most unpleasant time. But would it be worse than being sniggered at behind her back? Or worse than being thought an ill-mannered disgrace?

'Where do I start?' Caroline asked with determination, and was rewarded by a smile full of approval and love.

'That is the Bingley spirit.' Aunt Mathilda applauded.

~~B~~

The Earl of Matlock had spent Sunday in London to rest from his travels, and recover from the shock of seeing the state of affairs at Rosings.

Since there was nothing which he could do about his sister or his niece, he decided to join his wife and discover the state of affairs with his nephew.

Therefore, after a leisurely breakfast on Monday, he boarded his coach yet again, this time for the journey to Meryton.

He arrived just in time for tea.

While he washed off the dust of travel, he had a chance for a quick word with his wife. 'How goes your evaluation of Darcy's lady love?'

'Much better than I expected. She is a pleasant young lady, and better connected than Catherine gave her credit for.' Lady Matlock chuckled quietly. 'Do you recall Barrington complaining about the girl who keeps beating him at chess?'

'Yes, of course I do. He claims to be most put out by it, although I strongly suspect he is delighted to have an opponent who does not try to kowtow to him.'

'Indeed. I discovered that Miss Elizabeth Bennet is that opponent.' Lady Matlock smiled at the stunned look on her husband's face.

'Well, well, well. I think that any girl who is prepared to take on Barrington, even if she did not win, is a perfect match for Darcy. Tell me more.'

His wife complied, passing on all the information that she had discovered about their future niece.

'It seems that I was right. Darcy would not be taken in by some over-endowed fortune-hunter. I look forward to meet the girl.'

~~B~~

The Bennets came for tea to Netherfield. They were accompanied by the Duke, who had decided to stay for the wedding. And while he complained about being woken up by his godson at all hours, Mrs Bennet had discovered him in the nursery on several occasions, soothing her son.

They were welcomed by Miss Bingley and her nephew, and were soon happily ensconced in the drawing room, ready to partake of the refreshments provided.

Just before they could start, Caroline stood up and asked for their attention.

'It has been brought home to me how badly I have acted. I am sincerely sorry for most of what I have said to you or about you. Since occasionally I managed to say nice things, I will not apologise for that.' Caroline gave a weak smile.

'Charles, viewed objectively, Miss Bennet is a wonderful lady. If you love her and manage to win her love in return, I will try to be happy for you.' She shrugged apologetically. 'At the moment, that is the best I can do.'

Bingley took her hands and kissed her cheek. 'I am delighted that you are trying to change. If you can manage to finish what you have started today, I am certain that you will find much happiness.'

'Thank you, Charles,' she replied with a timid smile, before addressing the next person.

Mr Bennet leaves his study

'Miss Eliza, pardon me. Miss Elizabeth, I was jealous that you snatched the prize which I had considered to be mine. I now realise that Mr Darcy was never mine to begin with. He has always been his own man, knowing his own mind. He knew that I could never be what he needed. If I am honest with myself, and I am trying to be, you can give him what I cannot. I hope that you will be very happy together.'

'Thank you, Miss Caroline. I hope that you too will find such happiness.'

'Mr Darcy, my apologies for all the discomfort I caused you over the years. And while I could hope that you had ignored propriety and spoken up sooner, I doubt that I would have heeded your words.'

'I too am sorry that I spoke so harshly, Miss Caroline.'

'Do not trouble yourself over it. I have only myself to blame. But I shall try to improve.'

'I wish you luck in this worthwhile endeavour.' Darcy bowed to the lady.

Caroline went on to apologise to everyone else in the group, until she came to the Duke. 'Your Grace, I am ashamed of myself for trying to denigrate Miss Elizabeth, by referring to you as unsavoury.'

'Think nothing of it, Miss Caroline. Truth be told, I was thoroughly amused, and since you have already apologised to Miss Lizzy, there is nothing else to forgive from me.'

'Thank you. You are most gracious.' Caroline replied with a grateful smile. She also realised that as uncomfortable as the experience had been, it had not been as bad as she had feared.

She recognised that the gracious forgiveness she was accorded was what truly made these people ladies and gentlemen, irrespective of titles. Perhaps she could learn to be like them. It was a heady thought.

~~B~~

After the Bennets returned to Longbourne, the Earl requested the use of the library for a family conference, which included his wife and son, as well as Darcy and Georgiana.

'I am guessing that Richard has filled you in on Anne's activities?' the Earl opened the conversation.

On being informed that everyone was aware of her actions, Lord Matlock told of his visit to Rosings.

Although Lady Matlock was sad to hear about her niece's state of health, she was pleased that her son would be provided for.

Richard was torn between elation at the prospect of owning an estate, and embarrassment due to his elation. His cousin noticed the ambivalence.

'Richard, as Anne said, you were the only one in the family to show her kindness. Who else would she chose as her heir? I must admit that I feel ashamed for having ignored her for all these years, but because Aunt Catherine...' Darcy trailed off. It sounded too much like he was trying to make excuses.

Richard considered the situation. 'We all understand, Darce, and I suspect so does Anne. But I think that I should go to Rosings... immediately after your wedding,' he suggested.

'Thank you. I always hoped that you would stand up with me, when I got married. Although I would understand if you wish to leave earlier.'

'No, I will stay for the ceremony, but I think that I will leave immediately afterwards. If I ride to Kent, I can be there by evening.'

~~B~~

26 Netherfield Ball

The ladies at Netherfield and at Longbourn were busy preparing for the ball. In the meanwhile, the gentlemen too had matters which required their attention.

Since Darcy did not wish to go to London to see the family solicitor, he approached Mr Phillips to prepare the marriage settlements. They met in Mr Bennet's study to discuss the details.

Mr Bennet, who was aware of the purpose of the meeting had invited Mr Gardiner and Elizabeth to join them. While Darcy was pleased to see his intended, he was surprised that she was to be included in the discussion.

'I felt that since this concerns Lizzy, she should be present,' explained her father.

'I am grateful that you did,' Darcy replied, as he kissed Elizabeth's hand.

'Before you ask, Gardiner is here because he has been looking after my daughters' dowries, and he has the final say in whether they receive it. If he considers a man to be unsuitable, he is authorised to withhold the funds.' Mr Bennet informed Darcy, before turning to his brother-in-law. 'Do you think Darcy's character is adequate?' he asked with a teasing smirk.

'From what I have heard of him, I think he will do nicely for Elizabeth,' was the equally mischievous response.

Elizabeth rolled her eyes at her relatives' banter.

'I am grateful that you consider me worthy of your niece, but I was under the impression that Miss Elizabeth would only receive a share of her mother's portion. Not that I care about the money, since Pemberley produces enough income.'

'Bennet's mother left her portion in trust for her granddaughters. Instead of keeping it in the four percents, she asked me to invest it. So, instead of growing to ten thousand pounds in total, as Bennet thought it had, the initial six thousand pounds has grown on an average of ten percent per annum. Compound.' Gardiner grinned at Bennet and Darcy. 'Before you ask, Elizabeth's share is five thousand pounds at present.'

There was a stunned silence for a moment, until Bennet murmured, 'my mother was a wise woman.'

'I would not have cared if you were penniless, as some people have claimed, but five thousand pounds is a very respectable dowry, which will look good to the *ton*. Now the question is, what would you like to do with it?' Darcy asked Elizabeth.

'You are asking me?'

'It is your money.'

Elizabeth looked around, and saw approving smiles on the faces of all her relatives. She returned her gaze to Darcy, and after a moment's thought decided. 'I believe I would like to leave it in trust with Uncle Gardiner for our daughters, if we have any. Otherwise for our youngest son.'

'That is an excellent idea, Elizabeth,' Darcy was delighted that his bride was already considering the welfare of their potential children. 'I believe that based on Gardiner's success, we should invest the amount I had planned to settle on you, with him as well. What say you, Gardiner? Is that agreeable to you?'

'I can always use new investments to grow my business, Darcy.'

Elizabeth mostly just listened to the gentlemen discussing the amount, which Darcy was planning to settle on her, as well as her pin money and the provisions for their children; only speaking when asked if the terms were agreeable to her. Since the amounts were very generous, and she would have control of her money, she had no objections whatsoever.

When they finished their discussions, Mr Phillips wrote up one copy for them to sign, and promised to have additional copies ready the next day.

Mr Bennet leaves his study

Elizabeth was starting to understand why Darcy had been so very sought after by the ladies of the *ton*.

~~B~~

At Netherfield Caroline Bingley stood in her wardrobe and looked forlornly at her dresses.

She had been trying to work out how to have an elegant dress for the ball, but without funds, she could not get a new dress. She had considered altering one of her current dresses, But while most of them were excessively fashionable, she had come to realise that the colours did not suit her.

She was brought out of her reverie by a knock on the door, followed by the entrance of her aunt. 'You are looking rather lost, Caroline.'

Caroline sighed and explained her predicament. 'I simply cannot attend the ball, since I refuse to look ridiculous. I was such a fool wasting all my money on this.' She gestured at her London wardrobe. 'And I simply cannot wear a day dress.'

'In that case you might want to wear this,' Aunt Mathilda signalled Lucy to join them.

The maid was carrying a gown which Caroline had not seen before. The cut was fashionable and very much suited to her figure, and the pale blue suited her skin-tone. A subtle amount of lace enhanced the elegance of the gown.

Caroline gasped. 'This is exquisite. Where did this come from?'

'It was made by the local dressmaker,' Miss Bingley answered with a smile at her niece's response.

'You had this made for me?' Caroline asked, while gently running her hand over the fabric.

'Charles had this made for you. He was waiting for you to come to your senses, before giving it to you.'

'This is wonderful.' Caroline's eyes misted. She smiled at her aunt. 'I must go and thank him,' she exclaimed, before rushing off to suit actions to words.

Aunt Mathilda looked after her retreating figure with a fond smile. 'You are learning at last.'

~~B~~

All the preparations were finished and the guests started to arrive at Netherfield. As arranged, the Bennets, accompanied by the Duke, arrived early.

Since the ball was now being held in honour of Darcy's and Elizabeth's engagement, Kitty and Lydia had been allowed to come, after they had promised to be on their best behaviour. They and Georgiana would not be allowed to dance with anyone other than members of the extended family.

Darcy, who had been given advance information by Georgiana, who had seen the dress Elizabeth was wearing, took his bride aside and presented her with a necklace and matching earrings, set with pearls and emeralds.

'William, I cannot accept these,' exclaimed Elizabeth in consternation.

'Do you not like them?' Darcy asked worriedly.

'Not at all. The necklace is exquisite, but...' Elizabeth did not know how to explain that she felt overwhelmed.

Darcy reassured her. 'They were my mother's and she wanted me to give them to my bride.'

Elizabeth hesitated a moment longer. 'Since they are a gift from your mother, I cannot possibly refuse. Thank you.' She smiled at Darcy, then turned around, for him to place the necklace around her neck.

When she turned back, she noticed that Darcy wore an amused smile. 'You are the only woman I know, who would be reluctant to accept such a gift.' He bowed and placed a lingering kiss on her hand. 'You look wonderful.'

Mr and Mrs Bennet had watched from a distance. The lady shook her head as she watched her second daughter. 'I would never have thought that Lizzy could look so very beautiful and grand,' she quietly commented. 'But I believe she needs some help,' she added, since she had noticed the earrings, which were still in the box.

Mrs Bennet walked over to the couple with a proud smile. 'Would you like some help,' she offered, indicating the box.

Elizabeth gave her a grateful smile and said, 'I would appreciate it. While I am certain that William would be willing to help, earrings might be beyond his experience.'

'You are quite correct. I am happy to bow to greater experience.'

'Mr Darcy, you are exceedingly generous,' replied Mrs Bennet with a fond smile, without clarifying whether she meant the jewellery or his attitude.

'Whatever makes Elizabeth happy,' the gentleman murmured.

~~B~~

The rest of the guests had arrived and been greeted, and the first set of the evening was about to start.

Miss Bingley had been exceedingly flattered when the Duke had requested the first set from her.

Elizabeth danced with Darcy, of course, and no one was surprised to see Jane standing up with Bingley. The Earl led his Countess to the floor. They were followed by Mr and Mrs Bennet, while Richard engaged Mary for the first set. Even the Gardiners and the Phillips' joined the couples on the dancefloor.

Mrs Hurst chose not to dance, due to the lady's condition, but she encouraged her husband to dance the first set with her sister, who looked lovely and was glowing with pleasure.

The younger girls all stood at the side of the room, supervised by Mrs Taylor. Georgiana could not help but comment, 'do not William and Lizzy look exceedingly well together?'

Kitty exclaimed in surprise, 'I had not known how well Papa and Mama can dance.'

Lydia, who liked the look of a man in regimentals, paid particular attention to the two Colonels, and noticed Colonel Forster dancing with Charlotte Lucas. 'Why do the best officers dance with the plainest girls?' she asked plaintively, only to be shushed by Mrs Taylor. 'Sorry,' she murmured with a blush.

Luckily for her, she managed to watch her tongue for the rest of the evening, and enjoyed her first dances at a ball.

~~B~~

Jane danced the supper set with Bingley, and was having a lovely time.

When the music ended, Bingley drew her aside to ask quietly, 'Miss Bennet, may I be so presumptuous as to ask if you still have the final set available?'

'I have not yet promised it to anyone,' Jane replied cautiously. She wondered if Mr Bingley was trying to ask what she was hoping he would ask. Due to her sister's courtship with Mr Darcy, she had spent a considerable amount of time in the company of Mr Bingley, as the putative chaperone of the other couple.

It had given her a chance to converse with the gentleman privately, and to get to know him. While she had thought him a little immature at the beginning of their acquaintance, in recent weeks he seemed to take pride in taking control of his life.

Although he still asked for and listened to advice by Darcy regarding estate management, he had stopped asking for approval in his more personal sphere. She had even heard him tell Caroline, politely but firmly, to mind her own business.

Jane found that she liked Mr Bingley's company. When they had discussed books, the gentleman confessed that Plato's Republic was too highbrow for him. He found simpler enjoyments more to his taste. He had admitted that while he enjoyed watching performances of Shakespeare's comedies, he could not sit still long enough to read the plays.

Since Jane felt a similar inclination on this and other subjects, she considered Bingley to be a very comfortable match for her. That he was handsome and amiable, as well as an excellent dancer was a bonus. With him she felt relaxed, and yet, at the same time, there was an excitement when she was in his company. Ever since that time when he mentioned children, she had been letting down her guard.

Bingley looked hopeful at her response, and asked, 'would you allow me to request that set?'

Mr Bennet leaves his study

'Mr Bingley, I presume that you are aware what kind of a message this would send to our neighbours?'

'Quite aware, yes...'

Jane considered the wording of his request. 'What if I should not allow you to ask?'

'Then I would not ask, and let someone else have the pleasure of that dance.' Bingley appeared to not be happy about this option, but determined to let her make her own choices.

Bingley giving her that option, decided Jane. 'You may make your request,' she answered with a smile.

The gentleman returned her smile in equal measure. 'In that case, Miss Bennet, would you do me the honour, and grant me your hand... for the last set.'

'Yes, Mr Bingley, it would be my pleasure.'

'May I also call on your father tomorrow?'

'I believe both he and I would welcome this call.' Jane confirmed with shining eyes, as Bingley kissed her hand.

~~B~~

27 Wedding

Even though she had gone to bed late the night before, Elizabeth was up at her usual hour. She quickly dressed, and quietly slipped out of the house.

She was headed for Oakham Mount, since this would be the last opportunity she would have, to watch the sunrise from her favourite spot. Tomorrow she would be getting ready to be married.

Excitement warred with trepidation. In these few months she had fallen deeply in love with Darcy, and looked forward to their life together. But this meant that she would be leaving the home and family she had known all her life. Everything would be different. Would she be up to the challenge of being a good Mistress of Pemberley?

Would she be a good wife to William? Her Aunt Madeline had taken her aside and explained what she could likely expect on her wedding night. Her aunt seemed to think that there could be great pleasure for herself, while some of the innuendo she had heard from other matrons had suggested that it was an unpleasant duty to perform.

Elizabeth hoped that her aunt had the right of it. If the curious tight, tingly and melting sensations, which she had experienced on those few occasions when William had kissed her, were anything to go by, her duty would not be a duty at all.

She also wondered if William would be a good husband to her. Would he continue to treat her with respect and value her opinions? Once they married, according to the law, he would effectively own her, and she would not have any choice but to obey. Even the wedding vows stipulated that she must obey her husband. And obedience had always been difficult for her, at least if the orders had seemed arbitrary.

Elizabeth was so engrossed in her musings that she did not notice the gentleman standing in her path, until she almost collided with him.

'Judging by your expression, I hope that you do not have second thoughts about tomorrow,' Darcy said quietly, just before the collision, startling her from her reverie.

After recovering from her startlement, Elizabeth replied with an uncertain smile, 'not second thoughts exactly, but I was wondering what my future will hold.'

'Surely it will not be all that bad...'

'I will be leaving my home and my family, and everything will be new and strange. While something new is exciting, at the same time it can be rather frightening.'

'Do you not claim that your courage always rises at every attempt to intimidate you?'

'I do and it does, but I cannot help but wonder what kind of wife I will make, and what kind of husband you will be.'

'Perfect and doting, respectively,' came the smiling answer.

'I never realised how much of an optimist you are, William. I am certain that you have noticed that I am far from perfect.'

'True, but your imperfections make you perfect for me.'

He put an arm around her shoulders, and pulled her to him. 'All will be well. You shall see.'

Elizabeth relaxed in Darcy's embrace. 'Since you shall be in charge of my life as of tomorrow, I shall have to trust you to be correct.'

Darcy put a finger under her chin and raised up her face. He softly kissed her lips, making her shiver with that new sensation, which she experienced at his touch. 'All will be well,' he repeated, 'as long as we love each other, and are prepared to discuss problems, should they arise.'

When Elizabeth smiled at his assurance, Darcy asked, 'where are you bound? Not Oakham Mount by any chance?'

'Indeed I am.'

'I hope you will permit me to accompany you. I feel curiously protective.'

'In that case, I will welcome your company as I farewell my childhood.'

Darcy offered Elizabeth his arm, and they walked in companionable silence until they reached their destination.

As Elizabeth looked out at the view before her, she realised that she was looking at her past, while her future was standing beside her, offering his silent support.

That quiet support suddenly lifted the weight off her shoulders, and she looked at her future full of optimism.

Darcy noticed the change in mood, and could not resist that now brilliant smile directed at him. He pulled her towards him and kissed her until they were both breathless.

As he recovered, he murmured, 'it is fortunate that the weather is as chilly as it is, otherwise I would be tempted to tempt you; and you are very tempting indeed.'

His only answer was an impertinent smile.

~~B~~

Bingley too had risen quite early, and he presented himself at Longbourn as soon as polite visiting hours started, where he requested to speak to Mr Bennet.

Bingley, having been advised by Darcy, came immediately to the point. 'Mr Bennet, I would request your blessing to marry Miss Jane Bennet.'

'My blessing, but not my permission?'

'Miss Bennet is of age and does not require your permission, but we both would like your blessing.'

'What makes you think that you are worthy of my daughter?'

Bingley looked crestfallen. 'To be honest... nothing. But I love your daughter very much, and I will do everything in my power to make her happy.'

'And what do you think will make her happy?'

'I believe that being surrounded by a loving family makes her happy. Being near her favourite sister...'

Mr Bennet was pleasantly surprised that Bingley had judged Jane's character so accurately, and that he was more focused on love than material possessions.

'Love is all well and good, but it will not keep her fed and sheltered.'

'Sir, since Jane, I mean Miss Bennet prefers living in the country, I plan to buy an estate where she will be comfortably situated. Darcy has been teaching me how to manage an estate, and promised to keep advising me, should I need assistance. I can well provide for her material needs, and I cherish the thought of her gentle support.'

'I am concerned that you are both so good-natured that the servants will rob you blind.'

'Mr Bennet, I believe that I have grown up enough that I will not allow anyone to act in a manner injurious to your daughter. And you may be misjudging her. Yes, Miss Bennet is kind and gentle, and prefers to look for the good in people, but she is not stupid and will not be deluded. I believe that under her soft demeanour, there is a core of steel.' He now gave a chuckle. 'Also, my Aunt Mathilda would never forgive me if I did not stand up to anyone who would impose on me again.'

Bennet joined in the chuckle. 'I have noticed that she is a quite remarkable lady. I suppose some of that pepper must be in you as well. Very well, you have my blessing.'

Bingley almost floated, when he went in search of Jane, to tell her of Mr Bennet's agreement.

~~B~~

Mrs Bennet was delighted with the news that Jane was to marry Mr Bingley. 'Did I not predict that Mr Bingley would have the good sense to fall in love with Jane,' she cried.

'Yes, Mama, you did,' Jane blushed at her mother's exuberance.

The lady looked expectant. 'I hope that unlike Lizzy, you will give me enough time to plan a proper wedding.'

'We have not yet discussed a date...'

'Spring would be the perfect time. There will be plenty of flowers available, and we will have time to get you a proper trousseau.'

Jane and Bingley exchanged glances, and he nodded with a smile, knowing that his love liked to please her mother, and this was the time Mrs Bennet could show her daughter how much she was loved.

'Very well, Mama, but no later than Easter,' Jane agreed with the ecstatic matron.

~~B~~

Elizabeth and Jane spent their final night together. When they were curled up in bed, Jane could not resist teasing her sister.

'I told you so,' she said, reminding Elizabeth of her own prediction.

'I knew you would not be able to resist saying so,' Lizzy mock complained.

'I cannot help it that I am older and wiser than you.' Jane giggled at the face Elizabeth pulled. 'Are you happy?'

'Oh yes,' Elizabeth breathed, her eyes shining. 'Although I shall miss you. We will not be able to have these talks anymore.'

'You will be able to talk to William like this...'

Elizabeth blushed at the reminder of sharing a bed with her husband. 'Perhaps.'

Her sister noticed the blush and teased, 'or perhaps you will be too busy to talk.'

'Jane, how can you say things like that.'

'I just thought that you might be too busy sleeping,' Jane smirked.

'I think that talk of weddings has quite corrupted you. I suggest that we should sleep, before you get worse.'

'You are quite right, Lizzy. You need to sleep, to look tolerable tomorrow morning... and tempting tomorrow evening.' Jane smothered her sister's further protests by giving her a hug.

~~B~~

Mr Bennet leaves his study

Mr Bennet was waiting for Elizabeth in his library. He remembered all the times he had spent in this room, teaching Elizabeth and relishing her eager interest in the written word.

It seemed but yesterday when she had learnt her letters, and now she was a woman grown, and about to leave to start her own family. He chided himself for becoming maudlin, when Elizabeth entered.

'You look wonderful, Lizzy. All grown up.' He enfolded her in a gentle embrace. 'I am so proud of the wonderful woman you have become.'

'Thank you, Papa,' Elizabeth replied, reverting to her childhood appellation, which she had not used in years.

'Are you ready to start your life with that remarkable young man of yours?' Mr Bennet asked as he released his daughter.

Elizabeth, who was also valiantly supressing her tears, answered firmly, 'yes, I am.'

Mr Bennet offered her his arm, 'in that case, shall we go?'

Elizabeth took his arm, and they left the library. They were joined by Jane as they made their way to the carriage which was to take them to the church.

~~B~~

Darcy waited nervously in the church. Colonel Fitzwilliam had been teasing him all morning, trying to give him advice about what his cousin should do to please his bride. While Darcy ignored the unsolicited advice, his irritation with Richard's teasing had at least distracted him from his nerves. Now they were back in full force, despite his cousin's presence.

'At least your lady is punctual,' murmured Richard as the doors opened, and Mr Bennet escorted Elizabeth towards her waiting groom.

Mrs Bennet could not hold back her tears, as she saw the look passing between her daughter and the man she was about to marry. It seemed to her that both of them forgot the presence of everyone else, as Elizabeth made her way to the altar.

Mr Bennet could not resist a smirk, when he passed Elizabeth's hand to Darcy, and the man barely noticed him. Yes, those two deserved each other and would do well together.

Although it pained Mr Bennet to relinquish his favourite daughter, he was pleased that she had found a man, who cherished her as much as her father.

He was well content as he took his seat by Mrs Bennet, and took his wife's hand.

~~B~~

Miss Caroline Bingley watched the ceremony with envy. She had spent the last several years trying to catch Mr Darcy, and now he was marrying Miss Elizabeth Bennet, whom he had known for only a few months.

She wondered what opportunities she might have missed in her obsession with becoming the Mistress of Pemberley. In truth, she did not care a fig about Mr Darcy. His appeal had always been his wealth and position. Although his handsome features were a pleasant bonus.

As she observed the couple saying their vows, it was obvious that they married for love. Mr Darcy had never looked at her like that. At best he had been polite. In retrospect she recognised that most of the looks he had directed at her, had been laced with disgust.

When the vicar pronounced them to be husband and wife, the look of pure joy and reverence as Darcy bent his proud neck to place a kiss on his bride's lips would remain branded in her memory.

For a moment Caroline hoped that she would meet someone who felt this strongly about herself, but she chided herself out of becoming obsessed with a new objective. She determined that she would find herself a husband who at least liked her well enough to have a not unpleasant marriage.

~~B~~

'Mrs Darcy,' Darcy breathed as he smiled at his wife, who was now seated in the carriage with him, to be taken to Longbourn for the wedding breakfast.

'Mr Darcy,' was the equally smiling response, before Darcy carefully kissed his wife.

'It is now quite proper for you to kiss me improperly,' Elizabeth teased.

'I know, but if I do, you will need the services of a maid to undo the damage I will do to your hair, and your dress will become dreadfully wrinkled. And we are expected by our families,' Darcy acknowledged with regret.

~~B~~

Once the wedding breakfast was over, a convoy of carriages made their way to London.

The Duke's carriage led the way, followed by the Gardiners, and the Earl and Countess of Matlock, who also transported Georgiana and Mrs Annesley, who would stay at Matlock House for a week, to provide privacy for the newlyweds.

Mr and Mrs Darcy followed behind the others. While Elizabeth and Darcy enjoyed the privacy, which afforded them the opportunity to kiss and allow their hands to wander, the confined quarters and the chill temperature restricted their activities.

As pleasurable as those activities were, the journey to London was more than three hours, and eventually the couple resorted to conversation to pass the time.

Later that evening, Elizabeth happily discovered that her Aunt Madeline had been wrong. If anything, her aunt had understated the ecstasy to be found within the loving arms of her husband.

~~B~~

28 Epilogue

Immediately after the wedding, Colonel Fitzwilliam rode directly to Rosings. He arrived just in time to farewell his cousin, and he managed to raise a final smile on her lips, which remained after she breathed her last.

When he went looking for his aunt an hour later, Perkins informed him that Lady Catherine had just removed herself to the Dower House, and would not welcome any visitors. Even though Richard tried to see her from time to time over the years, she remained in seclusion for the remaining years of her life.

Richard informed the family of Anne's passing, but passed on her suggestion that since they did not visit her during her lifetime, they should not bother to succumb to hypocrisy, by attending her funeral. Mr Collins performed the service, which was attended by Richard and the staff at Rosings.

Although the staff, who had been informed by Anne that Richard Fitzwilliam was her chosen heir, were pleased to greet him, Mr Collins was disconcerted to discover the change in management, and that the Colonel expected him to minister to his parishioners, rather than spy on them. The parishioners on the other hand, were delighted by the change.

After arranging for his cousin's funeral, Richard rode to London to resign his commission, and to visit the family solicitor, to arrange for the transfer of Rosings into his name.

When he returned, the staff, at his orders, enthusiastically started to clear the house of the overly ornate furniture.

~~B~~

At the beginning of spring, Jane Bennet married Charles Bingley.

Since Mrs Bennet had been deprived of planning an elaborate wedding for Elizabeth, this wedding was as lavish as she could make it.

The whole extended family attended, to wish the couple well, and to celebrate their happiness.

During their wedding trip, they found an estate for sale, with which they both fell in love. By the time the lease on Netherfield expired, the Bingleys moved into an estate in a neighbouring county to Derbyshire, and Jane and Elizabeth, in addition to every other source of happiness, were within thirty miles of each other.

~~B~~

By the time the militia left Meryton, Colonel Forster too had found and married a lady who suited him perfectly.

Charlotte Lucas was thrilled when the distinguished officer asked for her hand in marriage.

~~B~~

It took several months, and the advice and help of his extended family, to turn Rosings Park into a pleasant home.

One lady in particular Richard often consulted about choices of colour and style.

As soon as the house was liveable, but needed the final decorating, Richard visited Meryton, where he courted a lady whom he had met during his visit the previous year. Mrs Bennet was astonished but thrilled, to have her third daughter marry a major estate owner, and the son of an Earl, no less.

'It is most peculiar. In the past I expected Jane to make the best marriage of all my daughters, while I doubted that any man could be interested in marrying an impertinent girl like Lizzy, or a plain one like Mary. And now Mary is to be married to the son of an Earl, and he owns a large estate. Lizzy is married to the nephew of that Earl, and his estate is even larger. But Jane is married to the son of a tradesman. Admittedly, he now owns an estate as well, but still...'

~~B~~

The following year, Caroline Bingley met a gentleman with a moderately large estate in Cornwall.

Sydney Salier

While he had no connections to the nobility, he was the leading landowner in his neighbourhood. Caroline decided it was better to be a big fish in a small pond, than a minnow in the ocean of the *ton*, and happily settled into married life with Mr Streatfield.

Her dowry helped her husband to improve on the estate, allowing him to provide good dowries to their two daughters, one of whom married a Viscount.

Mrs Caroline Streatfield was thrilled to have connections to the first circles at last.

~~B~~

By the time Kitty and Lydia came out into society, in the same year as Georgiana made her debut, both had learnt proper manners and comportment, and were accomplished in all aspects of being the Mistress of an estate.

Kitty, while still quieter than her younger sister, had learnt to stand up to Lydia, and had stopped following her around.

Although Lydia was irrepressible as she had always been, she had learnt to behave with decorum... at least in public.

Due to their well-connected brothers-in-law, they had the opportunity for a season in London, where they had many admirers.

Kitty met and fell in love with George Jeffery, the heir of a moderate sized estate, and they settled into the country to enjoy married life.

Lydia encountered a shy young man at a ball, who was being teased by some of the older students from his school, about his lack of dance-partners. Unable to resist annoying the bullies, she curtsied to the young man, saying, 'I am sorry for being late for our dance, Sir,' while smiling brightly.

While the young man may have been shy, he was not stupid. 'Not at all, Miss Bennet. It is I who was delayed by these... uh... gentlemen.'

He offered his arm and led her to the dancefloor. 'Thank you, Miss Bennet, for your kind assistance,' he said quietly, as soon as they were out of earshot.

'You are very welcome, Sir. I was afraid that you might take my forward behaviour amiss, but I cannot abide bullies.'

'Neither can I, but a ballroom is not the place to start a ruckus, so I had to put up with their teasing.'

'But why did you not simply ask a lady to dance with you?'

'Because every time I try to speak to a young lady, I start to stutter,' he shrugged in a self-deprecating manner.

'I have not noticed any stutter.' Lydia said in puzzlement, and was brought to a sudden stop, when the young man halted their progress.

He too wore a puzzled expression. 'I suppose it only happens when I get nervous,' he posited. 'And I always get nervous when trying to ask a young lady to dance.'

'That is curious, but I suppose it makes sense. But I wonder if you would answer two questions for me.' When he indicated that he would be pleased to do so, Lydia asked, 'how did you know my name, and would you tell me yours. I am certain we have not been introduced.'

He coloured slightly and stammered, 'I asked a f-f-friend ab-b-bout the n-name of the b-b-beautiful lady,' he nodded at Lydia, whose turn it was to blush. 'My name is Andrew B-B-Barrington, at your s-s-service.'

Within the year, Lydia was married to Uncle Reggie's grandson, and eventually, she became a most respected Duchess.

Mrs Bennet was thrilled that she had been correct about the chances of her youngest daughter.

Mr Bennet was pleased that the once silliest girls in all of England, had become so very sensible.

~~B~~

Georgiana was a little slower to make a match, but eventually she made an excellent marriage to a young Viscount who found her to be enchanting.

Her love of music continued undiminished, as it was encouraged by her husband.

She settled into an estate not too far from Pemberley, and the siblings found many reasons to visit each other, as well as the Bingleys.

Sydney Salier

~~B~~

Mr Gardiner's business became ever more prosperous, and he bought a larger house in a more fashionable area.

When her services were no longer required at Longbourn, Mr and Mrs Gardiner were pleased to hire Mrs Taylor as the governess for their children. She remained until the youngest girl was getting married. At that point she accepted the proposal of one of Mr Gardiner's business associates, who had courted her during the last year of her service.

Eventually, the Gardiners bought Netherfield, where they enjoyed a well-earned retirement, while their oldest son continued to manage Gardiner & Sons.

~~B~~

The Duke of Barrington, whose major estate was in Westmoreland, found a surprising number of reasons to visit Scarborough.

After many months, during which time their friendship deepened, the Duke proposed marriage to Miss Mathilda Bingley.

While the lady was thrilled and flattered by the offer, she explained, 'I am too set in my ways to contemplate marriage, as I like my independence. As a single woman I may not have many rights, but as your wife I would have none. I have no wish to become non-existent in the eyes of the law. In addition, I have no interest in status or in dealing with the machinations of the *ton*.'

Instead of bringing home a new Duchess, the Duke contented himself with being a *very* close friend of this independent lady. This friendship lasted for the rest of their lives.

~~B~~

Mr Collins, encouraged, or truth to be told, bullied, into more socially acceptable behaviour, became a surprisingly caring parson for the people of Hunsford.

He eventually married the daughter of a local merchant, and proceeded to have four daughters.

Fortunately for him, his wife was a sensible woman, who raised their daughters to be accomplished young women. Since she was also careful

222

with money, they managed to provide the girls with reasonable dowries, which helped them to find husbands.

On occasion, Mr Collins was heard to proclaim that he was exceedingly grateful that he did not have to provide an heir for Longbourn, and he eventually sent a letter of apology to Mr and Mrs Bennet for the attitude he had displayed on his one and only visit.

~~B~~

Mr Wickham did not fare as well as the family whom he had attempted to ruin.

Within months of his arrival at Marshalsea, he got into a fight with one of the other inmates. Although the injury he received was slight, it became infected and hastened his unlamented demise.

~~B~~

In contrast, Mr and Mrs Darcy both lived to a ripe old age.

They had several children who were taught to be as outgoing as their mother, but their father ensured that their impertinence was under good regulation.

When their oldest son was ready to run Pemberley, they took Mr and Mrs Bennet as an example and spent time visiting family, although they never stayed away for long from their beloved Pemberley.

~~B~~

When Joshua Bennet finished his education, he returned to Longbourn, where Mr Bennet quite happily handed over management of the estate to his son.

This coincided with Joshua's twenty-first birthday. The day after, Mr Bennet and his son agreed to break the entail on Longbourn, which had caused Mrs Bennet such distress. In future, in the absence of a male heir, a daughter could inherit the estate.

Joshua was of a more practical bent than his father. He enjoyed managing Longbourn, and a few years later he married the youngest daughter of the Long family. They proceeded to have a large and boisterous family.

Sydney Salier

Since Mr and Mrs Bennet spent much of their time visiting, they ceded the Master suite to their son, and shared the Mistress' suite when they were in residence. In return, Joshua ensured that Mr Bennet's library remained his father's domain.

~~B~~

Mr and Mrs Bennet lived out their lives in contented harmony. They enjoyed visiting their daughters and grandchildren, all of whom they spoiled shamelessly.

It was not until many of their grandchildren were grown up and had children of their own, that Mrs Bennet quietly passed away in her sleep one night.

When the whole house was peaceful, Mr Bennet at last retreated back into his study. Although he mourned the loss of his wife, he was grateful for all those years he had abandoned this beloved refuge.

~~B~~

The End

Books by Sydney Salier

Unconventional

An Unconventional Education (Book 1) – A P&P Reimagining

Unconventional Ladies (Book 2) – A Regency novel inspired by P&P

The Denton Connection

Don't flatter yourself – A P&P Variation

Mrs Bennet's Surprising Connections – Prequel to 'Don't flatter yourself'

It's a Duke's Life – Sequel to 'Don't flatter yourself'. A P&P spin-off

Don't flatter yourself – Revisited – The alternate version of this P&P Variation

Consequence & Consequences – or Ooops – A Regency Romance inspired by P&P

No, Mr Darcy – A Regency Romance inspired by P&P

Remember – you wanted this – A collection of P&P variations

Surprise & Serendipity – A P&P Variation

You asked for it – A P&P Variation with a twist

Made in the USA
Coppell, TX
31 July 2021

59735850R00135